RUTHLE

VAMPIRES OF BATON ROUGE: BOOK 4

Roxie Ray and Lindsey Devin
© 2022
Disclaimer

This is a work of fiction. Names, places, characters, and events are all fictitious for the reader's pleasure. Any similarities to real people, places, events, living or dead are all coincidental.

This book contains sexually explicit content that is intended for ADULTS ONLY (+18).

Contents

Chapter 1 - Francois 5

Chapter 2 - Maeve...18

Chapter 3 - Francois 26

Chapter 4 - Maeve...40

Chapter 5 - Francois 57

Chapter 6 - Maeve...75

Chapter 7 - Francois 91

Chapter 8 - Maeve...104

Chapter 9 - Francois 118

Chapter 10 - Maeve...131

Chapter 11 - Francois 143

Chapter 12 - Maeve...157

Chapter 13 - Francois 172

Chapter 14 - Maeve...184

Chapter 15 - Francois 193

Chapter 16 - Maeve...205

Chapter 17 - Francois 222

Chapter 18 - Maeve...231

Chapter 19 - Francois 248

Chapter 20 - Maeve...262

Chapter 21 - Francois 275

Chapter 22 - Maeve...291

Chapter 23 - Francois 311

Chapter 24 - Maeve...325

Chapter 25 - Francois 335

Chapter 26 - Maeve...350

Chapter 27 - Francois 369

Chapter 28 - Maeve...381

Chapter 29 - Francois 391

Chapter 30 - Francois 402

Chapter 1 - Francois

If I wasn't already on the route to being crazy, I would have told you the Ancients were trying to get me there.

I plucked at the lace frill on my sleeve. My Renaissance-style cuffs were hardly in fashion now, but I'd worn them long enough that probably the fashion would roll around again before I'd replaced my extensive wardrobe.

Well, it used to be extensive. Rack after rack of retro… Okay—vintage.

Merde.

Shit. *Vintage.* Who was I kidding? Retro and vintage were both far too modern to describe my sense of style. I wore *antique* clothes. Damnit. I was a living antique these days.

But clearly only the best, most valuable kind.

Most days.

I hadn't even had chance to get used to living free in the modern age. Not really. I hadn't truly existed outside the shadow of my father before Nicolas had imprisoned me, and my stay with Jason, such as it was, had been cut short. Irritation flared through me, but I quashed it.

It was a pointless emotion.

Stay with Jason. That made me sound like a guest, right? Almost honored, perhaps? Well, I wasn't entirely sure what I was to Nicolas Dupont and his family, but I guessed *honored* would never be a verb of choice in reference to me.

But they *had* offered me some modicum of freedom.

Almost.

Better than I'd had when I'd lived with Father, anyway. I hadn't really been a son or a subject. A servant, perhaps. Something necessary that he didn't really like.

I'd run The Neutral Zone in New Orleans, which maybe sounded quite free—running a club that various supernaturals used to congregate and iron out deals and keep the peace—but even that had been under Father's rule. It hadn't been true freedom. Then I'd been compromised in battle and captured by Nicolas.

Captured and *saved*. I shook my head again. It was weird to think of imprisonment as saving me.

But he had.

He was trying to cure me, or at least free me of the effects of the drug in my system.

Different freedom.

Only now, the Ancients had me, and they appeared to be carefully undoing Nicolas's work and returning the effects of the dead man's blood still in my veins. It was growing stronger with each passing day.

They didn't have access to the antidote in the same way Nicolas seemed to. Or they weren't sharing, if they did.

And they'd brought me full fucking circle.

When they first took me from the apartment where Jason and I were living, they'd holed us up in some antebellum mansion somewhere nearby. I hadn't recognized it. It was just a place that was still lucky to exist. A place that had smelled constantly swampy and damp, where fabrics were decaying and torn. Mold and spiders had been my constant companions.

Well, the spiders had until I took their legs. Raisins had always held more value than spiders, I found.

I didn't touch the spiders in this new residence they'd moved me to. They were bigger, but they were also familiar. Oh, and the residence wasn't entirely new, either.

They'd brought me back. They'd brought me *home*.

Another full circle.

Fuck. I'd fought so hard to escape the influence of Father, of my position as heir to his throne, of all this house meant, and the gardens beyond... Hell, always the gardens beyond.

"Putain." I swore aloud in French, the sudden sound harsh as I ground it out.

Those gardens. They were my torment now.

Ghosts visited me from those gardens.

I saw them each night. Originally, they'd only been visible through the windows. Wraiths, of mist wrapped in the sheerest of transparent fabrics, an ephemeral breeze keeping them from ever being truly solid. They'd flickered like the signal was failing, and I'd needed to blink or look slightly away to even see them.

These were the ghosts I'd created when I'd lived here. They certainly weren't simply conjured up by my crazed mind just now. They haunted me but they also kept me from being alone. They dwelt here. The last place they'd seen on Earth.

Where I'd killed them.

Where I'd buried them.

They drove me increasingly mad but they also kept me company.

Perhaps they kept me sane.

I'd killed these women and I'd buried them. They were as much prisoners here as I was.

And they were no longer satisfied with remaining in the gardens. One had watched me from the doorway last night.

I shivered at the memory. I'd jumped when I saw her, and she'd stood still, simply watchful, her gaze heavy and knowing.

They all had a familiarity. Whatever had drawn me to them in the first place drew me to them still. Perhaps that was their end game, to bring me over to join them.

Well, I was vampire, so we had a long game in front of us if that was the case.

Soon, they'd speak. Of that, I was certain. Their mouths often moved already but they were soundless, like a television I couldn't tune in well enough to align the audio with the visuals.

I laughed. I couldn't lip read. Maybe they were simply telling me what a slum my ancestral home had become.

"Oui, oui." I directed a disinterested wave at the latest ghost to appear, my frilled sleeve flapping against my hand.

She stood in the middle of the lawn, but my expansive gesture did nothing to sweep her away.

I didn't need any of them to point out what this place looked like, though. I could still see that much for myself. If the bayou had been busily reclaiming the previous place the Ancients had kept me, dust and age were waging a fiercer battle in my family home.

Every surface had a soft gray layer of old skin cells and other things I never wanted to know. Upholstery fabric was worn and thin. Paint flaked on the walls, and wood was silvered and scarred.

Some of the furniture bore rips and tears—even evidence of tiny claws and probably teeth. Sometimes I heard the scratching and gnawing, but it was a welcome relief to the silence.

When everywhere was too still, my veins ached with the passage of my blood, and my head pounded. I couldn't reach my state of vampire meditation anymore, the place where everything was silent and still. It was beyond me. I was in a perpetual state of alertness.

The Ancients still brought me blood, but never fresh. It was like they had a stock or a supply, but when I asked questions, no one answered. And it was always from a virgin—I could taste that, although there was an element of something old and bitter—and the blood was never from my mate. The one I'd just found before they moved me.

Found.

Then lost.

She was somewhere, but I was sealed in here by the same magic they'd used before, the barrier to the corridor outside invisible but more tangible than any door.

The door itself stood open, mocking me, but I couldn't leave.

Anger and rage fueled some of my desire to survive, now. My mate was out there. I needed to claim her. After so many years of so many mistakes, my life was mocking me.

Before, it would have been easy to succumb to the madness. Too easy. The house I'd fought to keep together for so many years seemed to be falling apart around me, although I was currently in the butler's quarters, below stairs—me, *below fucking stairs* in the servants' parlor—so I couldn't see the rest of the rooms.

Father had liked to keep things traditional, but stasis had claimed him so often that I'd eventually modernized one of the rooms for my own comfort, and now I had no idea what the Ancients were doing to my home. They were using it as a base of some sort but I didn't know why.

From the infrequent sounds I picked up, it was as though they were searching. Something they were doing systematically, anyway, in the upstairs rooms. I couldn't always hear them moving around, but I could *feel* when the house was empty of their presence, like they all had a signature that radiated around them. Something that spoke to me. Like I was plugged in to whatever circuit they were operating on.

Maybe the multitude of voices would be enough to stop the craziness threatening to engulf me because I couldn't become a savage. I couldn't give in to the dead man's blood trying to claim my system and my thoughts.

I brought the image of my redheaded mate to mind again. I'd seen her for such a short time.

So very short.

But her scent. That was the sweetest voice of all. It whispered and beguiled, and it begged me to hold on.

I needed to hold on.

For her.

For me.

I kicked my leg up over the back of the chaise and let my boot swing, the heel striking the dusty velvet with satisfying muffled thuds when there was a noise from upstairs. In addition to the noise, there was the usual signature I associated with the Ancients but also someone else… the new person was definitely different. Yet familiar.

Who were they bringing here?

My interest piqued, I stood and walked toward the enchanted doorway. I couldn't pass through the space, but I could see and hear and smell…

Sweet Jesus.

My gums ached then my fangs sliced through in a Pavlov's dogs' response to my captors being back and the fact that their appearance usually meant food swiftly followed. This was no gentle descent of hunger. One moment my fangs weren't there, then they were, taking up all of the space in my mouth. I grumbled as I breathed in a familiar scent and finally placed it.

A useless scent. And she had yet to acquire the full level of grace granted to her by her vampire side.

That strangely mingled smell of vampire mixed with born-shifter could only belong to Jason's mate. But why were they bringing her here to me?

Did they smell her unusual scent, too? Did they know what she was?

A hybrid.

I half grinned, and my fangs pressed against my lower lip. How long since we'd had a true hybrid amongst our number?

If only I could get… I almost tried to walk out of the room as the thought struck me. Father's library held many books, not all of them legible anymore, but I'd never seen such an ancient collection of paper. Some didn't even look like paper. Vellum. Human skin. I'd never had the patience to identify what the pages were made of, but now I had more than a passing interest in the contents of the books.

They could hold information I'd find useful—and not just about Jason's mate and how powerful she really might be if she could get her shifter side under control. But maybe even information about who the Ancients really were or what they wanted.

Why they fucking had me.

And if I found that information, I could escape. I could find my mate and rescue both of us from this hellhole. Because that was all that really mattered. She was the key to my whole future. Impatience wanted me to move fast, but I curtailed it. I wasn't in a position to act yet. Not if I wanted to be successful. And I didn't just want that—I *needed* it.

I scraped the toe of my boot across the floor, disturbing dust bunnies and grass seed that seemed to come in through the tiniest of gaps and cracks.

The scent of Jason's mate grew stronger, and when she appeared on the other side of my enchanted doorway, she was struggling in the grip of one of the white-blond excuses for vampires. They all looked like Father had looked after he rose from a particularly long stasis—like a light breeze would tear them in two or shred their thin skin to tatters.

But they were stronger than they appeared. That, and Jason's mate was doing a particularly good job at acting today as she seemed to try to wrench her way from the Ancient holding her.

She shrieked as soon as she saw me, which I assumed was more acting on her behalf because she was certainly stronger by now than she probably wanted them to know, but the sound was eardrum piercing, and I winced. She needed to tone the volume down if she expected anyone to believe she was still weak after her transition to vampire.

Still, if we were acting, I could do that as well.

"Bonjour, ma petite." I walked closer to her, knowing my grin was lascivious now as I played what I hoped was her game. "Have you come to join me, sweetheart?" I made sure my voice was a purr.

"Never." She spat the word. "I'd die alone first." She glanced at the vampire holding her. "Not with him," she pleaded. "Return me to the women."

The women… I tilted my head briefly as I tried not to react. Were the women also here? Had I been so distracted by the scent of the hybrid that I'd neglected to note the presence of my own mate?

I drew a slow inhale through my nose and there she was. Spring blossoms interwoven with the clean air of a fresh new day. She was pure hope. The idea I could start anew.

She was in the house. It was enough to drive a man mad. Surely as mad as Jason was going, given he was also apart from his mate. Still, at least she had a fighting chance, and more so if the Ancients didn't discover what she truly was.

She struggled a little more, and as I watched her, she narrowed her eyes like she expected me to do something.

I held my hand out in invitation. "What's wrong? Ma petite… We could be…" I paused and smiled. "Friends." The word was far more threat than promise, and I knew it.

We hadn't spent any time together before I was taken, and she knew nothing of me but my reputation.

And maybe if she had to die, then here, in this enchanted room with me, was better than anywhere else, but I also had no doubt that if she was taken back to the human women, to my mate, then she would protect her. My mate would come to no harm if she existed in the same space as Jason's hybrid mate.

I'd intended for them to take her away anyway, but now my purpose was renewed.

"Take her," I barked. "What possible use could she be to me? I need virgin blood." I sneered, baring my fangs, letting them both glimpse my madness. "And she is no virgin. I have no need of a companion, and one…so new…isn't fun." I made sure to slow my gaze as I trailed it up her body, as though I was assessing her.

"Not with him." She spoke again through gritted teeth before letting loose another piercing shriek. "I can keep the screaming up, you know, and it's all you'll hear if you leave me in this room."

The Ancient sighed and shook her before spinning them both away. "Very well, but good luck controlling yourself in a room of humans. This was the kindest option." He glanced over his shoulder. "For all of you."

My heart plummeted inside my body, leaving my chest hollow and aching. "Putain." The catch-all curse was as familiar as breathing as I whispered it.

I was essentially sending a fledgling vampire to guard my mate. I didn't know if her thirst for blood drove her or if her wolf won. My certainty that she'd protect my mate dimmed.

I could only hope the hybrid had enough continued self-control to keep everyone safe while I tried desperately to figure out a better plan to overpower the Ancients while we were sorely, clearly outnumbered.

Chapter 2 - Maeve

I glanced around. Somehow, after ten days of captivity where nothing much seemed to happen, I'd found my Zen. Or my PTSD or Stockholm syndrome, or whatever. My mood was very *que sera, sera...* I couldn't change this situation. And apparently, I couldn't fight it.

I just had to wait for whatever was going to happen next.

There were two of us here now. There'd been three, but they kept taking Ciara away. No, that was a lie. There were occasionally more than three, but only Ciara ever came back. She might not this time, though. I had no idea where they took her or why.

Of course, her being in the room with us was always interesting. She'd called the man they'd tried to put us with a vampire. I cackled out a laugh at the memory, and Penelope looked up.

"What's tickled you? One of the ghosts?" She rolled her eyes.

She'd left me in no doubt over how she felt about the paranormal. She was truly a disbeliever—even when I'd explained about my blog and all the things I'd heard and seen as a paranormal investigator.

Penelope joked about Ciara and the vampire comment when she wasn't here, even though I itched for Ciara to repeat her claims and explain to me why she thought the utterly mad man we'd met was an actual honest-to-God creature of the night.

But Penelope's jokes kept us sane. Well, sane-ish. For abductees. And as she said, she was *entirely* sane because she didn't believe in vampires. She didn't believe in ghosts or werewolves, either.

I'd asked her about it, and how—living here, in a city literally soaked in witchcraft and voodoo—she could continue to not believe.

She'd tossed her hair. Not just a flip. A full-on toss, the movement filled with unconcealed scorn, but her honesty was refreshing. She didn't give a shit what I thought about her opinion,

"So New Orleans has a creepy undertone, sometimes," she said, "but that's just the gruesome history of murders in the city and the numerous paranormal explorers and ghost hunters who crowd some of our oldest buildings with their vintage tape recorders and motion sensors. It's just dumb tourists who go missing while wandering unaccompanied around a cemetery or in the bayou. That's just asking for trouble if you ask me."

And I did ask her. Often. Because hearing her talk was better than silence. Even if everything she said went against everything I believed.

More than belief. I'd seen things, and my Granny used to tell me stories about Ireland. Stories about the fae folk and the other side. Granny had believed in it—and in her own abilities to read tea leaves and contact spirit guides. She'd *lived* it. She'd been wise and she'd always known things there was no way she could have known. But I'd learned not to question that.

And there's always been something comforting about it. The idea that something existed beyond our knowledge. Like we had a safety net. A hammock we lazed in. Something was wrapped around us, and it had the ability to keep us safe.

Of course, it also had the ability to harm us, so I kept investigating and exploring because that sort of knowledge was power. What else was out there? What did I need to protect against or avoid?

And why, apart from the fact Ciara had named him *vampire*, did I see that man's eyes in my dreams? Why did I feel turmoil when I thought of him? I needed to find out more.

Something about him called to me. Instinct told me he wasn't like the other, entirely cold beings in this house, even if Ciara didn't like him.

"It's quiet today." Penelope's face was drawn and pale. The correct term was probably *pinched.* Perhaps she even had a couple more gray hairs than she'd had two weeks ago. But I got that.

I'd spent the first half of our time here a wreck. I'd searched every corner of the room, looking for a way out. I'd banged on the windows and doors, and I'd yelled until my throat was raw and my voice was hoarse.

"I prefer it quiet," I murmured. "Maybe they'll forget about us."

"And then what? What the hell would we do when they've forgotten about us?"

"Escape?" I made it sound so easy.

"Haven't you tried that?" Penelope's tone was dry as she lifted an eyebrow.

"I'd try harder." After all, there must be something I hadn't done. There was always something new to try or do. That was how humanity advanced. Because we didn't give up. We weren't quitters. "I'd try something else," I clarified. The door had to give at some point. It wasn't like they'd magicked it shut.

Same with the windows.

"You think they'll feed us soon?" Penelope laid her head on the dusty pillow as she spoke.

I was pretty tired too, but we were both trying to keep to a normal routine. It would be too easy to lose ourselves to sleep and spending the days unconscious out of fear and boredom.

"I hope so." They rarely brought us much of nutritional value—mainly slightly stale bread or things that just tasted *old*, although I truly believed artificially yellow sponge cakes filled with fake cream might outlast the human race.

Still, we never left even a crumb. We needed the energy to stay awake.

There was a noise at the door. "Maybe that's a meal now?"

But we both scrambled to the places we always took when someone opened the door, partially shielded by the heavy furniture in the room.

"Get back in there then. If you can." The pale man with the impossibly blond hair shoved Ciara through the doorway, his show of strength unnecessary. He smiled, and my insides twisted at the malevolence playing on his lips.

"Damn you." Ciara almost spat the words at him, and rage seethed from her. "Damn all of you."

But the man's smile merely widened as he nodded. "And the same to you, my dear. Eternally, no?"

The door closed behind him again and Ciara wrapped her arms around herself, her face pale as she looked at us. "You both doing okay?"

I started toward her but she stepped back, pressing herself against the wall. I stopped and glanced at Penelope. "We're both okay. But where did they take you? Are you hurt?"

Ciara shook her head and she looked at the door like she could still see the guy who'd just brought her back. "No, they wouldn't hurt me. I'm not sure they can." She shivered.

"You're cold." Penelope stood and walked from behind the dresser. "Come and get in the bed. Get warm."

But Ciara shook her head. "I'm fine. Just a bit…" She grimaced. "I'm just a bit hungry."

Penelope threw her hands in the air. "Same, girl. These guys have a real problem feeding us, right?" Then she wandered to the window and looked out. "I don't even know what they want with us. Why are we still here?" She tapped gently on the glass. "I mean, it's obvious there are bodies buried out there. Look at the uneven ground. Are we next?" When she turned, her eyes were wide and fear-filled.

I shrugged.

"I'll protect you." Ciara's voice was gritty, her words full of determination, and I resisted the urge to laugh.

"You're no stronger than either of us. We're all tired. All hungry. Our best chance is making a plan to escape." I stopped speaking, though, because that seemed like such a dumb thing to say.

How would that plan look? Could we rush one of the guys the next time they opened the door? Break a window? Even if one of us escaped, the other two would be left here with God knows what in terms of life expectancy.

"That's Francois's garden." Ciara waved a hand. "I wouldn't worry about ending up in it. I *will* protect you."

My mind buzzed. "Francois?"

She nodded. "They put him with us at first."

Penelope laughed, the sound sharp and abrasive, caught between amusement and horror. "The guy you said was a vampire? The monster?"

I moved closer. This was the kind of information that would make my blog blow up.

But Ciara just waved her hand. "He *is* a monster," she said. "That much is obvious. You can see the garden. But for now, we should rest. If we're going to figure out a plan, we should all be strong." She lay on the bed, pulled the comforter around herself like she was a Tootsie Roll, and closed her eyes.

"But is he actually a vampire?" I whispered the words so Penelope wouldn't also hear.

I'd been called a crank many times for my obsession with the paranormal, but something about the way Ciara had reacted to the man before, and the way he'd behaved… That hadn't seemed fake. There had been an energy between them that I rarely saw. I liked to tell myself it was the frisson of truth. The same thing that got my spidey senses really tingling when I followed any lead I believed in.

"Ciara?" I whispered again, hoping to jolt a response from her but her eyes remained closed and she didn't move. I touched her because it was like she'd died, she was so still.

"Must be tired." Penelope's voice interrupted my thoughts of the paranormal as I watched the sleeping woman.

"Hm. Maybe," I said, and returned my attention to the door.

Surely someone would bring us some food soon.

Chapter 3 - Francois

I twitched. Had I slept? Found my silence? Surely not…
And if not my silence, then was I following my father? Was
stasis in my future? I shuddered.

If that slow death beckoned to me, I didn't want to
know. Vampires were eternal. Supposedly. Allegedly. But
stasis was other. I needed to research it. After all, the family
fucking madness had seemed to follow me like a fucking
dog.

I laughed, the sound loud as it bounced off the walls
around me.

And if madness, why not fucking stasis, too?

All the family curses. Why fucking not?

"Why fucking not?" I yelled the words out loud after I
thought them.

"Why fucking what?" A sultry voice spoke from the
other side of the room, and I jerked my head, to the right.

"What the…?" No one should have been able to sneak
up on me. I was a vampire. Had I *actually* been out? How
long far?

"Hello, Francois. It's been a while." The female
vampire sashayed from the gray shadows. She was another

relic I thought I'd left in my childhood. "You're all grown up now, in fact."

"Clémence?"

She laughed, and it was the same sound it had always been—husky, throaty…sexy—but now I at least recognized it as such.

"Yes, of course. 'Tis I." Her French accent was as pronounced as it had ever been, and the general tone of mischief she leant to her words almost made me smile. She's never failed to make me smile as a child.

"But why?"

"Because you need me, mon amour. You need me." She dropped her voice low. A soft croon.

I leaned into her touch as she ran her fingers through my hair, but I wasn't moved by her. My heart yearned for my mate. My body longed for the woman with the red hair and irresistible scent. A frail human, but she was mine.

"Do I?" I didn't just feign disinterest. I literally *was* disinterested.

There was nothing anyone could do for me. Not even Clémence.

"And why now?"

"Because, mon coeur…"

I almost laughed as she narrowed her eyes seductively. *Her heart.* I highly doubted I'd ever meant that much to her. When she'd spent time with me in France, I'd still been wet around the ears—a youngling. She'd almost been my nanny.

She took my hand and stroked her fingers over mine, although her touch did nothing. "You must have questions."

I sat up a little. "Questions?" Even as the word left my lips, a movement at the door caught my attention. Speaking of those damn ghosts… There she was. The one I saw most often. Almost solid today, in fact.

I squinted as a memory tried to surface. What had her name been? *Ma petite*? No… That was only what I'd called her. What I'd called all of them.

Every woman I'd tried to take as my own. All of them. Ma petite.

She lifted a hand and played with the ends of her hair where it curled against the white nightgown she'd ended her days in. None of the ghosts were gruesome, none with any injuries or blood splatters. Instead, they all wore the plain white I'd provided. They'd all been so beautiful and needed no other adornment beyond the delicate broderie anglaise and fine stitching.

I nodded even now, pleased with my decision-making skills back then.

"Oh, Francois…" The ethereal voice floated across the room, accompanied by a stream of icy air.

Oh.

Shit.

They spoke now? Was I never to have any peace?

Well, if nothing else, perhaps it was interesting. A distraction. I inclined my head toward her and Clémence followed the direction of my gaze.

"You annoyed by the enchanted doorway, Pookie?" She ruffled my hair again, and I moved away from her reach.

I shrugged, channeling something casual and keeping my frustration at being imprisoned in check. "Gotten used to it." Clémence looked slight, but she was powerful… And I was crazy, but I wasn't stupid.

"But no questions?" A soft, beguiling smile curved her lips.

The ghost at the door stepped forward. Damn it all. I just needed to remember her name.

"Lots of questions, Francois, remember?" The ghost's voice was like music. Silvery bells.

I nodded, and the ghost smiled.

Clémence shifted closer to me. "Need me to start you off?"

I nodded again.

"Well, the magical doorway's gotta stay. They don't trust you not to leave." Clémence chuckled as she spoke.

Apparently, I only needed to nod occasionally for her to believe I was present with her and not trapped in some kind of purgatory where my past haunted me.

"Why are they here?" the ghost asked, and then faded before I could say anything to her.

"Why are they here?" I repeated the question as I looked at Clémence.

She laughed and tapped the end of my nose with the pad of her forefinger. "You silly boy. Silly, silly Francois."

I waited expectantly. "Well?"

"They're—We're—the *Ancients*."

"Oui. Bien sûr... Yes, of course." I could agree with her until my days ended. But that didn't mean I actually knew what she was talking about.

She jerked back, her surprise evident. "You really don't remember?" she hissed.

"Of course they're the Ancients." But that was the only fucking part I *did* know. I waved my hand dismissively. "Fucking Ancient bastards took me from my apartment."

She threw her head back, her laugh this time drawn out and loud. "Putain! Sweet fuck, Francois. How can you not know? What the hell else have you forgotten?"

I shrugged and stood, forcing a laugh of my own. "How can I know that, Clémence? How does one know what one has forgotten?"

She looked me up and down. "Merde." She cursed again and whirled away before pacing back. "Shit. They've come for you."

"Come for me?" I raked a hand through my hair. "Yeah. I got that much because…" I spread my arms wide. "Here I fucking am, right?"

She sighed, filling it with every bit of exasperation she'd probably ever experienced in her very long life. "I don't have time for this."

"Time for what?" Apparently, I was full of nothing but questions now.

"To spoon feed you. Those days are long gone. Been there, done that." She examined her nails like she was bored, but I remembered Clémence's games.

I shrugged and dropped back into my seat. "Okay." I closed my eyes like I might return to my repose, allowing myself the smallest of smiles when she shook my shoulder.

"Wake up, you ancient French bastard."

"Ancient." I tsked. "That feels a little…harsh."

She grimaced. "Idiot. No, you are *an Ancient*. Well, you could be."

"Wh…?" I didn't even get the full question out. My voice dried and died away. What the hell was she saying? "Go away, Clémence. Get out if you've just come here to play." I motioned to the door. "Leave me with the rats and the mice."

She tapped her foot. "No. You need to understand this. Do you remember who your father was?" She crouched beside me, her gaze earnest, her hand grasping mine like she might believe I was at the very edge of my senses and she could prevent me from tipping over completely.

"Bien sûr. Émile Ricard, King of New Orleans." I kept the contempt out of my voice. The sometimes king. Otherwise, he'd left it to me. And he'd taught me to be cruel.

Was I still that man? Still so cruel?

Surely not. I'd found my mate now. I only needed to get to her and claim her, and then I would be changed forever.

But before I could examine those new ideas, Clémence spoke and interrupted my thoughts. "No, before that. Before he took you and your mother and fled to the new country, to America. What was he then?"

I shook my head. "My memory…" I tapped my temple softly. But I wasn't being entirely truthful. There were things I did remember. Small things.

Like Clémence. She'd brought me little treats. Mammals to suck blood from when Father was punishing me again.

That old bastard. He'd always been punishing me for one thing or another.

But I didn't remember everything. Why we'd fled… It was a blur of raised voices, stealing away as though our lives were in danger, and bloodshed. So much bloodshed.

Unexpected corpses everywhere. On the big ship we'd used to traverse the Atlantic, in the small area where we landed, then littered across the country until we found somewhere to settle.

But that had just been a disadvantage of being a vampire traveling internationally at the time.

Only why had we traveled at all? The more I tried to remember, the more the tattered thoughts slipped away. I glanced at Clémence, not wanting to ask her yet not wanting her to leave this room without her telling me what she knew.

"What has happened to you, little one?"

I flinched at the echo of the pet name I'd given all of my women… *ma petite*… but Clémence had at least anglicized it this time. And I was no longer her *mon petit*. I wasn't sure I ever had been. And I certainly had no idea of her role, now.

Why the hell was she even here? In my fucking house. And she wasn't ill at ease. She was comfortable here.

I ignored her question. I didn't need to tell her anything immediately. "How long has it been, Clémence?" I sighed.

She half-smiled. "Too long, je pense."

"You think?" I chuckled.

She nodded. "Yeah. I should have gotten here sooner. Look at you. Your poor mind."

I flinched away as she ran her fingers through my hair. I didn't want her touch. She was nothing to me anymore. Nicolas's parents had bought him a pet human. I'd had a grown vampire to take care of me. All the times Father had kept Mother to himself or abused her in some way— because there had been abuse. I couldn't remember it, but I was sure of it all the same.

It was one thing I was grateful I had no recall of. Mother was an angel in my mind. I didn't want her tarnished or hurt.

"Why would you have come sooner?"

"As soon as I heard about Émile's bouts of stasis, I should have come. They all need a caretaker when they're in stasis."

I looked at her. "I was his fucking caretaker," I ground out. I'd done all the work. All of it. Run New Orleans. Kept the old fucker hanging on. Looked for my cure.

"No." Her voice was hard, her smile thin. "You don't understand. *I'm* the caretaker. They're my responsibility. I keep them all alive. And now…now one is dead." She shrugged. "But he had an heir."

I watched her as my mind raced to catch up to the words she'd just said. "Say it all again, but make it make sense."

She stood and dragged a rickety old chair from beside a table, the wooden legs scraping across the flagstone floor. "I'm just going to say it. I don't have time to work out where the gaps in your memory are, so I'll pretend it's all one big gap."

I nodded, pressing my mouth into a line so I wouldn't interrupt her.

"Emile was an Ancient."

I breathed in hard through my nose. A reflex to hearing those words.

She pressed her hand to mine again. "He was an Ancient, and he ran away from their planned stasis. They have to sleep or they go mad. But we prepare for it. We keep them safe. We keep them nourished."

I almost laughed at the idea that those vampires upstairs were somehow *nourished*. They all looked like a stiff breeze would break them apart and scatter their remains.

"His bouts of stasis were involuntary, Francois. No one was controlling them for him. He was succumbing to madness because he was away from the others. They are stronger when they're together. They *need* to be together."

I still didn't say anything.

"But there's you." She looked me in the eye.

"Me?" I laughed. "What about me?"

"You're the heir. An Ancient, now, if you're suitable. It's you. Ancients are the oldest vampires. We're special. Our bloodlines are clear and clean, and we have right to rule, but we need our full number to be strongest."

"What?" But she wasn't lying. I'd known her long enough to know that. "But stasis? For me too? Fuck it all to hell. I was going to go mad after all? There was a family curse and it was still going to claim me? Turned out we could all run but we couldn't hide."

"No stasis right now." Her eyes almost glowed, the sudden light eager. "We have too much to accomplish to waste time sleeping. And we have to bring you to your full strength."

I almost gave in to more laughter, let her see the madman lurking beneath my façade. "And what am I expected to accomplish from these luxurious quarters?" I spread my arms wide.

"Well, acceptance of your position, initially. Then we need to dethrone the false king."

Ahhh…Nicolas.

Once, I would have set Nicolas on fire myself and danced on his ashes. But that desire had changed these past weeks and months. He was no longer my enemy. He was my savior.

Worse, he was the brother I'd always wanted. The brother I'd lost.

Hell, Loïc should have been the heir. He would have been a better one than me. He'd always done everything better than me.

All I had to do, though, was buy enough time to wait for Nicolas. Because he'd come. I'd watched him ride to the rescue too many times before to doubt he'd do the same this time.

He'd come for any of his people.

Even for me.

And I'd be ready to escape when any opportunity arose. I didn't plan to be a fucking Ancient, regardless of anything Clémence might expect of me.

Clémence patted my thigh. "I can see this is a lot to take in," she murmured. Then she clapped her hands and stood, her demeanor changing in an instant. "Bon! Good. Good, well, there's a formal dinner planned for this evening."

"Oh?" I narrowed my eyes. "For what purpose?"

She laughed, her good humor from earlier returned. "We need to ensure the local community knows their real royals. Only the Ancients should be here unchallenged. There will be plenty of local influential people in attendance. I'm told some of them could be quite…" She paused as if searching for the right word. "Tasty."

I shook my head again. I'd learned my lesson about shitting where I ate. Or eating where I took a shit or whatever. Anyway, I no longer mixed the two, and seeing as this whole thing was one big shitstorm, there would be no eating here today. Not by me, anyway.

"*You* are royalty, Francois. No longer the prince. You're the king. Doesn't that feel good? It should feel *great*."

"And the Duponts?" I asked the question as casually as I could. If Clémence was here and willing to share information with me, I needed to collect as much information as I could.

"Meh. Nicolas Dupont is a false king, and his family has no place here. They don't run things. But I think they'll get my message very soon."

"Your message?" But I already knew what it was. Ciara. She was the message.

She waved a hand like the actual message didn't matter, and I wasn't sure she was going to say anything else. But as she walked toward the doorway, she turned and smiled, the twist of her lips cruel. "We took the mate of Nicolas's servant. He was getting above his station, anyway."

I hid my wince. If Clémence had really known the Duponts, she'd have been aware that Jason was much, much more than Nicolas's servant. He was his sireling. He was family.

Vampires didn't often have blood family, so our families expanded to who we chose. Born vampires like Nicolas and myself were rare.

"Was that wise?" I nudged a little. If she was sufficiently enthusiastic about her cause, maybe she'd get careless and share more information with me.

"It's time the people in this swamp know who's really in charge. We control the supernaturals, and the humans are ours to do with as we wish."

I lowered my head so she couldn't see my eyes. "Merci, Clémence. Thank you."

It was better she thought I was in full agreement with her, or at least grateful for her attention. I needed to absorb any information she presented me with. But she couldn't know I wasn't onboard with the Ancients' plans.

I smirked after she left the room. It almost seemed like a I had something to live for after all.

Chapter 4 - Maeve

I sat and listened to the silence around me. Penelope had given in and fallen asleep in the bed next to Ciara, and now I was just watching them both.

Penelope fidgeted in her sleep, and occasionally she whispered or talked. She was rarely still, but that was to be expected. This was a stressful situation. No sign of *any* sort of trauma at would be odder.

Which brought me to Ciara. I glanced at where she lay, perfectly still. Perfectly quiet.

Perfectly… I floundered as I searched for a word that captured her best. Absent. It was like she wasn't even there right now.

I sat back. She looked perfectly human. But that was their thing, right? All creatures of the night *looked* human? But Ciara? It seemed so unlikely.

Still, there was something about her. Beautiful, flawless skin, clear eyes, a way she held herself and grace in how she moved.

And vampires were why I was here in New Orleans, anyway, right?

It had been one more lead for the blog. Maybe the big one that could prove everything Granny had always told me. I laughed quietly. Granny had always insisted I had *the sight* but I sure as shit wouldn't have made this trip if I'd foreseen being abducted.

Oh, the things I'd learned from Granny. Well, not so much learned as learned *about*. She'd told me so many stories in the summers I'd spent with her. She'd spoken of fae and leprechaun and other tiny folk, and at the other end of the scale, she'd mentioned creatures as big as giants— what any other person might laugh off as *bigfoot*—and I'd been fascinated by it all.

But while Gran had claimed to see them, even while we were together—sometimes she described the delicate wings of the fae as they danced their way over her worn kitchen table—I had never seen anything.

The ghosts were the most unsettling. The figures that she said visited us or stood behind me, or peered out from walls as we passed by. I didn't see any of those either, but sometimes the prickle of my skin as she described what she could see was worse.

Even now, it seemed the harder I looked, the less I saw. Yet I knew these things were out there. I just knew it.

And I wanted to prove it.

As I continued to watch Ciara, her eyes sprang open. The woman literally went from being asleep to being alert in the time it took her to open her eyes.

She sounded confused, though. "Maeve? Why are you watching me?"

I shrugged. "Just wondering, that's all."

She sat up slowly, careful not to disturb Penelope, and slid from the bed until she was opposite me, both of us on the floor. "What were you wondering?"

She seemed to have woken up even more beautiful, if that were possible.

"About you." I doodled my finger through the thick, dusty pile of the carpet. Once upon a time, this would have been expensive.

Hell, this whole room, although it was stuck in a time warp, probably contained more antiques than I could count.

"About *me*?" She laughed, although a flicker of unease crossed her face. "Not even about how we're all going to escape?" Her casual tone wasn't entirely reflected in the small crease that appeared between her eyes, and I shrugged.

"Can't you do something?" Vampires were supposed to have incredible strength, right?

"Me?" This time her eyes widened. "Do we even know how many of them there are? What they're capable of? How could *I* do something?"

I opened my mouth to explain I knew exactly how she could do something to help us, but I paused. Maybe I was better not to say how much I knew just now. If I told her that I knew she was a vampire, she could just shut me down with a denial, but if I remained silent for now, I could watch and learn so much more.

Instead, I changed the subject slightly. "How did you get here?" We'd talked a little but always Penelope was awake, and talking about her abduction always rendered Penelope almost speechless.

Penelope would describe the side of her apartment building being blown off and floating through the air, and that was all she would say before her eyes widened and filled with tears and she started to shake at the memory.

From time to time, she wouldn't even answer properly.

"Who cares?" Penelope always said it with a careless shrug. "No one would believe me anyway."

But those stories were my bread and butter. Forget the red topped tabloid magazines and the headlines about Elvis returning home to Jupiter or the latest woman to have Bigfoot's baby... Give me the small things. The events that should have been mundane except for that one thing that couldn't be explained. *Those* events were where I would find my truth.

Those were what I needed to propel my blog from being written in the shadows to being mainstream.

They were also what I needed to anchor my own belief to, because so far in my life, I was chasing fragments and silhouettes when I *knew* there was far more out there than that.

Ciara shrugged. "I was taken from my…" She hesitated. "My boyfriend's house. Well, it's where he lives, anyway. He'd gone to investigate a noise and I…I suppose I just wasn't there when he got back." She looked slightly haunted as she finished speaking, and she pressed a hand over her chest.

Vampires…vampires… I racked my brains. They didn't really have boyfriends. That wasn't the right language. Not as I understood it anyway. She'd have a mate. A fated or *true* one if she was very lucky. Maybe that explained her hesitation over the word.

"You been together long?" I tugged at a fiber of the carpet as I spoke, untwining it so it looked fuzzy and frayed. Hopefully no one would notice I'd done that. Not that it really mattered. Who paid attention to antique carpet in a kidnap house?

She cleared her throat. "I guess." Her tone was so noncommittal, so *deliberately* casual that I looked up.

Her face had paled and her eyes weren't the same shade of green they'd been before. They looked more red, but perhaps that was just a trick of the light.

"You don't know?"

She waved a hand. "It's one of those things where it hasn't been a long time but it feels like we've known each other forever, you know?" I nodded, but I didn't really know.

I'd never experienced any sort of instant connection or immediate familiarity with anybody.

My mind wandered to the man we'd been briefly trapped in the room with. Something about him, though. Something. I wanted…

I shook my head. I wanted to know more. Like I always did. Like I wanted to know more about Ciara. I wanted to know more about my situation but if I couldn't escape, I could sure the hell investigate and keep my mind busy so I didn't go crazy with it all.

"What about you?"

We'd all exchanged our stories before. I'd only really asked her to see if she might change a detail or an event. But she hadn't said anything specific enough for me to know, and now she'd switched the subject to me. Still, I could play along.

"I came to New Orleans for material for my blog. I run a sort of...sort of news and reviews type blog." I hesitated the same way she had before leaning on the lie I'd used before. "Food and restaurants and similar." It fit for New Orleans, and it was convenient and common enough that no one would really question it. "And I don't know why I followed the beautiful woman except she was all dressed up and looked like she was headed to the most popular, happening place. And if she was, that was where I needed to be." I chuckled, but it was hollow as I recalled my own stupidity.

The impossibly pale woman, her skin almost alabaster in tone, her hair white-blonde, had winked at me as her lips had curved into a smile of promise, and I'd followed her immediately. Hell, I would have followed her anywhere.

"It was like I lost my mind," I muttered. When I remembered it now, I couldn't even recall why I'd followed her. She hadn't said anything to me. One moment I'd been minding my own business as I tried to figure out which direction a nightclub I'd heard about was in, the next nothing had been more important in New Orleans than a woman I'd never met.

Wait, had she said something? I bit my lip as I tried to recall. Maybe just one word.

"Clémence," I blurted.

"What?" Ciara drew her eyebrows down into a shallow frown.

"I think she gave me her name." I shook my head and pressed a finger to my temple to ease a sudden ache there. "But it's all a bit blurry. Maybe she drugged me."

"Maybe." Ciara shrugged, and her stomach rumbled. She jumped to her feet, the movement so fast that if I'd blinked, I might have missed it, and she turned from me before heading to the door.

She banged on the heavy wood. "Hello!" she called. "Hungry in here. And I don't just get hungry, I get hangry." She banged again, and the door shook under the weight of her attack.

That was interesting, too.

Then she paused as though she was listening and stepped away from the door. "Someone's coming," she said.

I listened but couldn't hear whatever Ciara had. I didn't move closer to the door, though. Something in her gaze had changed, like she was hyper-focused now, and her cheeks looked pinched. The woman definitely looked hungry…and a little predatory.

Could I take her?

Hell, no. Not if she was what I thought she was, anyway. My curiosity about her was tempered by a healthy dose of caution about how much attention to bring to myself by asking questions.

Just as I was assessing my chances of surviving the day, the door opened and a woman I hadn't seen before dragged in a rolling rack of dresses. It stuck on the carpet and she tsked and half-lifted it to bring it the rest of the way into the room.

Two pale-faced women followed the rack into the room, their dark hair unkempt, purple shadows beneath their eyes.

"Right." The woman with the rack of dresses clapped her hands as she spoke and two huge men who looked like security guys on steroids blocked the doorway behind her. She glanced at Ciara. "Oh, hello, dear." But her tone was patronizing, her voice dripping with saccharine, the sweetness there artificial.

"I'm hungry," Ciara muttered.

"I see." And the woman narrowed her eyes like she really did see. She waved her hand toward one of the security guys. "A smoothie, I think." Her delicate gold bracelet glittered in the light where it dangled from her arm as she moved with a grace I'd never seen in my life.

She looked similar to the woman I'd followed before I ended up here—same almost translucent skin, same captivating inner glow, same white-blonde hair.

Interesting. They even had the same pale blue eyes. They could almost have been sisters, if coloring was the only thing that mattered. But their bone structure was entirely different. As I looked more closely at this woman, her differences to Clémence became more apparent.

"Bruno," the woman said to one of the security guys, "take Ciara to *eat*."

"Wait. I'm hungry, too." Penny stirred in the bed, rolling over as she spoke, her voice still rough and sleepy.

The pale woman laughed. "You can wait," she said. "We've got things to do." She nudged one of the brunette girls she'd brought in with her. "I'll start with you," she said.

"Wait."

After I spoke, the pale woman looked at me, and her eyes turned icy. I almost shivered, but I tensed my muscles and held her gaze.

"Who are you?" Okay, so my question wasn't much, but it was better than nothing at all, and I was supposed to be asking things and finding shit out.

"Nicole," she said, and it had perfect French pronunciation.

I nodded. I had no follow-up questions to ask, although I was totally curious why Ciara had been sent to get something to eat and the rest of us had to remain here.

"I'm Maeve," I said to the closest woman.

"Angelica," she whispered, and she nodded to the other woman with her. "And she's Krissy."

I nodded. "Sister?" I kept my voce down but from the way Nicole angled her head, she could hear every word, and she was listening.

That woman had the hearing of a bat, if that was the case.

And I was just asking the question to tick it off my list. Angelica and Krissy looked as if they could have been twins.

But Angelica shook her head as Nicole drew Krissy forward, toward the rack of beautiful dresses. "Nah, we're just best friends. Been inseparable all our lives. We do everything together." She smiled, but it was just a stretch of her lips. "Although this hasn't been our best experience. Being abducted wasn't such a great idea."

"At least you have each other?" I cringed as I spoke. That was a kind of shitty thing to say, but I often started my mouth up before I put my brain in gear.

"True." Angelica shrugged. "Although I'd rather Krissy didn't have to go through this. Look how thin she's gotten."

I glanced at the other woman. Both of them were far too thin, and it was the reason I'd made my mistake. Ordinarily, they probably didn't look at all like each other, but they were both so hungry and emaciated that they were the same shape now.

Nicole grabbed a floor-length black dress from the rack, and the thin fabric fluttered as she swished it through the air, the movement creating a disturbance in the air.

Penelope shivered next to me. "I'm cold," she whispered.

"You're hungry and tired," I whispered back. "Maybe if we go along with whatever this is, they'll feed us." I glanced at the security guy still by the door. There wasn't any point in making a run for it. He looked like he could snap two of us in half at the same time.

"But they've taken Ciara to get something to eat. Why not us?" Penelope's stomach grumbled as she whined, and I lifted my shoulders in a deliberate shrug.

I had an idea why Ciara's hunger was more pressing than ours, but I couldn't voice it. After all, I'd sound like a proper nutjob if I explained that if they left Ciara hungry, then *we* were probably the food.

"We'll get a turn," I whispered instead. If only I felt as sure as I sounded about that. "At least we have something to keep us occupied right now?" I shrugged again as I gestured toward Nicole and the other two women as Nicole pushed coat hangers to one side on her rack, sending floor-length dresses fluttering with the abrupt movements.

"These are gorgeous!" Krissy's voice was an excited squeal as she ran her hand over some of the fabric. "Which one should I try first?" There was something hysterical about her speech, something too bright-eyed about the way she looked at the dresses.

Was she acting or playing along, desperate to be set free, or were they somehow forcing her cooperation another way?

I stepped back, happy to let someone else be a guinea pig rather than me. All of the dresses were a little too black, a little too like Nicole had raided Morticia Addams's closet on her way here. They all looked funereal, and damn Nicole right to hell if she thought I was dressing up to attend my own funeral.

Or my own virgin sacrifice, or whatever the hell this was.

I cast a quick glance at the women in the room with me. What were the chances we were all virgins? It wasn't like anyone could tell these days or even that we pretended we could anymore. It was just another thing that didn't matter to anyone who was worth our time.

Krissy squealed again as Nicole held a dress against her thin frame. "Oh my God," she exclaimed, as she bunched the fabric in her fists. "It' so pretty!" She glanced up, her eyes alight with out-of-place excitement.

Angelica nodded. "Sure, hon. You're going to look like a princess." But she rolled her eyes a tiny amount at the end of her sentence as Krissy turned her attention back to the dress.

"Can I try it on? What's it made of? Is it expensive?" Krissy peppered Nicole with questions, and Nicole's beatific smile slipped to a strained tug of her lips.

"You all need to choose dresses," Nicole said, the words pointed as she included Penny, Angelica, and me in her audience. She laughed, but it was a grating sound. "You all get to look like princesses." Her voice was as sharp and fragile as ice, and I winced as it sliced through the air between us.

"Maybe we'll find our princes." Krissy looked down at the dress she held against her body as she swayed, making the skirt flare around her legs, like she was dancing at a ball.

Angelica started to shake her head, and I could almost feel her panic saturating the air between us.

But Nicole whipped her head around, her nostrils flaring. "Sounds like a plan," she purred at Krissy while she narrowed her eyes in apparent warning at Angelica.

I shuddered. Whatever was going on tonight wasn't going to be good.

Apparently, Angelica had read a warning in Nicole's expression, too, because she was as quiet as her best friend had been enthusiastic when it was her turn to try the dresses. Her movements were efficient, even though her face was pinched and her fingers formed skeletal claws as she gripped the luxurious fabrics in hands that shook just enough to showcase her fear.

I pressed myself back against the nearest wall, my heart sinking as Nicole eventually dismissed Angelica to the side and turned her focus full beam on me. Still, maybe better me than Penelope. At least I seemed primed to detect something really, truly off here. This wasn't just a normal abduction experience. This was an escape room on crack cocaine, and I hadn't put all of the puzzle pieces together yet.

As Nicole glanced between Penelope and me, seeming to weigh up her options, I stepped in front of my friend, shielding her.

Nicole smiled, and the tip of one of her canines glinted. "Your turn next?" She pointed at me.

I smiled back at her, hoping my effort was even half as mean as hers. "I don't think so. I'm not picking out which dress I die in."

As I spoke, the bedroom door opened, and Ciara was shoved inside the room. She looked between Nicole and me, not even taking a moment to recalibrate to her new surroundings.

"Everything okay?"

"Sure." Having her back filled me with fresh bravado. "I was just telling little miss Fashion Assistant over here that I have no need to be dressed like a reaper on anyone's account today."

Nicole snarled, the sound otherworldly, and her eyes dimmed to a deep ruby red, the color bleeding into the pale blue.

I gasped, but before I could move, Ciara had moved to stand between Nicole and me. It was like she'd beamed herself there somehow. I hadn't seen her take even a step.

Then, as soon as Nicole lunged forward, she was jerking back, clutching her cheek and Ciara was shaking her fist.

"God damn, woman," Ciara said. "Sharp cheekbones much?"

I burbled a nervous giggle at the obvious evidence Ciara had just punched Nicole—shit was definitely about to go down now, and it was maybe the last shit I'd ever see. Especially if we were, as I believed, in the middle of a nest of fucking vampires.

One of the guards jerking my arm cut my giggle off abruptly, and he yanked me toward the door.

"Get off me." The other guard had Ciara and she struggled against his vise-like grip. "Let me go, you bastard." She sent a couple of quick punches to his face and one landed, the resulting meaty sound wet and dense.

The guard growled, but I grew more docile, allowing myself to be pulled along. What the hell had I just seen? Red eyes? Glinting teeth? Movement too fast to be seen?

Hell, even if I was going to die here, I'd find out what was going on first.

Chapter 5 - Francois

A rumbling sound echoed down the hallway outside my room, and I glanced at the doorway. Wheels were turning out there. A cart of some sort. But when a woman—a vampire—I'd never met before rolled it into view, it was a cart full of garment bags.

I stood and swept a mocking bow of welcome. "Step into my parlor…" *Said the spider to the fly.* But I left those words unspoken.

"Francois." She greeted me with a slight incline of her head, her pronunciation of my name perfect.

But who the hell was she?

I smiled. It was a courtly smile. On the verge of being charming, even. I knew that. I'd used that smile often enough through my life to know the effect it had on women. "I seem to be at a disadvantage…?" I let the words trail off in question—a space for her to fill in her name.

She giggled, and the sound tightened all of my muscles and chilled my bones. It was needlessly girlish but it carried a dark, deadly edge underneath. Like she'd smile sweetly while she clawed someone's heart from their chest.

I had no doubt this woman could be a formidable enemy. I filed the knowledge away.

She tossed her hair back, and a wave of sickly, candied perfume washed in my direction, polluting the air around me. "Nicole." She giggled again before adding, "And I'm at your service." She almost purred the last part.

I kept my smile frozen to my face, despite the fact I had no interest in her. She was clearly vampire, but that wasn't the issue. Vampires often mated with vampires or simply used each other for fun. It was often a mutually beneficial relationship given that vampires were a lot less fragile than humans.

But I'd never been interested in having a vampire companion. I'd sought my mate to stave off family madness…and then I'd brought about my own madness in my quest to forget and remove myself from the lifestyle my father had created.

In short, I'd created my own fucking madness. By running from the possibility, I'd run to it.

"Francois?" Nicole's voice intruded on my thoughts. "Shall we begin?"

I renewed my smile to conceal my confusion. Why was she here? How long had I been in lost in my thoughts? I started to shake my head but nodded instead, stepping back a little to allow her farther into my space—but only as far as I decreed.

She tugged the rack of garment bags a little closer, and two male vampires lingered outside the doorway between her.

"Serge and Claude." She waved absently in their direction.

I glanced at them, taking in all I could in the brief moment, making my examination of them look casual and careless. Interesting. The burliest of them stood with his toes right against the doorway, but he ventured no closer. Did the enchantment keep him out as it kept me in?

Or did he simply choose not to cross? Most vampires couldn't work magic, and although we often employed the services of witches, there were still some among us who were suspicious and afraid. That was an interesting trait for a security guard.

"Don't mind Serge." Nicole spoke, answering my internal questions. "He's not long awoken, and there are still some things he's having a hard time with."

I filed away that information, too, and tried to redirect my focus back to Nicole. But it was difficult. The knowledge that my mate was nearby thrummed a steady and unfamiliar beat through my entire being. Hunger gnawed at my gut—for something more satisfying than whatever the Ancients kept providing me with.

My mate's blood would satisfy me. It would cure me. I *needed* her.

Nicole sighed and reached toward the rack, eyeing me as she did so. Her lip curled, revealing sudden distaste. "Maybe they were right about you," she muttered. "The mad prince. Perhaps your mind is gone already."

I remained quiet. It suited me for her to believe whatever she chose to regarding my intelligence or lack thereof. *Especially* lack thereof. I'd learn a lot more that way. Escape from the Ancients and the freedom of New Orleans from whatever reign they had planned would be a long game.

I wasn't usually so patient. Perhaps my time with the Duponts had taught me something. Father would roll in his eternal grave if he hadn't been scattered on the wind. His feud with the Duponts was longstanding and bitter, and I'd always bought into it and been a part of it—but when I considered it now, I'd never truly understood it.

New Orleans had been my home for a very long time indeed, though. No matter how long the Ancients' fought me, I'd fight back. I'd wait. I'd win. New Orleans belonged to no one but me.

Well, and currently Nicolas Dupont. But it had always been my city.

And I would save it.

"You have no idea of the power under your roof right now." Nicole spoke again as she turned her back to me, clacking impatiently through the coat hangers. Her voice was little more than a murmur but it was as if she'd forgotten that I was also vampire, that my hearing was at least as good as hers—if not better because I could almost guarantee I had age on my side.

Age didn't usually debilitate vampires the way it did humans. We usually grew stronger rather than weaker, frailer. In that way, my father's frequent bouts of stasis had been unusual. His weakness had made him vulnerable, so he had molded me.

But perhaps Nicole merely thought me crazy after all, rather than deaf—and either way unlikely to respond to her or maybe even likely to retain the information.

"Comment, mon ange?" I threw myself onto my chaise as I lazily asked her to repeat herself. I didn't need her to. After all, I was neither deaf nor crazy, but she didn't need to know that. Well, not *entirely* crazy, at least.

She smiled as she turned to face me, and it was extra bright, extra wattage, extra false. "I have the perfect suit for you to wear this evening."

I glanced at my frilled cuffs.

Her smile faded. "Something far more modern than you're wearing now. I can tailor it to you. Make the most of…" She chewed her lower lip as fleeting longing crossed her face. "Everything." She flapped her hands ineffectively toward me as her gaze dropped to my crotch.

I smiled although I felt nothing. Usually, if an attractive woman looked as though she literally wanted to eat me, my body responded. But not this time. My thoughts were only for my mate. "So. The suit."

She frowned slightly in response to my barely worded statement. "There are people for you to meet."

"Ah, yes." The party Clémence had mentioned. She'd made it sound important. "And I need a new suit?"

"Of course." Nicole's lip curled. "When I said there are people for you to meet, I meant there are *important* people."

"Mais oui…" I nodded as I agreed with her, deliberately playing dumb. "And I am dressed in my finest, oui?" I held out my arm, observing the dirt clinging to the lace as it partly concealed my hand.

She sniffed but didn't say anything, her disapproval plain.

I narrowed my eyes at her back as she turned and fussed with something still hanging on the rack. She wouldn't treat me like this if I was still Prince of New Orleans.

Her disrespect displeased me, and memories of my old life crowded my brain again. I could have been drunk on that power. Maybe sometimes I had been.

I opened my mouth to challenge her, but a pale woman flickered into being at the edge of my view, and I stopped. No, I'd been right before. I had to play along with whatever the Ancients wanted. It was my best shot at achieving a future. I looked directly at my ghost.

She was mine in all ways. She visited me, I'd created her. And now she'd brought me back to my senses.

"I'll change." I bit out the words but softened then with a deliberately slow smile. Something a little suggestive, in case she turned around. "Shall we see how I look, *chérie?*"

Nicole's back stiffened at my use of the endearment *darling*. "Take your time." She waved awkwardly toward the small bathroom.

I looked at myself in the mirror, laughing at the beliefs humans still held about vampires having no reflection. If only we were so easy to spot.

I held my arm out and grimaced at my cuff. It finished so…so…short. Where was the drape of fabric, the flamboyance, in modern clothing? Why were men no longer peacocks, presenting themselves in riches and finery, *offering* themselves to ladies? I shook my head. That much in life was a competition, surely? Although, I'd never found my princess or my mate before. So maybe the clothing didn't matter.

I knew exactly where my mate was now, and I still couldn't access her.

"Looking good, Francois."

I whirled around at the musical voice and the slightly grating laugh that followed it. "Maybe you should have updated your wardrobe before now."

I tried to focus on the ghost, but she was fuzzy.

"Eh…" I behaved like I was considering her suggestion, examining my sleeve again. "Non."

She laughed again, the sound less grating this time, like it was getting easier to do. "You need to be strong."

I shivered at the warning in her words, but when I started to ask for more details, she'd already faded from view, returning to wherever ghosts lingered—whatever I'd condemned her to. Perhaps she was still here, simply out of sight. I hadn't paid enough attention to that area of the supernatural community, and why would I have? Ghosts visited those they chose to, and they held allegiance to no king. They earned no place on the regular censuses I'd carried out. We were equally as useless to each other.

Except no longer.

My ghost seemed to have a use for me now. Or I for her. I couldn't tell yet.

I dressed as best I could in the suit Nicole had left me, studying myself in the mirror one last time before I returned to the butler's parlor to wait for my next instructions. Oui, I looked sharp. But I didn't truly look like myself. The man in the mirror, dressed in these clothes, was a stranger.

That realization jarred me. My entire world had shifted, and maybe nothing illustrated that better than this exact moment. Everything I knew had changed. Nothing was the same. Not even me.

I sat on the chaise as I waited, until a shadow loomed over me.

"Come." The voice was deep and resonant, but it belonged to a young vampire. I hadn't seen him before, but he was dressed the same as the guards from earlier.

It seemed the Ancients were very security conscious.

I sighed and stood. Showtime. I followed the vampire through hallways as familiar as my own face. *Mon Dieu*...I'd played in this house probably even before this guy was born the first time, let alone when he was turned, and now here he was presuming to show me the way to our destination.

The dining room, of course. The house had barely changed during my latest stay here. Part of me was relieved the Ancients hadn't ripped through and changed anything, but the other part of me was merely amused.

Of course they hadn't changed anything. If Clémence was right, and Father had been one of them, they probably all had similar tastes. I grinned. *Taste* was such a subjective concept. I'd only modernized one room in this house, but I'd had plans for more.

My nose twitched. It had been a long time since I'd smelled food in these halls. And it was interesting, because that suggested this dinner wasn't vampires only, although how humans factored into the interest of the Ancients, I couldn't say.

It was more information I could gather for Nic, though.

The young guard stopped just outside the dining room, and he almost bowed as I continued past him. It had been a long time since anyone had bowed to me, and I quashed the feeling of being back where I belonged. There was a seductive satisfaction there that I didn't want to take hold.

I glanced around the room of assembled people. Apparently, important people. A few were vampires allegedly loyal to the Dupont cause. I paid particular attention to them, memorizing their faces for when I'd have the chance to settle the score.

Unexpected feelings of loyalty for Nicolas rushed through me. I'd ensure the traitors in his house were dealt with.

But merde. When had I become as good as a Dupont myself? Merely a year ago, I would have accepted any bargain the Ancients presented me with. I would have secured my reign—Father's reign—at the expense of anything and anyone else. That would have been easy for me.

Only they wouldn't have helped control my blood like Nicolas did. They wouldn't have shown mercy. I would have been utterly theirs to command.

Perhaps Nicolas had allowed me freedom at his own expense. Certainly it seemed a little that way now. I could have been plotting to overthrow him all along. Did he doubt me? The thought stung.

I sat in the first empty chair I arrived at, more determined than ever to prove to Nicolas that I deserved a place in his territory.

The silence that had fallen when I entered the room became covered with chatter that escalated as each voice competed with the next to be heard, to make the owner the most important person in the room.

My nose twitched again. Not at the scent of food still drifting on the air from the kitchens, but from a sudden hint of warm bodies and perfumed hair. Human females. My fangs pushed at my gums, and I rubbed my hands over my face, seeking control.

They were led into the room, each unfamiliar, although I scanned each one, looking for the familiar curly hair that belonged to Ciara. Or the red flames that belonged to my mate, lighting my heart. Neither were there, and I breathed a small sigh of relief. That was a small mercy—although I tried not to consider the worse alternatives to them not being here.

The humans giggled, the anxiety on show as they twisted their hands in front of them before being led to empty seats. Each was seated away from the next. They were adrift in a room of vampires, and it was unlikely they knew.

Plates were set in front of the humans, and they glanced nervously at those of us not eating before their instincts took over and they forked large amounts of food into their mouths. There were no manners here. Simply pure, animalistic hunger.

There was another noise at the door, and two guards appeared. I sat up straighter. This day just grew more and more interesting.

When the first Ancient stepped inside, I inhaled. Not because I needed the breath, but because the surprise prompted an instinct older than I was.

Ruse, the man who'd just entered the room, looked around, his gaze lighting on me as he did. I fought the urge to shrink back, make myself smaller. Last time I'd seen him, I'd been a boy. I hadn't known what he was, only that he had power that rolled off him and chilled any room he entered. He'd been as good as my boogeyman.

He nodded, apparently acknowledging my flash of recognition, and I inclined my head in return. I was grown now. No longer scared of these powerful vampires. Out of the two of us, I was arguably more crazy, anyway.

Clémence stood briefly as she waited for Ruse to take a seat beside her. I looked more carefully at the assembled vampires. Aside from Nicolas's assorted traitors, I recognized more than I'd originally thought. Aleron sat a few seats down the table, his expression as disdainful as I remembered. He'd always looked at me as though I might infect him with some sort of disease, and I'd enjoyed tormenting him by wiping sticky fingers across his fragile skin whenever I found the opportunity.

Yet while I was no longer scared of these men and women, the ones with the thin skin and the dried-out voices who'd visited Father and held meetings punctuated by low, vehement voices behind closed doors, a shiver of something akin to fear ran through me when Ruse remained standing and Clémence retook her seat.

"Thank you for coming." Ruse sounded every inch the benevolent host. He held his arms out. "And thank you especially to our human friends, who might find our politics boring and our ways…unusual."

The human female closest to me paused in her eating for a moment, lifting her gaze to Ruse before her plate recaptured her focus again.

Pity replaced my fear. The *unusual* ways of vampires rarely ended well for humans.

"As you know," Ruse continued, "we're here to consolidate, to educate, and eventually…" He smiled coldly and looked carefully around as if to ensure we were all listening to him. "To celebrate. New Orleans and Baton Rouge will come back under our rule. No false pretenders to the reign. We are the old guard returned as rightful rulers, and we will usher in a new era, here in the Americas. We've already started. New York City has fallen."

There was a smattering of applause at this point, but I sat, listening, stone-faced.

Clémence glared at me, but I lifted one shoulder in a slight shrug. Political posturing had always bored me. It could be dangerous to appear interested now.

"Loyalty has already been pledged all over Europe." This statement earned him a few cheers, and he smiled in response. "Not that we're surprised, of course. Our homelands have always been loyal." He started to sit then seemed to change his mind, waiting a moment before he rose back to standing. "And it's loyalty I sense here in this room. We are all blood, after all." His glance at me seemed especially meaningful, and I fought to keep emotion from my face, instead nodding slightly again.

The movement itself meant nothing more than that I'd heard him, but Ruse didn't know that.

"But now—" This time he really did sit as he laughed. "We eat." He gestured widely with his arms, encompassing everyone at the table.

Nausea sat in my stomach. Our food was already at the table. Our food was eating.

At least Ciara and my mate weren't here. They weren't currently part of this ridiculous show in any way. I tried to see that as a positive even as I felt a nearly uncontrollable yearning to see my mate, smell her, taste her, hold her and keep her safe.

My ghost appeared by the door, silently watching. She'd told me to be strong but so far there's been nothing I'd needed to be strong about—

I stopped myself mid-thought as Aleron leapt from his chair, his face already contorted to that of a killer with prominent cheekbones and descended fangs. He ran, his movement almost a blur until he reached the female farthest from him. He took her into his arms and moaned long and low as his fangs pierced her neck.

There was no seduction here, no showmanship, no peacocking or wooing, and I stared at my ghost as I curled my fingers around the wooden seat of my chair, holding myself in place.

She watched me back without recrimination or bitterness as the room filled with the sounds of sucking and bliss. I couldn't look away. I didn't want to see what the others were doing. I didn't want to see anything else.

The human Aleron had grabbed had fought initially until her body slackened as the strength of his venom and its presence in her bloodstream wooed her into a false trap of safety.

My fangs pushed at my gums again, but I clamped my lips shut and closed my eyes as I fought to find my silence. I needed to will myself away from this room and the temptation to feed.

But before my self-control deserted me, the sounds of sucking stopped and I opened my eyes as the Ancients and other vampires let bodies thump to the floors and nearest surfaces. They'd drunk them dry.

I closed my eyes again, fighting the urge to order everyone from my house. They had to know the dangers, the risk of exposure. But I looked at my ghost and thought of my garden… I hadn't always been so careful.

As if summoned by an inaudible bell, several servants and more guards entered the room and they efficiently cleared the corpses, lifting them without any regard for the life that had once been contained within them. They were just skin sacks, now. They held no worth to anyone here at all.

I steeled myself against a wave of guilt. I'd been that way. Before Nicolas.

But I'd always reasoned that I'd had a purpose. I was searching for my mate, for a cure.

It wasn't enough.

I'd been a monster.

Perhaps I was still a monster but I had a new cause. I needed to find my mate and Ciara and we needed to get the hell out of here to help the Duponts. I couldn't fail on any one of those three things.

The stakes were too high.

Chapter 6 - Maeve

Guards led us through various hallways and corridors, and the smell of food emanating from somewhere teased my nose. My stomach grumbled in response, and I clamped my hand over it. We seemed to walk miles through hallways, but in reality, I was just shuffling and weak.

I pushed myself to take every step forward. I hadn't realized how much being in one room had impacted my overall fitness, and that was a worry. I'd never be able to overpower a vampire if I couldn't manage a short walk through an old house.

Because I was almost certain now that's what they all were. They seemed to match enough lore, anyway. And more than that…I just felt it. Like a gut instinct that I was somehow right.

Dad had always laughed when Granny had referred to her gut or feeling something *in her waters* and I hadn't fully understood what she meant, but I did now. It was like knowing a fact without any doubt it was true despite having no proof to back it up. I would have called it faith, but it was more visceral than that. There was no room for doubt.

A scream echoed from somewhere deeper in the house, and I flinched before looking around.

"What was—" I started my question in a whisper but Ciara grabbed my wrist, halting the flow of words.

She shook her head, her lips pressed together, her gaze boring into mine.

Okay…so talking was a bad thing to do. I automatically flexed my fingers as Ciara's grip relaxed and then I rubbed my wrist. Shit. There was some strength in that woman— which only added to my… I hesitated over the word *theory*.

Certainty. It added to my certainty that I was in a house of vampires.

I was a human inside a vampire nest, which made my situation unlikely to continue, if I was honest with myself. People in this house were already injured, dead, or dying, if the screams were anything to go by. There was no best outcome, either. Being kept as a blood slave would be no better than being drained dry all at once.

There was certainly an irony if I made the biggest discovery of my career—and could prove it to the world— but died to do it and before I could tell anyone at all. I almost rolled my eyes at myself.

Dying wasn't an option then. If I could prove vampires existed, I was going to damn well stay alive to do that.

The guards drew us down a corridor that sloped downward, and the air became damp. Damp but not truly wet, which was interesting. Anything below ground level here should have been flooded, but we appeared to be approaching some sort of sublevel.

I trailed my hand against the rough stone wall, and it almost vibrated under my fingertips, sending a hum up my arm. *Magic.* The word appeared in my head and it was another certainty—the same way I knew I was among vampires. Some instinct deep inside me just understood things no rational person would ever believe.

And anyway, how else could I be in an underground room in the bayou? It just didn't happen. What was that saying about excluding the impossible, and whatever remained, no matter how improbable, being the truth? I almost laughed at myself. Perhaps it depended on what I considered the difference between impossible and improbable.

Although… Sherlock Holmes and me. We would have made quite the pair.

The guard stopped in front of a low wooden door set into the wall. The earthy, damp scent was replaced by something sharp and tangy, something almost coppery. I could taste it, and it irritated my tongue. It was as if I'd been sucking on pennies, and I swallowed against the bitterness of it, coughing as it caught at the back of my throat.

I glanced at Ciara. She'd wrinkled her nose and looked almost frozen somewhere between disgust and horror. Her gaze darted between the door and the guard, and her chest no longer rose or fell, as though she'd stopped drawing air in, like she didn't want this smell inside her or she didn't want to risk taking in a breath.

A stain had formed at the small gap where the door met the floor, as if liquid had crept under the threshold, before absorbing into whatever porous material the floor was made of, and it was too dark and shadowed to tell the color, but I could guess what that liquid was.

The guard flung the door open and gestured into the small room.

Ciara hesitated.

"Get in there, wolf," the guard snarled, and half pushed her through the doorway as she tried to step over the dark stain.

It still glistened wetly in some patches, and I stepped over it as I followed closer behind Ciara. She still seemed the safest person to stick with, although I had a hard time drawing my breath now, and my blood rushed through my ears, creating a pounding sound that drowned out most other noise.

"You okay?" Ciara's words were muffled and muted as she looked at me.

I watched her lips move but my nodded response was automatic as I surveyed the room we stood in. There was a drain in the middle of the floor, and more dark staining soaked into the floor around that.

Other than that, there was one small bed—barely even a bed—in the corner. It had some sort of rickety frame and a mattress so thin it might have been steamrolled into shape. There was a rust-spotted, time-marked mirror on one wall and also a bucket in the corner, and I wrinkled my nose.

Two of us.

One bed.

One bucket.

Lots of stains.

This room was so different from the faded elegance of where we'd been kept before. And where the hell was Penelope? Were they picking us off one by one? I swallowed. What chance did that leave me?

"What the hell are you thinking?" For a second, Ciara's eyes seemed to blaze red. "You can't just put us in here.

They'll come, you know. My mate will come. What do you think you're going to do then? You can't explain this away." She gestured around the small room with her arm.

I shivered. *Small room* was a kind way to describe it. It was little more than a dungeon.

The guard laughed as Ciara folded her arms and scowled at him, her eyes returning to that dull red color.

"Stay here." The guard laughed again as he reached for the thick, wooden door to pull it closed behind him.

Ciara made a frustrated noise as the door thumped shut in the thick wall, and she closed her eyes as though willing her patience back into place.

Her hands were fists at her sides, and I could almost see her counting, seeking that imaginary ten that too many people believed would make any situation okay again, but she was perfectly still.

"So." My voice came out louder than I'd intended as I walked and sat on the bed. Exactly as I'd expected, it was hard and uncomfortable, but I attempted to look comfortable as I lounged against the wall.

There'd be a plan. If Ciara was what I thought, there'd definitely be a plan.

Hopefully, though, the plan wasn't using me as her food source as she waited for rescue. I glanced at the drain. It seemed a current possibility.

Ciara glanced at me before putting as much room between us as she could, leaning against the wall, her hands behind her back. "So...?" She raised an eyebrow as she prompted me, and her eyes had returned to their usual, familiar color. A *human* color.

"What's the plan?" I shrugged. I hadn't rehearsed this part. I was full-on winging it. "You going to drain me dry?" Well, shit. Winging it didn't mean ramming my foot so far into my mouth that I choked on it.

Ciara's mouth opened. Then closed. Then opened again.

But only air came out before she closed it a final time and just looked at me.

It was a hard stare, too. Like I was suddenly sitting in front of my high school principal, and that had never been a pleasant experience. The memory of her royal blue shoes—shoes that never matched any of her outfits—and the sound they made as she'd stalked the hallways or moved around her huge desk to sit behind it and stare at me for the billionth time across an ocean of wood—

haunted me for a moment, and I lost my ability to string words together.

"The drain…" I mumbled. "Stains. Red eyes."

Ciara tilted her head as she watched me, but she didn't speak.

I closed my eyes. Something about her gaze was a little unnerving. The laser focus, perhaps, although I didn't feel like prey. More like she was studying something she didn't understand.

"What's the deal with the eye color?" There. A sensible question. "And what's a mate?" I added, although I had a pretty good idea. It was self-explanatory, and a term I'd only really come across in refences to the supernatural.

Sometimes, it made me think that finding my exact other person would be a bonus far exceeding the existence of repeated wading in the swamp of online dating. There seemed to be nothing to catch in there but cooties.

Yes, the idea that fate would provide all I needed in a man was…reassuring. As I considered the supernatural world, an image of the mad prince returned to my thoughts. There was something about him… despite his *alternative* dress sense. He definitely needed dragging into this century.

I grimaced. Not that I was offering… Not that I was offering *at all*.

I pushed him from my head. I didn't have time for intrusive, unwanted thoughts about men I didn't know…even if something about him piqued my interest. My *professional* interest, of course. Only ever that.

Ciara sighed and looked down at the floor. She looked down so long that it seemed she wasn't going to say anything in reply.

When I grew uncomfortable, and shifted my position, she finally refocused her attention on me.

"It's a lot," she said.

"What's a lot?" I worked out a kink in my left calf, massaging the spot idly with my fingers.

"If I tell you, it's a lot to process." She spoke slowly, like she was saying each word as the thought occurred to her. "I know it's a lot to process because it was a lot to process for me. Even…" She hesitated and blew out a deep sigh. "Even knowing everything I already knew." Then she laughed, almost looking embarrassed as she rolled her eyes. "I think I only *thought* I knew some of the stuff." She nodded and grinned as she looked right at me. "I know a hell of a lot more now."

I pinched myself to keep my excitement in. "New rule, Ciara. If you think it, you have to say it."

She wrinkled her nose. "What? Why?"

"Because there's a lot you won't tell me if you don't take that rule seriously." I focused on still seeming casual, even as anticipation hummed through me.

I was on the verge of something big. It was like she was about to confirm every legend I'd ever read. The air in the room had thickened like even the building was waiting, and the magic I'd felt before buzzed against my skin, heightening my expectation.

"A mate is…" Ciara still spoke slowly, her brow furrowed, and I withheld my sigh.

This wasn't the interesting part, damnit.

"A soulmate, I get it." I waved my hand as I interrupted her. "But I suppose the real question is… Why say *mate* instead of *husband* or *boyfriend*?" Those were the normal words, right? The ones that society more usually used and expected as ways for describing significant others, really.

"Because—" She stopped. "It's a different commitment."

I raised both of my eyebrows. "Longer?"

"Forever," she whispered.

"I think maybe you need to just tell me everything." I needed to hear her say the damn words. I didn't want to put them in her mouth for her.

She sighed before sinking to the floor, looking graceful even as she drew her long legs up against her. "I'm not exactly human."

"Whoop!" I fist pumped before I could stop myself from making any sudden movements or openly celebrating.

"What?" She tilted her head again.

"I knew it," I mumbled. "I knew there was something here. It's the reason I came. Continue." I gestured, suddenly all regal and gracious like I could actually tell her what to do, but really just trying to style out my ridiculous show of enthusiasm.

She lifted an eyebrow. "Like I'm not human at all."

I held my overactive fist in my other hand, anchoring it in my lap. But my enthusiasm spilled out of my mouth, instead. There was no containing it. "I knew it! Vampire? You're too fast and too strong to be fae. And your eyes are red sometimes. And I assume people around here…" I glanced at the drain and the staining on the floor again. "I assume they drink blood."

The corners of her lips twitched like she was withholding a smile. "You already have theories?"

"Theories?" I scoffed. Theories and hypotheses and suppositions. And a damn blog full of proof if only more people would read the thing. "There are things that I *know*." And again, I couldn't explain it. I did just know. "Somehow."

"Mmhmm." But she didn't look convinced. "Well, whatever you think you know, the things I'm about to tell you are probably going to blow your mind."

I shook my head. "Absolutely not. I can handle vampires." If I'd expected her to be shocked at my use of the word, I was disappointed.

She merely raised an eyebrow. "And shifters?"

Damnit. I fist-fucking-pumped again. I couldn't help it. I mean, talk of vampires was one thing, but to have Ciara confirm shifters for me as well?

Holy shit. What a win. I could prove two of the biggest things I'd ever investigated.

"What kind of shifters?" I asked my question like that mattered. She could've been about to introduce me to the world of snail shifters, and I wouldn't have given a shit.

She sighed again. "Look. I can't lie. This isn't a good situation."

I nodded, agreeing with her. This was a shit situation. About as shitty as situation could get.

"This is a death situation," I said. "I know what it is. So you might as well spill, right? Dead men tell no tales, after all." I followed my corny line with a dark laugh, and Ciara winced.

"There's every chance I *won't* die, though." She looked almost apologetic.

I puffed my cheeks as I blew out a sigh. "The perks of being an immortal vampire."

"I'm half wolf shifter." She lowered her voice to the point I almost had to lip read.

"A hybrid?" I squeaked out the words. "Holy shit, Ciara!"

She motioned with her hands—the universally accepted *lower the volume* gesture, and I waited a moment before speaking again, barely moving my lips—as if that made a difference somehow.

"Do they know?"

She shrugged before speaking in the same barely there voice as before. "I'm not sure. Sometimes I wonder how they can possibly not know. Other times, they seem clueless." Then she adopted a more normal tone. "You're not reacting the way you should be."

It was my turn to shrug. "I thought I'd said I'm a paranormal blogger?" Maybe I shouldn't reveal everything about my history and Granny. Just an overview of recent events would do for now. "I investigate the supernatural and anything out of the ordinary. I've been low key following events at a local nightclub for a while now— maybe you know it? It's called Nightfall." I barely waited for her confirmatory nod before I continued. "But then I saw some grainy footage of this…guy…something falling…but not really falling, you know?" I struggled as I tried to describe the video I'd stumbled across late one night. "The guy looked like he was being lowered. It was controlled. Sometimes he hovered. There was a blown-out apartment behind him. Anyway, I came as soon as I could."

"And how's that working out for you?" Ciara half chuckled as she asked the question.

I made a show of glancing around. "So far, the accommodation isn't getting a five-star rating. Not sure about this New Orleans hospitality I'd heard about."

Ciara laughed. "We're usually better than this, to be honest. Maybe not my pack—we're not very open to outsiders, but New Orleans is built for tourists."

"So what gives? Who was that guy? The flying one?" I had so many questions, and we had nothing but time to kill.

Now that Ciara had started to open up, it was time for me to get my answers.

"Oh, that was Francois." She sounded pretty off-hand about it.

"He can fly?" That was a part of the lore I'd never believed. The whole vampires turning into bats or just flying like witches without brooms was a bit too superhero-esque for something so dark and…well, dead.

"No." Ciara laughed again. "We don't fly."

"I didn't think you did. Glad to be proved right on that. So what was going on? Magic?" I hadn't thought they were magic-users either, though.

"Mmm." She nodded. "You're here at a bad time, to be honest. It's a long story, really, but the Baton Rouge King took over New Orleans, and we should have had stability, but some older vampires have waged a challenge. We don't know much about them—they're called the Ancients—and they have powers we don't. They seem to be able to wield magic. They've come to take over, though."

"Shit." The word came out on a breath, and my nervous anticipation ramped up to almost excitement levels. "I know I should be scared—like really scared—but I'm already facing death in the face, right? What does it matter the kind of vampire who brings that about? Tell me as much as you can. Will we be rescued?" I hadn't meant for that question to stop me in my tracks, but it did. "Yeah. Will we be rescued?" The excitement inside me died down.

Ciara's brow furrowed. "You have no idea how badly I want to tell you yes. I know they'll try. I'm the sister of the alpha of the local wolf shifter pack. That means he's the head, basically. Like their king or their boss. He's in charge. So we should definitely have some angry wolves on the warpath." A fleeting grimace crossed her mouth. "I hope. But even if they can't help, my mate is the sireling of the King of Baton Rouge and New Orleans. That means that the king—Nic—turned him into a vampire." She explained the various terms like I didn't know anything at all. After a short pause, she nodded. "You know what? They'll come. I'm sure of it. They're planning and strategizing and they're on the way. I have absolute faith in that."

But I shrank down a little on the uncomfortable mattress. I'd never been someone who relied on faith. I believed in things I could prove—hence the blog, hence the evidence gathering…hence this goddamn trip to New Orleans.

I stared at the closed door and I stared at the drain in the floor. The mirror reflected my despair back at me, the reverse image of the room mocking. This was a very, very bad situation indeed.

Chapter 7 - Francois

The room was empty of humans and their remains now—technically and actually devoid of life. The other vampires moaned their satisfaction like the drunks I'd seen in The Neutral Zone, when that had been my club, before Nicolas put Sebastian in charge and changed things.

I stiffened in anticipation of a wave of regret, but I felt nothing. Literally nothing. I no longer cared about ruling New Orleans or being the center of political machinations here. I'd been Father's stand-in during his times of stasis, and I'd thought I wanted to be his heir… But maybe I hadn't.

Maybe I *didn't*.

I glanced around the table. Especially if being his heir meant being an Ancient.

Their paper-like skin seemed to glow almost eerily in the lengthening shadows of the early evening. I'd never really noticed the same characteristics in Father. But of course he'd shared them. It was all so clear now that I could look back, untainted by living in that moment.

Ruse stood, the movement abrupt as he didn't even attempt to conceal his vampire speed. I'd grown far more used to lazy movements if I was trying to conceal my true nature rather than scare local humans away.

"And now for a tour," Ruse said, his voice booming with fake geniality, a fang peeking from under his top lip. "Francois, if you would be so kind?"

If my attention had been wandering before, I focused on him now. He expected me to give them a tour of my home? What was I? The after-dinner entertainment?

He narrowed his eyes at my silence, and pain shot between my temples.

Then I also stood, my movements jerky and uncoordinated as I fought against whatever force was compelling me.

"Now, now, Francois." Ruse's voice remained cheery, but his face was hard, without a trace of amusement. "I'm sure you'd like to show us around this lovely home."

"Indeed." I gritted my teeth as pain flashed through my head again. "Where would you like to start? Upstairs?"

Ruse shook his head. "Oh, no, I think the lower floors are far more interesting. Particularly anything subterranean in this city. Impossible rooms belonging to impossible people, don't you think?" He looked around the table, inviting the rest of the Ancients and guest vampires to share his enthusiasm. "Impossibilities proving just how much is possible for our kind here." When he nodded, everyone around the table nodded along with him—even me, although again, my movement wasn't my own.

"Right this way." My teeth were still clenched as I left the table and walked toward the door, barely even pausing to ensure I was being followed by the collective in the room.

I wasn't a good tour guide. I didn't keep up an interesting patter of family anecdotes or facts about the house. Ruse had an ulterior motive for wanting to look around, and he probably wasn't truly interested in any of the past my family had built here.

I reached the door that led to the basement. Only basement sounded too grand. The rooms were barely serviceable. They'd been speedily and roughly carved into the spaces beneath the house before being enchanted by magic strong enough to keep them dry. Even with that protection, there was still an undeniable odor of damp and swamp, like nature hovered, threatening to retake what we'd stolen.

"Why down here?" I paused with my hand on the doorhandle and spoke my first words since leaving the dining room.

Ruse shrugged, his grin malevolent. "Humor me."

Aleron sneered behind him, the slight movement of his mouth almost making his thin skin rustle. "Just like his father." His voice was little more than a wheeze. "Too much independence in him. Not enough thought for his family."

"Open the door." Ruse bit out a command in the same tone my father had always used, and my hand moved as if by itself, pushing the handle down and opening the door.

A wave of cooler air met us, a sweet scent twined in the usual damp aroma, and my nose twitched. I walked toward the source of the scent as though compelled, although I was fairly sure Ruse wasn't doing anything this time.

"What's this space?" Aleron interrupted my instinct to keep moving forward as he touched my shoulder to get my attention.

I flinched away from him then consciously relaxed. Showing them any weakness at all was a bad thing. But sudden adrenaline thundered through me, as if the situation had just ramped up, and I didn't entirely understand why.

I swallowed and waved an arm, trying to channel my usual disposition. "Oh, the holding cells." I cringed a little as I spoke, at the memories of the humans I'd held down here.

So much waste.

I'd only seen potential. Each of those humans could have been the one. *My* one. Except they weren't.

And they never would have been.

My one had shown up here without any guidance or…encouragement from me. Fate had brought her right to my door.

I almost laughed.

Useless. Fate had brought my mate to my door when I couldn't even access her.

My need for a well-timed Nicolas Dupont rescue grew ever more fierce. I'd seen him do it before. He'd fucking come for Leia's father, for fuck's sake.

But of course he'd come for Leia's father. Leia was his mate.

I was not his mate.

And I'd killed Leia's father.

Fuck. *Putain.*

I inhaled again—slowly, deliberately. My mate, she was down here.

"Next left, Francois."

I automatically reacted to Ruse's instruction, opening the door at my side before walking into a tiny viewing room. Immediately, goosebumps rose on my arms.

I'd spent many hours in this small room. Lurking. Watching. Plotting.

"Where are we?" Aleron sounded almost gleeful as he entered the small space. "Oh, my…" He merely breathed the words as he glanced toward the small viewing window.

It was a two-way mirror, and anyone on the other side of the wall had no idea they were being watched.

I looked up, my gaze focusing like a laser on the two women on the other side. Ciara…She was there. They'd put her in with a human. Poor human.

But…not any human. My nose twitched. That was definitely my mate's scent.

I looked at the redheaded woman on the small cot. Even as I recognized that she was too thin, lust sparked to life in front of me.

"Now this is a feeding frenzy I'd like to see." Clémence spoke quietly. "That one has far too much control." She nodded at Ciara, and I made tight fists as I fought the growl of ownership that threatened to rumble through me.

Ciara had control. The idea was like a balm that soothed a little of my tension. Maybe my mate would be okay.

But I couldn't function on maybes. I needed to be sure of it.

A flicker of movement in the cell caught my attention, and then a barely formed ghost sat next to my mate on the bed. She drew her knees to her chest and tucked her arms around her legs, a pose that was all too familiar from the way she'd sat in that room before.

This was different, though.

She wasn't all out of hope. She *was* my hope.

"Do you know why they're here. Francois?"

Lost in my thoughts, I jumped at Ruse's voice. My mouth dried, but I forced out an answer. "Food?"

He laughed, but when Ciara glanced toward the wall between us, he lowered his volume. "Oh, Francois." He pouted a little, the expression ridiculous on his face. He tutted. "Non, mon ami. Non."

I shuddered as he called me his friend. I'd never be that. Not while he was trying to overthrow Nicolas, and certainly not while he held my mate in a cell.

Every fiber of my being vibrated with the need to tear the wall between us down and rescue her. Claws began to form from my fingernails, the tips digging into the skin of my palms. I bowed my head in case my features started to change. I couldn't afford to lose control just now and I couldn't let the others see.

"Your father—" Ruse adopted a tone like a genial grandfather might use to tell a favored grandchild a bedtime story, but I wasn't comfortable or ready for him to begin.

There were too many other thoughts crowding my mind.

"Émile," he said unnecessarily—like I'd forgotten my own father's name. "When he left us, he had with him an important book."

"Oh?" I tried to sound midway between couldn't care less and somewhat interested. Like it didn't matter to me at all, but still, the more information I could learn, the better.

Clémence glanced at me, the look in her eyes sharp. "You need to pay attention to this, Francois. You're the heir, and it's in your best interests to help us reform." Her gaze clouded a little. "Imagine the power we can amass when we are one again."

I nodded. "I see what you mean." I couldn't have cared less what she meant.

"If I can continue?" Ruse intended to continue whether I granted my permission or not, so I remained quiet. "Quite simply, we need that book back. So…" He gestured to the two-way mirror. "You can see that we've already made use of your little dungeon set-up. The vampire in there is the mate of one of the Duponts, and she's also the sister of the local wolf shifter alpha, I believe." He passed and examined his nails. "That makes her really quite valuable."

When I didn't immediately respond, Clémence answered and looked at him with the kind of reverence I would have expected to have been reserved for if she saw a god walking among us. "Indeed."

"The human is…probably expendable." He frowned. "But she has fire, so we brought her, too. If we can push the vampire into losing control through her, all the better. Eventually, she'll turn on her." He shrugged, making it clear how little that fact bothered him, and I couldn't smother my growl this time.

Clémence gave a lazy, throaty chuckle, but her fingers were steel around my upper arm. "Why such an *interesting* reaction to the fate of a human, I wonder?" She tapped her free forefinger against her lips and raised one perfectly shaped eyebrow.

I shook her hold from me as I took a step away from her. Then I let my fangs show. "Simple hunger, my sweet Clémence."

She grinned and touched the tip of her tongue to one of her own fangs. "I think I know what you mean."

I almost sighed in relief—the last thing I wanted any of these vampires to know was how important that human was. She'd become my whole world the moment I saw her, and I needed to hide that fact from them if I didn't want them to have anything to use against me—or her.

Humans who belonged to vampires, who were destined to be their mates, had always been used as leverage. After all, we were territorial creatures with very few scruples. Being long-lived shed a lot of the minutiae of being human. Over time, we simply learned to live without regret. Without compassion at all, really, for some of us.

I'd been headed in that direction myself before Nicolas had shown me unexpected kindness.

Aleron watched me. Damn that man. He always watched me, and there was always something like suspicion in his gaze. He was trying to catch me out. The Ancients might have told me they needed me, but Aleron certainly didn't *want* to need me. And maybe he'd do anything to prove to the others that I didn't belong.

"Simply put, Francois," Aleron said—as though he'd decided to handle this negotiation now. "If you don't get that book for us, both of these females will die."

My rage screamed inside my head until I couldn't hear anything else. It took me a moment to regain control.

"Then why have you taken a Dupont mate? Do you not think that will bring Nicolas Dupont to our door before we've discovered the book's location? Not to mention the local wolf shifter population. Do we need a house overrun with wolves?" Even to my own ears, I sounded dismissive. I needed to sound dismissive.

It would be dangerous to sound too invested.

"Wolves?" Aleron laughed loudly, not bothering to conceal the fact we were here. "Fucking *wolves*? We've been putting those dogs down for years. But they just won't stay down. Too many pups. No, let them fucking come. This way, we can eradicate the whole pack at once. Still, if you don't want to be distracted by the New Orleans pack, I suggest you find our book quickly."

As he looked away like he'd grown bored of our conversation, and I stared at my mate in the other room. Hell, the stakes were rising. I had a mate to protect, a book to find, a pack to prevent from slaughter… How could I do all of that? The Ancients didn't even feed me properly. Any moment, my madness could reclaim me.

"My mind…" I blurted the words, clutching at straws as my mate's scent teased my nose. Could the rest of them not smell this? I was lucky if they couldn't.

"What's on your mind, mon chou?" Clémence ruffled my hair. "You always were a sensitive soul, even as a child."

"Dead man's blood."

She retracted her hand as she gasped. "What? You've tainted your blood with a drug?"

I nodded. "I'm the crazy prince of New Orleans, didn't you hear?" I cast her a sidelong glance.

Her eyes were wide, her lips slightly parted. "But now…" She paused. "Now I don't even know if you can fulfil…" She looked at Ruse, and he shrugged.

"There's a method I've been using to keep things at bay." I raced ahead, speaking before I could think about the wisdom of my words. But if there was a way, *any* way…

"Oh?" Clémence lifted her eyebrow again.

I nodded. "The blood of virgins. I keep the madness at bay by drinking the blood of virgins." There was more to it than that, and I was pretty sure Nicolas had been dosing me with something, too. Probably the cure, but never enough to quite cure me, although even that assumption wasn't enough to make me hate him.

I was still alive because of him, and now I'd found my mate—she was right in front of me, close enough to keep and protect if I could only get close enough.

"We *all* like the blood of a virgin, honey." Clémence gave her throaty chuckle again as she drawled her words.

I shrugged. Again, I needed them to think I didn't care. "It keeps my mind working. It's medicine, pure and simple." And this virgin was my mate, too. Perhaps she'd even be my cure. I'd always believed so.

My steps shuffled slightly as I moved forward. "There's a virgin in there, and I want her." I turned to Ruse. "And if you want me to find your fucking old book, you want me to have her, too."

Chapter 8 - Maeve

"Why haven't you eaten me?" I almost didn't have the energy to speak. When Ciara looked at me, her eyes that dull red they'd become permanently now, I continued. "I mean, why haven't you drunk all of my blood?" It would have been a mercy now.

At least, that was what I told myself.

"How many days…?" I let my question trail away then tried to lick my lips with a dry tongue so I could finish asking it. "Have they…have we…?" I sopped again as confusion disturbed my thoughts. I didn't even know what I was asking now.

"I think four days." She answered the question I hadn't asked first. How fucking long had we been here? Four days.

Four? They were a blur. Sometimes people came in and shoved stale food at me. Sometimes they just came in and watched, like I was an experiment.

Perhaps I was. Maybe they were also wondering why I wasn't dead. Which brought me back around to my first question.

"My blood…"

She nodded. "I know. Your blood." Then she laughed. "I could eat you, if you liked. But I think my wolf wouldn't be too happy. She's holding out."

"You don't drink?" I had more half questions than full ones, it seemed.

She shook her head, then nodded, then just wrinkled her brow in confusion. "I don't know how to answer that. I mean yes, I drink. But Jason is different. I don't drink to kill. My wolf likes you. She wants to protect you." She shrugged. "I'm not going to drain you dry."

I huffed out a laugh. "But we might not be rescued."

The corners of her mouth turned down and although she fixed that with a smile, her voice was smaller when she spoke again. "They'll come."

I didn't have the energy to shake my head to disagree. But four days? In the stories Ciara had told me in the first few hours we'd been in here, it didn't seem like the new king of the vampires took four days to do anything. She was a new vampire, but she wasn't new to the supernatural world, so I'd trusted her judgment on that.

But with so long passing, maybe something had gone wrong. A rescue attempt might have failed. Wouldn't that just be my damn luck? If my own damn curiosity really had finally gotten me killed because the vampires who were supposed to rescue me—the vampires I was so hellbent on proving existed—couldn't even get their shit together for a rescue mission.

"So…" I tried speaking again. It was too much energy, but there was a lot more I wanted to know.

Only Ciara's eyes widened and she shook her head. "Shush." She waved her hand in a *keep it down* motion, and fear clutched my chest.

Someone was coming. She always knew before I did. I automatically made myself smaller and closed my eyes. Well, nearly closed them. I could watch the door through a tangle of eyelashes if I kept my eyes open just the barest amount.

"What's up?" I whispered the question when nothing happened immediately.

She looked at me. *Company*, she mouthed, and her mouth pulled into a flat line of displeasure.

That meant it was one of the oldest ones. The Ancients. She'd told me enough about them that they weren't the unknown, anymore, but they weren't any less scary for that. In fact, Ciara said there was still a hell of a lot the Duponts didn't know about them, so maybe that made them scarier still.

It was like a whole bunch of ancient gods had returned to Earth and they wielded thunderbolts and controlled the seas. Humans had never seen anything like this before—and worse still, neither had the vampires who'd lived among us for so long.

No one knew how to deal with this new threat. Hell, humans hadn't even dealt with the old one—the fact the paranormal existed in the first place.

And that was partly because no one had listened to people like me. How many times had I tried to warn them?

She tugged me to standing. "It's not a good idea to just lie there this time." Then she moved us into a corner and stood partly in front of me as the door opened and two of the vampires stepped inside.

An Ancient came in first, and power so fierce rolled off him that my knees buckled and I gripped Ciara's arm for support.

Then another vampire stepped in behind him and the energy in the room changed. There was something beguiling now. Compelling, maybe. And a flutter in my chest…at my damn core. I drew in a breath that sounded like a gasp in the confines of the close walls.

And that was before I even saw him. I wanted to walk out from behind Ciara and offer myself to the vampire who'd just walked in. But that made no sense at all.

"What the hell are you doing here?" Ciara saw him before I did, and her head turned slightly to the side before she spoke again. "Why the fuck is he here?" She stepped back, sandwiching me more firmly between herself and the wall.

Squashing me, actually. She must have forgotten her strength, again. She was like an immovable object, a slab of stone someone had positioned in front of me, and I struggled to draw a full breath.

"Ciara. You're too close." I pushed against her with my palms, but she was solid, a deadweight. "I can't breathe."

"Sorry." She threw the word over her shoulder as she moved away. "He doesn't belong here." Again, she seemed to be speaking to the Ancient who'd entered the room first.

"I disagree." It wasn't the first time I'd heard one of them speak, but their voices always made me shiver. They chilled me from the inside. "We make the decisions here, or did you forget? And we appear to have a little stand-off in this room, so we're fixing that. If you have no use for the virgin, *we* certainly do."

I gasped louder this time and immediately regretted that I'd made Ciara step away. A shield would have been welcome, because really? My sexual status was on full display now? My face heated even though I had no embarrassment over it. It was just no one else's business but mine. And certainly no business of anyone I wouldn't have told myself.

The chuckle that emanated from the ancient was raspy. "Oh, we know everything, my dear. We're simply surprised that you haven't yet been devoured." He chuckled again before his tone changed as he addressed Ciara again. "Now step out."

Ciara didn't move.

"You're still only young, despite your connections. I suggest you do exactly as we tell you."

With a strangled yell, Ciara flew from in front of me before hitting the wall on the other side of the room and sliding down it.

"What the…?" My fingers curled at the base of my throat.

Ciara hadn't moved on her own, and she hadn't been dragged. The Ancient in here with us was capable of magic. I remained where I was, unwilling to seem reluctant or disobedient but unsure what was expected. If I hit a wall at the same speed as Ciara just had, I'd be broken.

"If we hadn't already agreed, Francois, I'd be tempted myself."

I looked beyond the Ancient staring at me with hunger and some degree of curiosity in his gaze, trying to ignore that he saw me as a food source.

At the edge of the room, Ciara stirred and sat up, putting her back to the wall, but I didn't look directly at her, didn't check to make sure she was okay. Instead, I looked at the second vampire in the room.

Looked at him like I'd hot-glued my gaze directly to his body.

He was the most beautiful man I'd ever seen. His eyes captured and held me…like I was drowning in impossibly pale blue depths. He almost looked related to the Ancient, but he was so much more vital. The blue of his eyes was darker and held more fire…a glimmer of something…madness.

Yes, that was it.

Francois… the mad prince.

I'd seen him before, of course. The time Ciara had named him as vampire and before that…when I watched footage of a man held in a magic spell outside an exploded apartment.

Ciara was right. Why the hell was he here? And why couldn't I tear my gaze from him? I glanced over his clothes, almost wishing for X-ray vision. Everything was exquisitely tailored, and everything clung to him in all the right places, even if it did look a century or two out of date.

History had never been my strongest subject—something I was starting to regret now that I was dealing with beings so old—but the style suited him.

"Don't just stand there." The Ancient grabbed my arm, and I yelped as his fingers curved around me like iron bands, grinding against my bones and pinching my skin.

Francois hissed, and his eyes narrowed as they flashed red.

I shuddered at the expression of his hunger. But there seemed to be more there than simple appetite. I didn't get to look for long, though, as I switched my attention to keeping myself upright instead of merely being dragged in whatever direction the Ancient was headed.

Ciara started to yell behind me, but the sound became muffled when the Ancient waved his arm and the wood door slammed shut behind us.

I twisted and tried to pull away before gritting my teeth. "I can walk fine on my own."

But Francois continued like he hadn't heard me—except his grip tightened slightly as we ascended the narrow staircase back to the first floor.

The subterranean feeling dropped away as the decaying grandeur of the rest of the house replaced it. Even the air smelled different up here. The dampness was gone, replaced by a drier mustiness, like old trunks filled with historical clothes or pages of leather-bound books, their spines broken and unreadable.

He led me to a doorway, and suddenly we were in the heart of modern day. The future, even. A state-of-the-art television graced one of the walls, and someone had spent a lot of money in here, furnishing it with expensive but comfortable-looking seating.

I swallowed, my mouth dry as I stopped looking at the décor and finally noticed the inhabitants.

Four other ancient vampires sat in the room, draped artfully on the sofas and chairs as though someone had arranged them there for a photoshoot. Their hair was impossibly pale, their skin almost translucent, their eyes a ghostly shade of blue that I wasn't sure even existed elsewhere. In some lights, there was almost no color there at all; in others, I wasn't sure if I'd imagined it because it was a sheen or a flash like in an opal.

Fear mounted inside me. Not a surge, but a gradual creep. The vampires in this room looked lazy and well-fed, like lions basking on a rock. Almost like they didn't kidnap women at all. Almost like they were harmless.

The Ancient released my arm and thrust me away from him in one movement, and I lost my balance, falling against something hard and unyielding.

"Oof!" The air rushed out of my lungs, and an arm curved around my waist, holding me steady.

Shit. I hadn't landed against any old hard and unyielding thing. I was flat against the chest of Francois, who truly looked like a colorized version of all of these faded vampires. Before I could catch my breath, we began to move, my feet barely touching the floor as Francois took me back through the doorway.

Damn, I was weak. My head lolled against him, so I couldn't even fight this time.

But did I want to? This wasn't dangerous. Adrenaline wasn't running wild through me. My body told me I was safe and I didn't need to worry.

And my mind wasn't putting up much of a fight.

"What's the matter. Francois?" One of the Ancient's voices echoed through the cavernous entrance hallway after us. "Don't you want to share your meal?"

I should have stiffened. Should have pushed him away. Should have run.

But I didn't.

I wanted him to pick me up, cradle me against his chest. I wanted to be safe in his arms.

If I shook my arm to make him let me go, it was a token effort, but I couldn't be sure I even made that.

We headed toward a staircase that curved to a wide first step against the scuffed wood floor. Once upon a time, these boards would have been polished and gleaming, but any glamor was missing completely now.

Just as I thought we were about to climb the stairs, Francois veered to the left through a doorway I hadn't noticed.

"Oh." The sound that left my mouth was long and drawn out as I lifted my head to look up at the tallest of the bookcases. Each shelf was packed with books—the kind I'd thought of earlier, but each was in beautiful condition. Nothing in this room was remotely out of place, even though some areas in the rest of the house looked as though they'd been the setting for a fight scene or police search, with ripped fabric or overturned furniture.

This room, however, remained untouched. Perhaps vampires didn't read. Or maybe they revered books enough that they didn't want to damage them.

Francois pressed me into a leather bucket chair. "Stay there."

I glanced at the door. Could I make it? But that question brought me back around to the other awkward question in my head. Did I want to? Stepping back out of the library would only reintroduce the sense of danger I'd felt everywhere in this house except for when I was with Francois.

"Non." His French accent was enough to melt me, but actual French language. "Non, mon ange. C'est trop dangereux. It's too *dangerous*." He emphasized the last word as he watched the doorway himself. "Besides, I would catch you before you got three feet." He chuckled and the sudden light in his eyes suggested he might quite like that game. "Mais non, I need you to stay with me until I can get us out of this mess."

I watched him, careful not to react. I needed a blank expression while I absorbed his words and tried to unravel their meaning. But my head was foggy. I was hungry. What did he mean—he was going to get us out of this mess? He was a vampire. One of them.

He was dead bang center in this mess. Why did *he* want to get out?

"But…" I shook my head. There were too many questions and maybe not enough time. "Why me?" Okay, so I hadn't intended to start with that one.

He glanced up. "Hmm?"

I cleared my throat. "Why did you take me from that room? There are other women…" I waved my arm vaguely in the direction of upstairs. I couldn't be sure there were other women anymore. I could be the last one left.

"Oh." He returned to perusing the books in front of him, trailing his finger over the old spines as he narrowed his eyes and half-mouthed titles to himself.

I'd just settled into the silence when he spoke again.

"Because you're my mate."

I looked at him, but he was still facing the books.

"But do not tell them that. They believe you are simply…my sustenance."

"Sustenance?" Again, there were too many questions running through my head, so repeating his last word seemed to be the easiest thing to do.

"My *prize*, mon ange. One granted in advance to help me find this damn book they think is hidden somewhere in this house."

I glanced up at the shelves again. Looked like I could be here for a while if he was searching for one book. Talk about a needle in a haystack.

But things were really so much worse than that. Surely no one ever wanted to be called a *prize* by a vampire. And certainly not *sustenance*.

But the word that interested me most was *mate*. That word applied to Ciara...but not to me. I knew enough to understand what it meant, and regardless of how beautiful this man was...of how safe I felt with him...I was no vampire mate.

I swallowed my anxiety but it lodged in my throat. Perhaps I'd been safest in the dungeon room with Ciara after all.

Chapter 9 - Francois

Merde. I'd stumbled at the first hurdle. Hell, *stumbled?* I'd pretty much turned and run the entire other way. Here I was, combing through rows and rows of books, and reading and rereading their titles without really seeing them because all I could actually think about was how to rescue my mate from the Ancients.

I needed to get us out of here. Failing that, I needed to get *her* out of here. I couldn't leave her to the fate I'd witnessed in the dining room—the fate that had played out for multiple women over the past several nights.

The Ancients had drained so many women. And always with so much theater, treating them like honored guests at first. The women never bought it, though, and the bitter note of their fear in the air made nausea roil in my stomach.

I'd refused to partake each night, citing each time that it needed to be a virgin, better from the vein. When one of the women was discovered to be a virgin, and Abel had offered to share her, I'd said I preferred to take my feeds in private. That I'd grown used to creating a blood slave… That I needed a seduction. I'd fumbled for excuses in the end, and they'd laughed, but times had changed, so I'd seen the confusion on their faces. Perhaps they were out of step that my way was the new way.

They didn't argue.

I'd tried to lay a claim on both women down in the dungeon, but Ruse had merely laughed.

"What would you want with a Dupont mate? She's tainted." One corner of his mouth had twitched downward.

"But she's a Dupont. I think I could be the one to taint her. Imagine a rejected Dupont mate." I'd raised my eyebrows, putting lascivious meaning into my words, even though it pained me to say them when my mate was so prominent in my thoughts. The idea of another woman in my bed, on my tongue, on my cock… It was almost intolerable.

But Ruse had shaken his head. "I don't think so, Francois. One virgin slave should be enough. You aren't starting a harem." Then he'd chuckled and lifted a shoulder. "Perhaps if you find the book, I'll think about a greater reward."

And there it was. My entire value to them had been reduced to one book my father had stolen and *potentially* hidden here, somewhere in the house. Apparently, I'd know it when I found it.

They hadn't even given me a good description, but their old minds were sometimes clouded when they hadn't long awoken, so perhaps I shouldn't have been surprised. Father was often the same way when he emerged from stasis.

"Not so hasty, Ruse." The memory of Clémence disagreeing with Ruse's idea of a reward still had a visceral effect on me, and I stiffened at her voice in my head.

She knew something was up. She watched me often, seeming to focus when I spoke like she might catch me in a lie or at least unpick something not quite the truth. But I tried to stay close enough to what I believed that she couldn't detect anything untoward.

Still, she watched, even if she didn't declare herself. She couldn't afford to be wrong. After all, they no longer had my father. They only had me—and that was enough to make me feel sorry for all of us.

"Do you even know my name?" My mate moved in the chair behind me, and the soft leather rustled beneath her.

I grunted something that didn't answer her either way. Did I know her name? Had I? Perhaps I'd lost the word somewhere in my head.

"It's Maeve," she supplied, and I relaxed completely, like that word completed something in my head and my heart. It brought me home.

Maeve, *my* Maeve. Sitting in a room with me. My mate. I had everything I needed now.

Except no. My gums itched where my fangs pressed against them. Being so close to her without being able to properly explain everything to her, or touch her or kiss her or *claim* her, was torture.

If I claimed her, I'd start the mate bond. She could be mine forever. And her blood should cure me. I'd always believed my mate's blood would cure the family sickness…then the madness I'd brought on myself with the dead man's blood I'd become addicted to.

She could be a living, breathing cure, my ability to live again. I avoided looking at her. I needed to bring myself back under control and focus on my task. Even the urge to breathe her in, to draw her scent deep into my chest, was dangerous. She had the power to distract me completely from my task.

That damn book. "Merde." I swore aloud, the sound ugly, and Maeve moved again.

"What?"

"I can't find the book." But it was so much more than that. Only I couldn't tell her that life was shit and I still hadn't died yet.

I couldn't tell her that she was the first good thing to happen to me…maybe ever. I couldn't tell her that I was so used to my life being crap that I wasn't sure finding my mate was even real.

Instead, I leaned even closer to the books like that would suddenly allow me to see everything better. It was imperative that I found it. Now that I'd shown such an interest in Maeve, they'd be watching. Even if they didn't know exactly who she was to me, she could become leverage in whatever game they chose to play next. Especially since Clémence definitely didn't trust my motives at the moment.

I needed to watch my step even more closely now.

I closed my eyes briefly. *Hurry up, Nicolas. All past sins are forgiven.* I wasn't sure I could rescue Maeve on my own, no matter how much I wanted that glory all for myself. I wanted to be her only savior. The only worthy man.

"What did you mean before?"

I half turned at her voice. She was very pale, and there were purple shadows below her eyes. They hadn't treated her very well at all. Remorse wove fragile tendrils through my chest. I knew the signs of mistreatment because I'd been so guilty of it myself in the past.

As if on cue, my ghost appeared by the library door. "Your human is hungry." Her voice was stronger now.

"Hm?" I automatically responded to the ghost, but it was Maeve who answered me.

"Before, when you said I was your mate, what did you mean?" Maeve's eyes closed briefly before springing back open and she laughed, waving an arm. "Sorry. I'm pretty tired."

Her arm wave washed her scent over me, and I stepped back, looking between Maeve and my ghost as if to figure out who should get my attention first.

"Frankie." Maeve snapped her fingers, suddenly more awake. "What did you mean."

First... "Frankie?" I wrinkled my nose. No one had ever called me that.

"You don't use that?"

"No?" For some reason, I framed my absolute horror as a curious question. Mother had named me Francois and it was perfectly good, but... I grinned at Maeve. "Only you."

"Great. Now, the mate thing?"

I shook my head. Humans. Why did they never understand this stuff? I'd explained the same to each woman before her, even though I'd been wrong every other time. "You were created by fate for me. You belong to only me. We are destined to be together for eternity."

For a moment, Maeve looked bored, like she'd heard all that before, but then her already pale skin paled a shade more. "What? You mean as your personal juice box? The others think you're in here draining me. What does mate mean to you, exactly?"

The more she spoke, the stranger her accent sounded. She definitely wasn't local, but it was like the sweetest music I'd ever heard. Everything about her was magical and amazing to me—in a way that no other human had ever been before.

I'd been getting it wrong for so many years. So wrong. So many years.

"A mate." I stopped looking at the books and glanced at Maeve. She really was beautiful.

"She's hungry, Francois." My ghost's voice was an annoying buzz in my ear. Like a mosquito.

"Yes, a mate." Maeve stopped, confusion taking over features as I flapped an irritated wave at my ghost. "What are you doing?"

"Thinking," I replied, although my lie wasn't smooth. "My mate is someone who will save me, become my most treasured love, live with me as an equal." I smiled as a familiar title caught my eye on the bookshelf before I finished speaking, and I reached for the book and then flipped it open.

Maeve stood, her joints cracking quietly as she did. "Love? Are you actually joking? I don't know you. But you're a vampire. Newsflash." She spread her hands like she was creating a headline in front of herself. "Vampires fucking exist."

I chuckled at her unexpected outburst. Maybe she was really as fiery as her hair.

"Bien sûr." I nodded. "Of course. Vampires *do* exist, mon ange, and everything I have told you about being a mate is just so." She captivated me more the longer I looked at her. She really was my angel. My fiery angel.

I glanced back at the book in my hand, but Maeve plucked it from my careful hold and slapped the covers closed. "Sorry, Frankie. I don't believe in fate."

I sighed. I'd done this all wrong again. She was my mate, and I needed her to believe that. "Je suis désolé. I'm sorry, mon ange. Truly I am. I didn't really want to tell you like this. But could I leave you in a dungeon?"

She didn't answer, instead narrowing her eyes as she watched me.

"No matter." I shook my head. "Just because you don't believe in fate doesn't make it any less true. How would we have found each other, if not for the fates?" I touched her cheek gently, and although she flinched at the sudden contact, she didn't step away. "Now, can you read French?"

She nodded. "Un petit peu. I took some in school."

I laughed at her telling me *a little*. If I could imagine French lessons in school, she probably knew how to say she'd broken down and would like three slices of ham, or something equally as obscure.

"What are you looking for, anyway?" She slid the book she'd closed back onto the shelf.

"A very old book."

She raised an eyebrow as she watched me. "Here, in this room full of very old books?"

"Seriously." I chuckled. "That's all they told me at first, too." And Clémence had only just revealed more details. "We're looking for a spell book. An old one, filed with dark magic. It's one my father stole from them."

Her lips parted. "Wait. Your father stole from the Ancients? How did he pull that off?"

I glanced at a row of books. "He *was* an Ancient. Apparently, he…defected and took a souvenir." I drew another book out of its place.

"That doesn't look like spells." Maeve peered around my arm as I flipped through it, looking at the familiar illustrations I used to see almost daily as a child.

"Oh, it's not. This is a book of children's stories. Maman used to read them to me." My lips curved at the memory of my mother and her embrace as she read aloud.

"What are the spells for?" She sounded curious now.

"They're dark ones." Clémence had mentioned a resurrection spell and rediscovering their true power. Perhaps she hadn't expected me to join those dots, but apparently, they'd decided to return to the source—that the heir, and his crazed mind, wasn't good enough for their exclusive little club.

"What do the Ancients want?"

I glanced at her. The question seemed innocent enough, but it was a dangerous one to ask within these walls, with the Ancients so close by. It was even more dangerous to answer.

I took hold of her elbow and drew her close to me, lowering my head so I could murmur right by her ear. "They wish to claim the world. To destroy life and create a world of vampires for them to rule. At full power, they are gods. We'd be nothing but their pawns."

She stepped away. "And you're helping them?" Her eyes blazed with icy flame. "How can you help them?" She hissed the words, and I shook my head. "I won't."

She returned to the leather chair and dropped back into it.

I leaned against the bookcase and folded my arms as I watched her. I took in every line of her form, every feature of her beautiful face. She was mine. It might take some work to get there, but she'd realize that, too.

"If we don't help them—" I kept my voice low "— they'll kill us both and just ransack this entire house or turn an army to search for them. Currently, I'm useful. I'm the more expedient option. So I'll play the game to keep us safe. To keep *you* safe, Maeve."

A pink blush rose up her cheeks, but she tossed her hair over her shoulder and looked past me, her jaw set. "You say that like you care." Her eyes were ice chips as they met mine.

"Maeve." I sank lower until I sat on the floor. "You're my mate. I've been waiting for you for a very long time. If I can rescue you, I plan to, and I will do whatever that takes. Even helping to find this book."

"And I get no say at all? We aren't dating. We don't even know each other, and you're in here talking about forever and *treasured love*?" She shook her head, her brows drawn down. "It doesn't make any sense in my world. I don't have the research on this." She said that last part quietly, like she was speaking to herself now.

I shook my head, too. "There's no arguing. When a vampire senses their mate, it can't be challenged or changed." But I couldn't push her much further on this—I didn't want to push her away completely.

She scoffed before standing up, muttering under her breath. "Crazy vampires."

I turned to hide my grin. Somehow, I felt a whole lot less crazy when I was with her.

"This will keep us safe? You're sure?" She walked to a bookcase I hadn't searched yet.

"As sure as I can be. I can't fail to be useful."

"Okay." She nodded slowly. "Let's go then." She stooped to look at the lower shelves, and I watched each of her movements.

My ghost was right. Maeve needed sustenance. Especially so before I could feed from her.

Trying to do that would deplete her energy reserves too far, but feeding was essential for our mating bond. I needed to take care of my mate.

We both needed to be at full strength if we planned to escape. Being united as vampires would grant us the best chance.

My mouth watered and my fangs ached at the thought of drinking from her, but now wasn't the time. I needed to continue the search and make a plan.

My thoughts were becoming circular again. I focused on the books in front of me, skimming the titles, grazing my fingers over the leather, hoping to ground myself again.

It wouldn't be long now. I'd already survived this far. I could do a few more days or weeks. Especially now that Maeve was at my side.

Chapter 10 - Maeve

Francois was watching me. I could sense that much.
Even with my back turned, my skin prickled with awareness
of him. Every movement he made, every squeak of his skin
over the books. It was like being in a crazy hyper state, and
I was kind of sick of it.

A mate? What now? Ciara had told me she had a mate.
I knew what one was. But I wasn't the same. I was human.

And it sounded very serious. Worse than marriage
because it was literally forever. These were immortal
beings. The chances of *until death us do part* dropped
phenomenally when I considered pretty much eternal life,
right?

And… yeah. There was the fact I hadn't actually slept
with a man yet. I'd been quite looking forward to the whole
try before you buy part of life. I just hadn't reached it yet, too
focused on my work and trying to get people to take me
seriously. No one seemed to really understand my blog or
get the importance of it. But the joke was on them now,
right?

I nodded in agreement with myself as I looked around a library in a house full of vampires. Yep. The joke was sure on everyone who hadn't believed me.

Still, why, if I couldn't choose my own guy, would I give myself to this fruit loop? Even as I thought the unkind words, I regretted them. And it was like some kind of instinct forced me to want to unthink them. Like this vampire mattered to me on a level I couldn't understand.

They probably called that Stockholm syndrome, right? Because here I was, kidnapped and trapped in his house.

Only he was trying to rescue me, or so he said.

I reread the last few book spines again. If I kept getting lost in my thoughts, this would take days. But I was conflicted. There was so much I wanted to know. Especially as Francois seemed like he'd be receptive to me.

Plus, the danger didn't feel as imminent now that I was out of the dungeon room and I had a protector. I could afford to find out a little more.

"What's it like?" I asked.

"Hm?"

I repeated my question. "What's it like?"

"What's what like, mon ange?" He sounded distracted, and he kept calling me *my angel*. That should have been weird, but it warmed my insides in a way I didn't want to explore too much.

"Being a vampire."

"Oh." He chuckled. "I don't know. I was born this way. It's normal." As I turned to watch him, he gave a huge shrug. "I don't know another way."

I nodded. That sounded almost normal. How could he answer my question if he had nothing to compare it to? I'd spent my whole life researching, though, and never had an opportunity like this. "But do you like it?"

His laugh this time was short and sharp. "Ah, an entirely different question, non?"

I smiled in reply. It *was* a different question. Designed to find out much the same, though. I just had to get him talking. I watched him, taking in the shape of his mouth, the vivid blue of his eyes, as he appeared to consider his answer.

Finally, he exhaled softly. I already knew he didn't really need to breathe. He'd probably acquired the skill by mimicking humans for so many years. That piece of information had come from one of Granny's many stories, and so many other snippets of things I knew seemed like they were nipping at my mind, though. But how many of them would Francois confirm?

An actual born vampire, too, when all of our legends seemed to focus on creatures of the night who ran around sinking their fangs into humans. A shiver ran through me at that thought, and I touched the side of my neck.

Francois's eyes widened and he turned his attention to the next shelf. "Uhh…" He touched one of the books. "Some days it's fine. But it's hard to actively like something every day when the years begin to mount into the hundreds. There have been tough times—"

"Wars?" I suggested.

He grinned. "Those too. But vampires aren't immune to personal problems, either. It might not be quite as different as you suspect."

"But you eat people." I sounded a little more accusatory than I'd expected.

"Maybe only if they ask nicely."

My cheeks warmed at both his words and the suggestive smile that accompanied them, and I looked away.

If I could just access a computer or, hell, even paper and an envelope, I could get this story out there. Finally. My big scoop. An actual interview with an actual vampire.

I'd be able to tell the world about the threat in this house, living among us. The FBI or SWAT could come and rescue me. I'd be free or die trying.

My blaze of glory.

I sighed. Who was I kidding, right? No one would believe me still. I was just one more kook with a blog and a batshit crazy family. I'd tried so hard my whole life— detailed reports, footnoted essays, lighthearted clickbait articles, social media videos of varying lengths, ghost hunting tours... But nothing had worked. No one believed that they couldn't see.

Except me.

And that was because Gran didn't lie. When she said there was a spirit peering over my shoulder at the book I was reading, I'd read slower, turned the pages more carefully, because I wasn't the only one enjoying the story.

Only now, I didn't need Gran's word. According to this vampire, I was destined to be his supernatural wife for the rest of eternity.

"Can you die?" It was the next natural question. Exactly how long was eternity?

He raised an eyebrow. "Sounds like the answer to that should be a trade secret."

I laughed. "Legends are vague, right? Garlic, mirrors, daylight..." I waved an arm. We weren't exactly standing around talking in a darkened room. "Some things clearly aren't true."

"Mon coeur, mon ange. My heart. Take my heart and you take my life." He patted his chest softly. "Mais bien sûr, you already have my heart."

Before I could blink, he was right in front of me, his chest pressed to my breasts, his head tilted as though in question. My gaze dropped to his lips. I wanted... I leaned a little closer. Just one touch. I yearned for that. I'd never wanted anything more.

He gasped, the sharpest of inhales and for just one moment I thought he moved. I thought he might...

But then he was gone again and we both returned to our search, my breathing uneven and noisier than usual. Francois cleared his throat and busied himself at a bookcase, his back to me. What had I just wanted? And what had he meant? The idea that, of course, I already had his heart sat somewhat uneasily in my thoughts. Was it really so easy for a vampire to love?

Gran would have known. Somehow, she'd have known the answers to all of my questions. If she could see me now... I laughed, suddenly glad she couldn't see me now. I'd be disowned. She'd always told me my curiosity would get me into trouble one day—one more thing she was right about.

Like Francois, I touched the leather as I picked out the titles of the books. My French wasn't perfect—far from it, and some of the old typefaces were hard to read. Either too decorative or worn from years of being handled.

"Wait." I passed the pad of my thumb back over the burnished gold words. *Formules Magiques.* Maybe calling the spell book *Magic Spells* was a little on the nose, but it was worth checking.

I drew it carefully from the shelf. It was surprisingly heavy for one of the smaller books here. Certainly not as impressive as the old grimoires I'd seen and read about.

I opened the cover and an electric shock tingled through my fingers and shot up my arm. My knees buckled, and I cried out.

Francois was immediately in front of me, again. "Maeve, are you okay?" The way he spoke my name was like a caress.

"I…" I paused while I did a quick mental assessment of myself. "I…I don't know." My hand still tingled, prickling with something new and uncomfortable. Like I'd brushed against a plant that had stung me in warning for getting too close.

"Let me see?" He held out his hand, and when I started to pass him the book, he tutted his impatience. "Non. I don't care about the paper. Only you. Where are you hurt?"

I juggled the book under my other arm and held my hand out for his inspection. He took hold of it carefully, before turning it so he could see my palm.

I gasped. "What's that?" A perfect star shape sat in the center of my palm, like it had always been there, but I'd certainly never seen it before.

He ran the tip of his forefinger over it, and I shivered at his touch. My body almost hummed at the sensation, and I wanted to feel his touch elsewhere. All sorts of elsewhere.

It made no sense, but something drew me to him anyway. I stood perfectly still while he looked at my hand, and I almost willed him to look up. To kiss me.

I shook my head as the heavy book still under my arm pulled me back to reality, and I withdrew my hand from his grasp.

"I'm fine." But I was already mourning the loss of his touch.

I couldn't tell him that, though. I didn't understand what I was feeling, and I didn't want him to know or get the wrong idea.

Instead, I handed him the book. "Could this be the one?" I pushed my hair behind my ears as I tried to regain my composure, and I waited for his response. He opened the cover without seeming to feel so much as a spark, never mind a shock like I'd received, and he read a couple of the first pages.

Then he looked up, and the grin that captured his mouth was slow and…sexy. "I think you've found it. And so soon!" He laughed then stopped the noise suddenly and glanced toward the door. "We must copy as many of these spells as we can before we hand the book over."

"Why?" Our job was done now, surely. We could get on with the business of making our escape. Wasn't that the deal? "Aren't we leaving now?"

"Soon, mon ange. But I can't just hand over this book without knowing some of the spells."

"What will you do with them?" A different thought occurred to me. "Do you have magic, too?"

He shook his head. "No, not me, but I might have a witch who can help us…if she gets here in time."

"Wait." I shook my head. This was all getting confusing. "I thought the plan was two steps. One, find the book of spells." I gestured to it. "Ta-da! Two, escape." I pointed at him. "That's your part."

"There are maybe a few more steps in between those." He moved his forefinger and thumb apart about an inch.

"But really, not a lot." He had the grace to look sheepish, though.

I tapped my foot, suddenly tired again. It had been okay when I'd thought I had a goal. Find the book, get to go home. That much had been simple. Only now Francois said it wasn't so simple.

"Okay. So what needs to happen?" Damn, I'd kill for a Coke or a sandwich or a beignet.

"We need to copy as many spells as possible so I can examine them more closely—or Kayla can—when she gets here."

"And who's Kayla?" Jealousy was a deceptively soft dart inside me.

"Oh." He looked up and rubbed his forehead. "Oh, she's Sebastian's mate."

"And Sebastian?" Were all of these people also in the house with us? "Is he here?"

"Malheureusement, non."

"And why is that?" I agreed with him that it was unfortunate that the people he seemed to be relying on for our escape weren't with us, though. I racked my brains. Had Ciara mentioned Sebastian or Kayla? Were they familiar names?

I had no idea. I was almost too hungry to focus.

"Nicolas's brother, but we're getting ahead of ourselves." His eyes widened and he took on a more frantic look as he hurried to a big, old desk in the corner of the room. He set the spell book on the leather inset into the top. "I think they plan to resurrect my father. It's very dark magic."

"Your father is dead?" That conclusively answered my earlier question about whether vampires could die, then.

He nodded, the movement abrupt. "Oui. For some months now. Time is…" He waved distractedly. "Immaterial. If they resurrect him, he won't be pretty, and maybe when they get what they want, they'll even put him back. They certainly don't trust him. Not after he left…" His voice trailed off as he opened a drawer and started clattering through the things he found in there.

"What are you looking for?" I started to approach him before I stopped. My stomach grumbled.

Francois stopped what he was doing and looked to his left for a moment, tilting his head like he was listening before he nodded. "I will find you something to eat as soon as we finish here. We must hurry. I need to find paper and pens." He continued to rummage through the drawer.

"No, we don't." I shook my head and walked to the desk.

He looked up, one eyebrow arched.

"Just show me the pages you want me to remember. Read me the words. I have a photographic memory—I can remember everything we need." I leaned against the closest bookcase and watched him.

He smiled just a little. "So we can do this together? You're in this with me?"

Shit. The hope on his face physically hurt me. But I couldn't lie to him.

I shook my head slowly. "I need to get out of here. I need to get Ciara out too. I'll do anything for that. But I can't promise to stay with you if I might miss an opportunity to go."

He sighed and looked down at the book on the desk. When he raised his gaze, sadness lurked in its depths. But he tightened his mouth and nodded. "Bien." He waved me closer. "We'll begin."

Chapter 11 - Francois

"Mon Ange, allow me to feed you." Usually, I'd only spoken those words in misguided seduction, but now my ghost wouldn't leave me alone.

She was like a fly I needed to swat, but even I could see that Maeve was both hungry and exhausted. What if this didn't work? What if her memory wasn't all that she claimed?

"Okay." She nodded, and I was glad she hadn't protested. We had a lot to get through, and she kind of looked like she might expire with immediate intent.

I slipped from the library and to the kitchens, keeping my eyes open for wandering Ancients and their guards. There was no doubt in my mind that they expected me to simply obey their orders and remain in the library, but I had a mate to take care of. I couldn't yet risk trying to leave the grounds yet, though, as I had no doubt they'd altered the wards and would know the moment we departed.

The Ancients had hosted so many humans lately that the cupboards were well stocked, and I loaded my arms with fruit and snacks. I didn't know what to offer her, so I wanted to offer her everything, show her that I could provide anything she needed.

Besides, this was a welcome distraction, in a way. We'd found the book too quickly. It meant our time together would be shorter than I wanted, and at least feeding her would extend that. Even Clémence couldn't argue with me keeping my blood slave alive.

I hurried back to the library, and Maeve's eyes widened when she saw me. "Wow. Is all of that for me?"

"Anything for you," I replied, the words tripping off my tongue, my casualness betraying how much I meant them.

She ripped open a bag of chips. "Okay. I'm ready." She nodded at the book, and I opened it to the first page.

"How many can your memory hold?"

She grimaced. "More than I want to think about. But how much time do we have? Do you just want to find the relevant ones, or don't you know which those are? Do we need all of them?"

I shrugged, unsure of which Kayla would find useful.

"All of them it is, then." She drew a chair closer to the desk and sat down. As I turned each page, I murmured the words aloud. By spell four, I chuckled.

"What?" She turned her head and looked up at me.

"It's a good thing I have no magic. I would have already broken your bones, made you waste away, and turned you into a cockroach."

She laughed too. "At least I'd survive a nuclear war. Come on, we have a lot more to go." She bit into a cookie.

It seemed to take hours to read through the book, Maeve studying each page as my voice rose and fell quietly with the lyrical words. We were nearly at the end of the book when she spoke again.

"Have you read one that sounds right yet?"

I shook my head, caught between being frustrated by and glad about that. If this was the wrong book, we'd need to restart our search, but if this time was the only chance I had to court Maeve, then any extra moments I could glean were important.

"No," I said. "There has been nothing about resurrection just yet."

"Maybe that's not their plan?" Her voice was quiet.

I shook my head again. "I don't know what else it would be. I think, originally, their plan was for me to step into my father's footsteps. I'm the right bloodline. But I'm…" I stopped. Broken. I was fucking broken, but I didn't want Maeve to know that just yet. Not before she'd accepted me.

"You're what?"

"Not suitable." I looked away from her. If I continued to gaze into her eyes, I'd spill all of my secrets. I wanted to share everything with her, and that was an instinct more dangerous than I'd realized. "Let's continue." I turned the page, and she readjusted her position, ready to concentrate once more.

"Rise of the dead," I read out loud in French, and my stomach clenched. "I think this is it." I hadn't meant to tell her. Not right away. But there was that instinct to overshare again.

"Really?" She grinned and leaned even closer to the page.

"Yes." I scanned the lines, reading the words. "It talks about how to bring back a vampire—even one turned to dust." There seemed to be no limits to the spell. It was the most powerful one I'd read so far.

"Dust?" Maeve wrinkled her nose. "Okay. Let's get this thing in." She tapped the side of her head, and I recited each of the evil words.

They left a bitter taste in my mouth, and when Maeve moved in her seat, I took the opportunity to breathe in her scent.

This whole process was moving too swiftly. If we found everything the Ancients wanted, what then? Could I still guarantee Maeve's safety?

I hadn't understood Nicolas's protectiveness of Leia before, and I'd underestimated the reactions of a vampire whose mate had been abducted.

Those days I'd held Leia, I'd believed her to be mine. I'd believed in my madness. But I'd been wrong.

I'd been wrong so many times, and now I'd give anything to keep Maeve safe.

I didn't know how yet, but I'd do anything in my power to protect her or reach my final death trying.

When I breathed closer to Maeve's hair, the desire to claim her thundered in my veins. I existed for her, and she for me. I wanted her blood in my body. The impulse was almost too great to resist, but I drew away. I had to resist. Our mission here was important.

We couldn't let the Ancients resurrect Father and complete their goal. Nicolas was a good king, no matter what they believed, no matter their own ambitions to rule.

"Do you have that one?"

She looked away from the page, deliberately meeting my eyes and began to speak. Her voice was like music. She repeated the spell to me, word and accent perfect.

I nodded. "Bon." Good, yes, it was good. *She* was amazing. Not that I'd ever doubted my mate would be anything but amazing. "Let me look through the rest of the book." She was amazing but she was also tiring. Food hadn't been enough. She also required rest.

All of this concentration had to be taxing for her.

If I could find something in here that would take the Ancients down... That would be the best prize of all. They could have as many spell books as they wanted if the key to their downfall was secured in my mate's head.

I closed the cover. "There's nothing else," I said.

"You sound disappointed?" She concealed a yawn behind her hand.

I shrugged. "A little. But..." I looked toward the window and the darkening sky. This had been too quick. But what if it was also too easy? "What if this is only *a* book? They told me that my father had stolen a book. Would you leave a stolen book in full view, on a shelf in your library? Where anyone could find it?"

She frowned. "Probably not."

"Exactement!" Yes, something was definitely wrong here. I narrowed my eyes at the book like it could reveal its secrets.

"So, now what?" Maeve was still watching me.

It had been a while since anyone had looked to me for answers rather than simply expecting me to obey their orders or instructions, and a small measure of pride filled me. "Je pense que…" I started, but Maeve laughed.

"Maybe in English, Frankie?"

I smiled at the name she called me, although my cheeks heated. When I was distracted, which was more and more these days (although for a different reason now that I was trying to think of a way to protect Maeve) my thoughts often came in a mixture of French and English. Like they couldn't make their minds up what to be. "Okay. I think that we should keep this book a secret for just now. We clearly haven't found the one my father hid."

"Are you sure?" She wrinkled her nose. "If that one has the spell they want in it, maybe it's the right book?"

I shook my head and slid the book into a drawer then clapped my hands together. "Non. You didn't know Émile Ricard. He was dangerous and cunning and vicious and diabolical. He wouldn't leave something so precious lying out in plain sight. And if he risked everything to steal something from the Ancients as he absconded from their group, it was definitely precious." I looked upward like I could suddenly see through the floors above us. "I think we need to search the whole place."

"What do you think it has inside it?" Her eyes were wide, her voice a whisper.

"I don't know." I knew what I hoped, though. "Maybe a spell to end all of this?"

She nodded. "Then we need to search. When do we start?"

I chuckled and touched her hand fleetingly. I craved the feel of her skin. So soft and warm. I wanted her pressed against me, to feel the softness of her lips under my own while I buried my hands in her hair. I wanted her to surrender to me, to want me.

I wanted to claim her.

"Are you sure you want to do this?" A moment ago, she'd thought only of escape.

"I think it's my only chance to get away," she said. Then she rubbed the bridge of her nose. "And this is all fantastic information and evidence for my blog. Like I *knew* you existed, but now I have proof. People *have* to listen now, right?"

I started to shake my head. My poor, sweet mate. No one could know about the supernatural world…but perhaps now wasn't the time to discuss that with her. She was happy and she wanted to help, and that was perfect. I'd get to spend more time with her.

Instead of answering her question directly, I changed the subject. "The last thing that can happen is bringing my father back." I grimaced. "And not just for the power they would create."

I couldn't imagine a world with Father back in it. We'd never been what people would call a happy family. Then Loïc had met his final death and Mother had become a shell of herself and Father had become increasingly callous and cruel. His bouts of stasis had been more regular and longer, and after each one he woke up a little bit crazier, taking greater risks, caring less about who he hurt. He had become entirely selfish and self-absorbed.

I'd assumed that was the way of all vampires of such age, but Father had been hiding a secret. He was an Ancient, and he was apart from them, so maybe that had added to his downfall. It would have been ironic if, in his quest for success alone, he's achieved the opposite and weakened all of them. Now I simply had to ensure the status quo remained this way.

Maeve leaned closer to me, the warm aroma of her skin interrupting my thoughts. "Do you have a key for that lock?" She nodded at the drawer I'd just put the book inside. "Just in case anyone else comes snooping."

I nodded and produced a key from where I'd always hidden it, under the desk. She watched me lock the drawer then grabbed the key and pushed it inside her bra cup.

"No one will come snooping now," she whispered.

My mouth dried. "And if it's me who wishes to unlock the drawer?"

Her cheeks turned a pale shade of pink. "Then I might give you the key back."

"Or I could find the key myself...?" I let my suggestive declaration trail off as we locked eyes.

Her cheeks reddened and her lips parted, her pupils dilating. My whole future and my existence existed in the depths of her gaze, and I gripped the edges of the desk to keep myself from taking her in my arms.

I blew out a short sigh, the moment she dropped the key into her bra replaying in my head, and walked as fast as possible to one of the bookcases I hadn't checked yet. Putting some space between us was necessary now.

My father wouldn't have hidden the book here. I'd been right before—that certainty was like iron in every muscle fiber. He wouldn't have hidden it in plain sight. That was too risky and too plain stupid. If he had anything in any book that could harm the Ancients, that would also have harmed him. I'd be lucky if he hadn't destroyed it.

He liked to have the upper hand, though, so he'd probably kept it as some sort of leverage. He was arrogant enough to believe he'd be able to control it, anyway. He'd never have thought someone could take it from him and use it against him in any way. Turned out he'd been right about that.

"We should finish checking in here," I mumbled. "Just to be sure."

She walked to my side and stood silently, checking the shelves. We continued working in this way, methodically, her trailing close behind me in silence, until I stepped back.

"I don't think there's anything here," I murmured.

She pulled a face. "Doesn't look like it. Where next?"

Before I could reply, Ruse swept through the door, deliberately seeming to make enough noise to make his presence known. He could have walked as quietly as a light breeze, if he'd wished. He could have lurked and eavesdropped for hours, if he'd wanted.

Luckily, none of the Ancients seemed in a hurry to regain some of their vampire mastery. Either that, or they didn't believe it was important. After all, why should gods have to tiptoe?

"Anything?" Ruse bit the word out, a scowl on his face.

Maeve pressed herself half behind me, seeking my body as shelter, and my ego swelled.

"Have you found it?" he prompted when I didn't answer straight away.

I shook my head. "I didn't expect it to be the first place I checked. And possibly the library is a little too obvious. But you never know. Still, there are many more books to check." I gestured at the bookcases, some we'd looked at, a few we hadn't.

Ruse rolled his eyes. "Come now, this is your library, is it not? Don't you know the contents like any owner would? You should be able to locate one simple book."

I laughed. "Ruse." My tone said *really?* "I've been sick for years, I've been running New Orleans during my father's prolonged absences, and I'm required to remember the full catalog of my family's library?"

When Ruse's scowl didn't shift, I changed my tack.

"No, there are far too many books. I'd be at risk of forgetting some of them if I didn't check each one. Besides, do you really think I was concerned with a book that I hadn't even known the importance of? I was far too engaged with thoughts of finding my mate and virgin blood." I stopped speaking abruptly, but it was too late.

Maeve gasped quietly behind me, and some of her warmth faded as she drew away.

Ruse narrowed his eyes to slits and watched me thoughtfully for long, uncomfortable seconds. Finally, he nodded.

"As you say. You were otherwise occupied. How is the search for the cure for your madness coming?" As he spoke, he switched his focus to Maeve, and he smiled cruelly when her breathing became uneven.

I stiffened, but if he noticed, he didn't comment.

"That's long enough for today." He cast a glance at the table that held all of Maeve's wrappers from earlier. "I see at least one of you ate today? I trust you're enjoying my hospitality?" His voice was deceptively soft, not the benevolent host he was portraying.

The unspoken words were the ones suggesting he expected something in return for his generosity. The faster I got Maeve to safety, the better.

She couldn't stay here. Not now that Ruse was watching her as closely as they watched me. "I trust if you *had* found something or you had any *other* news, I'd be the first to know?"

Over my finally dead body. But I smiled, almost as consummate a liar as Ruse. "Absolutely."

Chapter 12 - Maeve

"I'll send a guard," the Ancient said, and the new interest with which he looked at me seared my skin.

It was like I was something valuable now, and I didn't like it. Before, I was pretty sure I'd just been the human attached to Ciara. My existence almost didn't matter. But now that I was the human attached to Francois, I apparently mattered a lot more.

Almost before he'd finished speaking, one of their creepy vampire guards emerged from the shadows. They were like blocks of stone. Eerily silent blocks of stone.

Their grip was immovable, too, even though I tried to shake off the one who grabbed me as he clamped his fingers around my wrist.

"Back to where she came from," Ruse ordered.

"What? No... But..." Francois spluttered his disagreement. "You said... You *promised* me..."

"Ahh." Ruse shook his head like he was sorry about something. "We had a deal, Francois. I believe *you* also promised *me?*"

"I haven't finished looking." Francois began tossing books from the shelves, and I flinched as they landed on the floor, silently offering my apologies to the leather as it smacked against the wooden boards.

"There's always tomorrow," Ruse said. It was as though he was placating a child—and maybe he was. I had no idea as to the age difference between the two vampires. How old were the Ancients, anyway? I made a mental note to ask Ciara.

I didn't fight too hard as the guard led me across the room. There was no sense in earning myself bruises, and I'd at least eaten today.

"I'll see you soon." Francois looked at me as I passed him, the anguish in his eyes obvious.

For some reason, there was an answering pain in my chest, but perhaps that was just because I saw my freedom disappearing into one of the giant shadows lurking in this house. I swallowed against the sense of loss.

That part made sense, at least. I'd tasted freedom today, with Francois. And I'd tasted…temptation? It was something else I didn't want to explore too closely because surely it was more like professional curiosity. I'd learned today. And now I was going backwards. They were taking me back as a prisoner.

I walked with the guard back down to the level below ground and the damp, musty smell filled my nose. It wasn't unpleasant. It reminded me of growing things and life, which was ironic when it was paired with the metallic smell of blood that lingered in the small room.

The guard shoved me inside and Ciara looked up. Her eyes were still the dull red color.

"You okay?" She spoke first.

I nodded and waited for the door to close behind me, signaling that the guard had gone. I had so much to say and so many more questions to ask. But I could start slow. "I spent today in the library with Francois."

Before I could say another word, Ciara was right in front of me, and she grazed her fingertips over my neck, ran her hands down my arms. "Did he hurt you? Did anyone bite you? Did *Francois* hurt you?"

"What?" I stepped back and laughed. "No. No way. He… I… Why would you ask th——"

I stopped talking as she clamped me against her in a hug and I couldn't breathe anymore. I patted her back to let her know and she relaxed and loosened her hold.

"Sorry. It's just…" She lowered her voice. "It's Francois. He might be one of the worst ones here."

"Really?" I ignored the doubt in voice. After all I'd only spent one afternoon with him. Why would I know him better than Ciara? But something inside me didn't believe in the Francois she described.

I might have ignored the doubt in my voice, but she picked up on it. "I'm serious. He's a crazed vampire who kills every virgin female in his path." She gave me another once-over then a hard stare. "You really are lucky you weren't bitten, you know." She still didn't seem convinced that I hadn't been.

I tugged at the neckline of my T-shirt showing her both sides of my neck. "See?"

"Hmm." She frowned. "Just stay away from him in the future, then. Keep yourself safe. You've been lucky."

"What did you mean?" I walked toward the cot. The mattress was still grimy and covered in stains.

"That he's dangerous?" She sat in her usual position. Back against the wall, eyes on the door.

"No." Not that. He hadn't felt dangerous at all. Well, maybe a little. But good danger, like if I let myself go, I could get burned in the best of ways. I could feel alive. I could dance in the fire and emerge stronger for it. I'd never felt that kind of suppressed potential. "What did you mean, he's *crazed*?" He'd seemed distracted sometimes, but entirely lucid and not like he couldn't control himself. "He didn't seem any different from the others…" I stopped as I rethought that. He was a lot different than the others. "Or, well. He told me some stuff, anyway." I glanced away.

"What do you mean?" Ciara climbed to her feet and joined me on the cot. "What has he been telling you? Anything we can—" She lowered her voice. "Use?"

I shook my head. "Maybe not. I don't know."

"What sort of things did the two of you talk about then? By reputation, he isn't exactly socialized these days." She leaned against the wall and curled her legs underneath her.

"He talked about his father a little. And we looked for a book. And..." This part felt like the most important, but it was also the information I wanted to part with least. I wanted to keep the information to myself, like it was special if I just kept it safe and hidden. But I needed to trust Ciara. She had such faith we could be rescued. "And he called me his mate."

Ciara gasped. And so much echoed in that sound—shock, curiosity, horror. "He did? No. Absolutely not." She tilted her chin, defiance in each line of her face. "No." She repeated the word with vehemence. "No. *This* is what he does. He hasn't changed at all. You can't. You can't believe it. After all these years, Francois Ricard, the crazed prince, the ruthless royal... He thinks he's going to get his happy ending. After so much fucking destruction in his wake." She shook her head slowly, the motion part sadness, part disgust.

"What do you mean?" I hadn't expected such an extreme reaction. I wasn't entirely sure what I *had* expected. Maybe for Ciara to explain more of what Francois hadn't gotten around to.

"I bet there's a lot more he hasn't said." There was something in her tone that couldn't be argued with, but I didn't want to argue. I wanted to know whatever it was she thought I was missing.

"I'm sure there's a lot I don't know," I agreed. "I mean, some of this is new to me." Even after believing in vampires for years, it was very different than suddenly having all of the answers I'd sought right at my fingertips.

She raised an eyebrow. "Honestly, Maeve. There's a lot you couldn't even have dreamed of."

"Like what?" My words came out as more of a challenge than I'd intended, and she sighed before looking upward as if for some divine guidance.

"Where do I start?" She moved and stretched a little. "Francois has killed many, many women. Out of all the local vampires, it seems like he's the only one who has actively *hunted* for his mate, but I thought he'd know by now that these things can't be forced. I have no idea what he's doing with you, except..."

"Except what?" I didn't mean to be pushy, but really? It was hard to wait for someone to unravel a whole story when it was as important as this one.

She rubbed her face and sighed again. "You know how the Ancient referred to you as a virgin earlier?"

"Yes." I tried not to be embarrassed, because really, I wasn't, but it still wasn't generally public information.

"That's the key," Ciara said. "The most sought-after vampire mates are virgins in two ways."

"Two ways?" If my voice came out squeaky, it wasn't on purpose. Just how many in the hell ways did vampires like to take people?

She chuckled. "Never had sex, never been bitten." Then she waved a hand. "The never been bitten part is negotiable. The mate instinct doesn't always discriminate. One of the vampire mates I know was a thrall before she mated. But I digress."

My head spun a little. That was a lot of information packed into one short block of speech. "It's preferable?"

That was a stupid question, really. But being female was a glorious contradiction these days. Virginity was equally lauded and shamed. Society seemed to value *purity* while shaming *inexperience*. And I certainly landed on the inexperienced side of the fence. I was just awkward and weird enough to not be massively attractive to most men.

And the guys I *had* met were also bloggers, but more the tinfoil hat-wearing variety, even deeper into conspiracy theories than I was, and that had never felt like the direction I wanted to go. Especially not if they thought the government was watching.

"It's just a thing. Lore, I guess. You know what, I've never thought to question it. I suppose it's weird, but all of the recent mates were virgins, from what I know. I was, anyway."

"Really?" She had no reason to lie to me, but there didn't seem to be a reason why someone so attractive would have been left on the shelf, so to speak. Was there a shelf these days? Did society still go with that myth? I nodded. Yeah. There was still a fucking shelf.

I was sitting front and center on that shelf.

Only…my heartrate increased…not anymore. Someone finally wanted me.

Said he wanted me.

Only he was a vampire and…that complicated things, right?

"Yeah. I had a very hard time in my pack. I was human, they were wolf shifters. They were strong, I was weak. They were bullies, I was the sister of the alpha." She grinned, but it was weak. "It was complicated."

"Not anymore, though?" Her life seemed only positive now—except for the whole prisoner thing.

"True." She extended the word like she didn't want to actually say it. "Jason claimed me and he also brought out my wolf."

"So you're happy? Have everything you ever wanted?" I couldn't see the negatives in what she was telling me. "And you're immortal as well?"

"I think we need to talk about a few things," Ciara said, and when I turned toward her, she was watching me carefully.

"Oh?" This really sounded like the kind of talk I didn't want to have.

She nodded. "Yeah. I know the kind of things in your head right now, I think. I mean, on the one hand…A vampire, right? Only the most powerful being around, and there's something about them. That hint of danger combined with something possessive and territorial. It's an intoxicating combination. But on the other hand…a *vampire*. They bite and feed and they *kill*." She watched me a beat longer before speaking again. "Francois is a killer, Maeve. He killed any woman he thought might be his mate—in his search for his mate. He's been a desperate man in the past."

My face turned cold as though the blood had all drained away. "Yes, but he said…" He said I was his mate.

She nodded like she could read my thoughts. "I'm sure he told every other woman buried in his pretty garden of secrets that she was his mate, too. What makes you think you might be different?" Her tone was gentle but the question hurt, shaking my newfound confidence that I was both wanted and might escape from here. "Francois is a madman looking for a cure. He's been that for decades, always hoping the next virgin he finds will be his true mate and her blood will cure his family madness. It never has before." Her voice was so empty of hope that I focused anywhere but her face.

How the hell did I expect myself to be any different than the women who had gone before? But I kind of did. Wasn't that the downfall of women everywhere? We'd always be different, always be the one to change him, always be the one he loved best or more or be the one he wanted to be better for.

Ciara rested her hand on my forearm. "Be careful, Maeve. Seduction isn't just an artform for vampires, it's a way of being."

I nodded and changed my position, curling into a ball as I rested my cheek against the grimy mattress. The room didn't matter and the cleanliness didn't matter when it felt like the last drop of hope had just been sucked directly from me.

***

I slept. On and off, in and out, and time passed but I didn't know what time I woke up or how long I'd been asleep for.

My stomach grumbled as I moved, and Ciara gave me a small smile.

"What time is it?" I asked her.

She shrugged. "I don't know. Time we got out of here, but it's been that time for a while."

As she finished speaking, she looked toward the door, and my hunger disappeared as my stomach clenched, anxiety tightening inside my body. Someone was out there again.

The door opened and a guard stepped inside. "Both of you," he said, and Ciara glanced at me.

We were slow to respond to his command, and the guard moved fast, suddenly hovering in front of me before I could react and hauling me into a standing position.

Ciara was also on her feet before I saw her move. "Let go of her." Her face contorted and the redness in her gaze brightened but the guard only laughed.

"Oh, yeah, fledgling? On whose say-so?"

"It's okay, Ciara." It was far from okay, but at least she' be with me today, and if either of the two vampires in the room with me today spilled each other's blood, I couldn't guarantee what would happen. I'd truly be on my own, though and that would be bad.

I needed Ciara with me.

She shook her head, the movement frustrated, but she remained quiet, following behind us as the guard led me from the room. We walked quickly through the house, and my chest lightened as the route became familiar. We were near the library again. I hardly dared hope that they might take me back to Francois.

I couldn't look at Ciara. If I did, I'd give away too much of myself. She already disapproved of how much I thought of Francois.

Hell, *I* kind of disapproved of it. I barely knew the man, although something in me trusted him, which was ridiculous—especially after all Ciara had said. There was no reason to trust him and every reason not to.

But I couldn't help the small bright light of hope that he lit inside me.

As we entered the library, Francois stepped forward, his arms out like he might hug me. "Maeve." But he recovered himself and stepped back as his gaze passed over the guard and Ciara.

Ciara hissed quietly and stepped back, knocking against the nearest bookcase.

"Ciara." Francois nodded, courtesy in every line of his body.

As the guard left the room, I looked at Ciara.

"You need to remember what I said." Her eyes were earnest as she looked at me.

"What's been said?" Francois glanced between the two of us. Then he rubbed a hand over his face. "I suspect I can guess."

Ciara nodded. "And it's all true. The craziness, the killing."

Francois nodded, too. "But it's all changed now. I've found my mate." His eyes glowed with reverence as he switched his focus solely to me. "My mate can cure me."

My throat dried. Ciara had told me the cure was my blood but I needed to hear it from him. "How can your mate do that?"

"*You*, Maeve. You can cure me. Your blood can cure me."

"You need my blood?" All of it? Was he going to kill me, too? I backed away as he held his hands out like he could draw me back.

He nodded, his discomfort clear to see in his gaze. "After we mate and I feed on you, I will be cured. You'll heal me."

Whatever had seemed romantic yesterday was suddenly a lot less so. The idea of this man feeding on me to cure himself felt colder than the romance I'd projected on being wanted. I'd been a fool.

Of course he only wanted me for how I could benefit him.

"You can't know that, Francois. Look at your previous failures. You thought each of those women could cure you, too." Ciara stood beside me, her support obvious.

But Francois shook his head. "It's different this time. I feel it here." He touched his chest briefly. "I've found my true mate. The future is inevitable." His focus remained on me. "There's no way we could reject each other. It's never been done." He laughed shortly. "Mais oui, bien sûr, every vampire who's been through the process seems to fear that their mate will reject them, but it's never happened that I've seen or can recall. Mates who find each other always end up together." He moved a little closer, and I stayed perfectly still.

It was as if he'd bewitched me. I was enchanted by him, despite what he was saying.

"I'll wait until you're ready, Maeve." His voice was soft. "I'll wait as long as I possibly can, but if you ever see me change, you must run. I'm not in control when the madness takes over."

Chapter 13 - Francois

Every word seemed forced from me. The truth—such an ugly truth—didn't come easily. And it put the focus on the wrong reason for wanting a mate. Like her only use to me was her blood, like I'd just sullied every other mated vampire pairing out there.

The blood cure wasn't everything in my heart, and I wanted to express myself fully, to say everything that needed saying, but now wasn't the time. We had too much to do, and Ciara was looking at me as if she wanted to personally remove my heart and assure my final death.

I wasn't sure I could blame her, but she couldn't argue that I hadn't looked after Maeve before. She'd returned fed, at least. I hadn't been able to keep her with me or protect her in the way I most wanted to—in the way our bond demanded I needed to.

"We're looking for a book of spells." Maeve murmured the words quietly to Ciara as she walked to one of the bookcases we hadn't looked on yesterday.

Ciara followed her, unease clear in her stiff movements. She cast a glance at me over her shoulder like I might pounce on either of them.

I wanted to protest everything she thought to be true, but I couldn't really blame her for her mistrust. I'd done all of the things she'd said. I'd probably done more, but thankfully those memories were hazy, and I didn't have to relive those past misdeeds.

The knowledge of them was enough. And being back here meant no escape. The ghosts still appeared to me daily, the strongest one among them speaking to me like she had some sort of right to comment on and guide my life.

Perhaps she did. Perhaps she had more right than anyone to interfere, seeing as I'd ended her opportunity to experience everything for herself. Regret was heavy inside me. But I couldn't change the past. I couldn't go back and make myself a better man. I could only focus on the future.

On my mate. On our life together.

I walked the opposite way to the women, finding a bookcase in the back of the room. It was almost out of sight but not quite—far enough away to allow the women a sense of privacy, if that was what they needed, but close enough that I could still watch over Maeve and ensure her well-being.

The books here weren't grouped like the others. Every other bookcase seemed to have been arranged by someone with a very particular kind of library-based OCD, but here the books were neither arranged by height nor color nor seemingly even by subject.

As I stood and contemplated what to do, a light breeze brushed over my right cheek, but I was standing away from the windows, and those weren't even open. It wasn't as though the house had air conditioning, either. Father had never favored modern inventions.

He'd always been secretive, though. And I'd always believed there might be secret passages and rooms here. Certainly I'd hoped so as a child. But I'd believed I'd searched everywhere. I'd probably avoided the library, though, but only because the dusty attics full of sheet-covered furniture and abandoned antiques held more appeal for my explorations.

I glanced at my feet. Another thin, ornamental rug with faded colors. I'd heard many times that the more worn they were, the more value they held. The rug butted right up against the base of the bookcase, and anticipation skittered over my skin—the kind I'd always felt as a child but thought I'd long grown out of. Did this house still have secrets to reveal to me? I bent down before lifting the edge and peeling it back.

Keep going, Francois. My ghost's voice was distorted as she flickered briefly into view, but then she was gone again.

I hadn't needed her encouragement, but my excitement definitely grew, and it grew again at the scuff marks I revealed on the wood floor. I glanced up at the bookcase. Was it truly a bookcase or was it a door?

I glanced at where the women were. The temptation to shout my findings was great but too many people in this house had super hearing now, and any one of them could have been stationed just outside the door—Ruse, especially. He'd taken far more of an interest in the search for the book than I'd expected.

I pushed the rug back into place and strolled to where the women were. I didn't want to alarm wither of them or let them know I might have found something.

"Maeve."

She glanced up as I whispered her name.

I beckoned to her, and she grinned before approaching me. Ciara touched her arm briefly like she might hold her back, but I caught her eye and signaled for her to come closer, too. Her reaction was the opposite of Maeve's and her revulsion was almost a visible physical ripple under her skin.

I waited until they came closer. "I think I found something." I barely spoke the words, but Ciara's eyebrows lifted in response, and she turned and whispered against Maeve's ear.

Maeve's eyes gleamed, and I grinned at her before turning and trying to remain casual as I returned to the bookshelf and rug.

"It's here." I pushed the rug back again to reveal the scuff marks. "I think it's a door."

"The bookcase?" For a moment, Maeve drew her eyebrows down in a vision of perplexity, but then she almost jumped. "Hell, yes!"

I motioned her to be quiet, and her cheeks pinked.

"Sorry," she mouthed. Then she whispered like I had. "Hell, yes! Of *course,* the bookcase. Eat your heart out, Scooby Doo!"

I grinned at her enthusiasm.

"We need to open it."

"On it," Ciara replied as she started lifting books in turn. "One of these has to be release the mechanism, right? Isn't that how it usually works?"

"Absolutely it is." Maeve started working up the case from the bottom, moving books and running her hands over the wood. "We're looking for any strange catches or niches or dents in the framework of the shelf. It might just hang on a hinged book."

Ciara nodded. "Okay." Then she grimaced. "Wait. I might have found something." Her grimace quickly expanded into a grin. "Yep. This is definitely something."

As she finished speaking, there was a soft click. And the shelf moved, swinging towards us the smallest amount as whatever had held it fully closed released.

Maeve covered her mouth. "It *is* a door." She glanced toward me. "Not that I ever doubted you."

I tugged at the edge of the open bookcase and a waft of musty air raced toward us. Maeve coughed and turned her head.

"Oh my God," she murmured. "How ancient is that space? The air tastes like dust."

A torch on a wall a little way down the passage flared to life and I blinked.

"Magic," Maeve whispered, as I looked beyond the torch to the ethereal vision of my ghost. She smiled faintly before fading from view.

Ciara and Maeve hesitated at the entrance to the passageway, Ciara's posture one of distrust, Maeve's more like uncertainty.

"Oui. I can go alone," I muttered. "You needn't come." This was too dangerous a situation to plunge my mate into. I didn't know what was in here.

As if the words had galvanized her into action, Maeve sprang forward. "Nope. Nuh-uh. Not happening. I've never seen anything this amazing. This is proper haunted house stuff."

As she moved away from the open door, she grabbed the torch and held it slightly aloft. "There are stairs." Her whispered words were clear to hear, and she didn't stop or turn around before starting to walk down them. I sighed at her complete lack of self-preservation before following her.

"Oh, no, you don't." Ciara's grim sing-song behind me brought me pause as she fell into step, her breath almost teasing against my neck.

I should have laughed. I was following my mate so that no danger came to her, and Ciara was following me following my mate to ensure that no danger came to her.

If she hadn't already been mated, I would have believed that he didn't even know what the bond felt like.

As we took a step forward, she spoke again. "Better close this in case anyone comes into the library while we're gone."

The passageway was plunged into near darkness, the torch bobbing away from us as Maeve descended with the only light source. Still, Ciara had the right idea—we didn't need to be joined on this quest by any of the Ancients.

"I've never been here." I fought to keep my voice low, and I trailed my hand along the wall to my right as we walked. "I didn't even know this existed."

That had probably been Father's plan all along. He would never have expected me to find it, and he certainly hadn't tried to tell me about it—even after some of his longer bouts of stasis, when it had looked as though his final death was close.

When we reached the bottom of the steps, we entered a small room, a windowless chamber, really, and another two torches flared to life with unnatural fire. The entire room vibrated with a type of magic that prickled against my skin and my first instinct was to run.

Maeve sucked in a breath. "This room *hurts*," she murmured.

"Witch magic," Ciara replied, not even looking to me for an answering nod. When she did look at me, there was derision in her eyes. "I have no idea how you didn't even know there was a whole secret room in your house, though."

I shrugged. "Witch magic," I replied. If they could put whole basements in New Orleans, they could certainly create rooms in pockets of space that didn't appear to exist.

"But why?" Maeve stood in the center of the room, still holding the torch she'd brought with her.

"Safe room?" Ciara twisted her mouth as she looked at the various shelves in the space.

I shook my head. "Back-up plan." The longer I stood here, the more sure I was. Father had created this space to ensure he could defeat the Ancients if they ever came for him. "There's nothing here but stuff to fight, oui? It's where he planned to have a last stand if he ever needed one. We need to check what's up here."

Maeve nodded and handed me her torch, her fingers grazing against mine as she did. "See if you recognize anything?"

"I won't. But I might know something important when I see it." That was some hope. How the fuck was I supposed to know anything about Father's previous life when he'd never breathed a word of it? Had he confided in Loïc? My brother was the true heir, after all. I was just the failure who came next.

I almost laughed. I was the failure who was still here. That probably said everything I needed to know.

"Wow." Ciara spun around, a large black sword in her hand, and she wielded it like she was a professional. As she pointed it at me, I backed away, the movement instinctive and automatic.

Power radiated from the sword in waves, filling the air with black magic with every movement Ciara made.

"What the hell?" Maeve paled and swooned a little.

"Put it down." I bit the words out as I reached for my mate. She was only human and didn't have the same natural defenses against magic that we had. "Come to this side of the room." I gentled my tone as I spoke directly to Maeve, and I took her hand, enjoying the warmth of her skin as her fingers curled around mine.

Ciara hissed but I didn't even look at her.

"Put it down," I said again, my tone milder this time. "We should avoid touching anything until we know what it does." I kept my admiration for how well she'd handled it to myself. Father's room seemed dangerous, though. There was immense power up here; it was almost like I'd been sitting inside a nuclear bomb this whole time.

I led Maeve to a crooked set of shelves above some sort of old, dark wood desk. Maybe a desk or perhaps a preparation area for spell casting, but Father had never given any indication that he could cast. He was an Ancient, though, so he could have simply hidden the ability. There were certainly things I hadn't known about him.

"What's this?" Maeve jolted me from my thoughts as she spoke.

I glanced at the book she was pointing to. She'd made the wise decision not to touch it. Or maybe it wasn't her decision at all. As I reached to pluck it from the shelf, it took all of my concentration to even touch it as the book itself seemed to repel me. If Maeve hadn't pointed it out directly, I might have even glanced right over it.

I set it on the desk and opened the cover. It behaved much better now that I'd lifted it from the shelf, but there was still a residual feeling of unease lingering inside me as I turned the pages.

The spells were written in Latin, and my use of the language was rusty, but key phrases I hadn't known I remembered jumped out at me. "I think this might be exactly what we're looking for."

"Really?" The glance Maeve gave me was filled with such expectant hope that the desire to kiss her was almost overwhelming, if not for the fact that Ciara was here and I didn't want my first kiss with Maeve to be a public event.

I nodded, still holding myself back from dipping my head closer and claiming her lips, ignoring when her gaze lowered to my mouth like she knew and wanted the same.

"I think this book might have the information in it that we need to kill the Ancients." I stopped and tilted my head, considering. That was a very bold claim. One I might not be able to back up. "Or at least incapacitate them until we know what to do in the future. I just need to get it to Kayla and see what she makes of it."

"Hurry up then. What do we do if one of them goes looking for us in the library? I closed the door but I couldn't replace the rug. None of them will need to be Sherlock Holmes to find our location if they're really looking."

"Let me just check for anything else that might help us in the fight ahead." I turned to the next set of shelves, but a loud bang sounded from the top of the stairs and the magical flames all flickered.

We'd run out of time.

Chapter 14 - Maeve

I jumped at the loud bang from the top of the stairs, and glanced in the direction of the sound before moving closer to Francois. It was instinct. The knowledge he could protect me, *would* protect me, radiated through my whole body.

I didn't question it. I simply knew.

He wrapped an arm around me, drawing me tight against him until a second bang echoed through the chamber, seeming to shake the whole space.

"What are they doing?" Ciara's eyes were wide as she reached for the black sword again. "Maybe I can hold them off."

"Non." Francois's reply was short and sharp. "We need to leave. There's no telling what they could do with the power and the artifacts in here." Then he turned to his left. "What should I do?" But he was talking to shadows. As if he'd received an answer, he grabbed a satchel from a hook on the wall and began putting books and artifacts into it. "Check for a door," he said to me. "My father wasn't so stupid as to trap himself in a room without an escape route."

I started touching surfaces and shelves, looking any kind of catch or mechanism, but panic took over and I fumbled, my desire for speed slowing me down.

"I can't find one." My voice came out quiet and thin as tension tightened my throat. I was going to let everyone down by not finding a way out.

Footsteps on the stairs chilled me, and I almost didn't dare turn around. The Ancients were coming, and I was about to die. Their pale faces glowed eerily in the dark, and I didn't recognize the one at the front.

"I told Ruse not to trust you," he snarled.

"Aleron." Francois still nodded his head like the man deserved respect, but perhaps that was strategic. He said nothing else and simply waited.

I itched with the need to run, and Ciara seemed to vibrate with a similar need to act.

The vampire Francois had called Aleron laughed, the sound cruel, and it was like needles slicing against my skin.

"No one move." He stopped at the bottom of the stairs. "I see you've found what we wanted." Then he stepped forward. "I'm going to kill the women. We have no further use for them now that you've performed as exactly as we need."

He was a typical storybook villain, monologuing his next moves, and Francois snarled as he stopped speaking, moving into a fighting stance, like he might attack the group of powerful vampires on willpower alone.

I twined my fingers with his, drawing him closer to me, and I glanced at him, signaling that he should look at the floor. It wasn't out of deference. I just needed his attention not focused on the vampires so that he could contain his temper in case losing that also unleashed his madness. I had nowhere to run if that happened.

And he'd warned me.

I'd need to run.

As I focused on Francois, though, Ciara made a howling sound next to me, and the noise of bones cracking and tendons snapping was like a riot of bullet fire. Then she leapt forward, her speed a blur, and she slashed her newly appeared claws across Aleron's face, slicing his delicate skin so that blood gushed from the wounds.

Her eyes glowed an unearthly blue, and she snarled, the sounds those of a wild animal.

Aleron produced a perfect white pocket square and held it to his face as though he needed to clamp his flesh back together, but instead of grimacing in pain, he closed his eyes and appeared to bask in it.

Francois stepped forward like he was going to control Ciara, and when she turned to slash him too, he raised his hand to defend himself so her claws ripped across his palm instead.

"Very good, Ciara." He smiled, even though his cheekbones became more prominent and his eyes turned deep red.

I started to move away. Was this the moment Francois had warned me about? Did I need to find distance? Surely I was caught between something bad and something worse in here. There was nowhere to go.

Aleron opened his eyes and chuckled. "Well, well," he said, as he watched Ciara readying for another attack. "A hybrid," he murmured. "I did wonder. How very rare." There was something insidious in his admiration. "And how very fortuitous. We might have use for you after all."

But before he could move, Francois clamped me to his side and yanked Ciara closer to him, squeezing her so she couldn't get away until she cried out as her claws pierced her own skin.

"You can't stay here." His gaze never left hers and their blood mingled before the drops fell onto the floor.

As I watched, runes lit around us, forming a circle of glowing symbols with the three of us standing in the middle and Aleron and the rest of the Ancients standing outside. There hadn't been enough room for them to mount a full attack, and now it looked as though they wouldn't get chance.

"No." Ciara tried to draw away as the word of protest left her lips, and the glow in her eyes faded as panic replaced the light. "What's happening? What have you done?"

I mimicked her movement, straining against Francois and yet staying molded to his body like we were one being.

Aleron stepped forward and I gasped as he loomed closer, but then his lips moved and I couldn't hear anything he said. He raised his fists and beat against a barrier that I couldn't see.

I turned to Francois but before I could ask him anything at all, all of the air was sucked out from around us, and my ears filled with a whooshing sound. My hair floated wildly, obscuring my vision, and the floor beneath me dropped away. I plunged downward, hurtling at speed until everything stopped in an oddly soft landing.

"What?" I looked up, expecting the Ancients to still be watching from outside whatever bubble Francois had just created, but we were somewhere new, somewhere I didn't recognize.

"You okay?" Francois reached toward me, ready to take my hand and help me up from my knees.

As I stood, he swiped at my jeans-clad legs awkwardly, dusting dirt and debris from me, and I smiled a little. He was a sweetheart really.

"I'm okay." I said the words he wanted to hear as I gave myself a quick mental check to see if it was true. Aside from having no clue what had just happened or where we were, the words felt pretty accurate. I wasn't hurt, and the Ancients weren't here. Both of those things were a win. "Where's Ciara?"

"Here."

I turned around to face my friend. "Oh, thank God." I almost pulled her into a hug but there was something still almost feral about her, and I hesitated, suddenly very aware of my own fragility. How many times had I cheated death now? I'd known monsters existed but it was different to be standing among them. I probably needed a little more self-awareness and a sense of self-preservation.

"Where are we?" As Ciara asked her question, I glanced around the small room we were in. It was another windowless chamber, but there was a raised stone table in the middle, and there was a smell of nature. Torches lowed around the edges of the room, illuminating pale stone.

"My father's resting place. He spent each stasis in here. I'd known there was a portal from the gardens but it doesn't surprise me that Father had more than one— particularly as a built-in escape route." Francois glanced at me briefly. "It's a good thing you thought I should study the floor or I'd never have seen the circle there." Then he shook his head. "Mais…thank goodness it only needed family blood to activate it. We need to hurry, though. This isn't a good enough hiding place. And if my father was truly an Ancient, there's also the chance their blood could grant them the same passage through the portal. They won't be far behind us no matter how they discover our whereabouts. We aren't safe yet."

A shiver ran through me at his words. How long had it been since I felt truly safe? Even as a child, Granny's stories hadn't really disturbed me. I'd felt secure in what she could see and what I couldn't. The veil had protected me, but now that had truly been lifted and the monsters were real, encroaching into my world, and I couldn't unsee them.

Francois looked at me, meeting my gaze, his eyes soft. "This is going to be faster if I carry you."

"What? I've been able to walk for a most of my life. Run, too." I wasn't really sure why I was arguing, but I hated the idea of being inferior to anyone. Or being infantilized. I glanced at Ciara, and she nodded.

"It's true, I'm afraid. Vampires can move very fast, and it's our only hope of outrunning the Ancients. Allowing you to walk or even run would just slow us down." She paused. "Or you'd just get left behind—"

"Which I can't allow. I must have you with me." Francois interjected his thoughts and Ciara nodded approvingly as if the idea of allowing me to straggle behind the two of them had only been to test Francois.

"Well, if it's the only way…" I swallowed as the idea of being so close to Francois tightened my chest.

"It is." He nodded decisively, and I moved behind him, expecting him to bend down so that I could climb onto his back. "Non, mon ange."

He turned and scooped me into his arms before cradling me against his chest—the position seemingly effortless for him, while I frantically thought light thoughts.

Ciara raised an eyebrow but nodded. "Ready?"

"Oui."

I glanced up at the set of Francois's jaw and the way he nodded. I wasn't sure if he was a man racing toward freedom or marching to his execution.

"Where are we going?" I hadn't asked before, which seemed remiss of me.

"Home." Ciara opened the small wooden door and the blast of humid air from outside swirled into the small room.

"We have to go. We're crossing magical wards, and anyone in the house will probably know." Francois darted forward, and his burst of speed stole my breath. Scenery passed by in a blur, but night had fallen and we were shrouded in darkness. Countryside gave way to suburbs before becoming the vibrant New Orleans I'd expected to arrive to, and neither Francois nor Ciara showed any sign of slowing as they swerved from the main streets to back alleys to complete our journey. Eventually their pace slowed and Francois put me down.

"We walk now," he said.

But we didn't walk long before we were all standing outside a nightclub, the queue to get into it stretching down the street and around the block.

I looked up at the sign above the door.

"Nightfall," I whispered.

Chapter 15 - Francois

I'd never expected to be so relieved to step firmly onto Dupont territory. Not even the knowledge that I used to command this space bothered me. I no longer wanted that sort of responsibility. Non. I wanted the protection only the Dupont royalty could offer. And we *would* be protected here.

I would be safe here, but more importantly, my mate would be safe here. Some of my worry slipped away.

The doormen stepped aside as Ciara swept past, his eyes widening. Her hurry seemed to increase the closer she got to the interior of the club until she was practically pushing patrons out of her way.

I cast my gaze over the new interior, the twinkling lights in the ceiling capturing my attention before a movement on one of the balconies overlooking the stage drew my gaze.

Jason pushed away from where he'd been leaning on the balustrade, watching the clientele and the singer, and he rushed down the stairs. Jason and I had been roommates when I was abducted by the Ancients, but he wasn't interested in me now.

He looked like hell, too, scruffier than usual, his face haggard. His cheeks were gaunt, and his eyes were haunted.

He rushed to Ciara and swept her into an embrace, holding her as though he never intended to let her go again.

"Ciara." Her name was mournful on his lips. "They had the whole place guarded with some sort of magic Kayla's been trying to unpick. We couldn't get to you... Nic wouldn't let me come back alone. I nearly ended up in his cells for trying."

When Ciara buried her face against his chest, I looked away.

I wanted that level of intimacy and connection with Maeve.

And I completely understood how he must have felt when he was unable to rescue Ciara. Sympathetic, impotent rage rose inside me, but I squashed it down. It served no purpose now. I'd returned Ciara to Jason and all could be well.

When I looked at Maeve, her entire focus had been captured by the people milling about and dancing. Some were grinding against each other, others were a hair's breadth away from feeding. Her eyes widened and she turned to me.

"Vampires?" She merely mouthed the word.

I nodded. "All flavors of the supernatural, I believe."

"*All?*" Her eyes widened more and she took a small step forward like she wanted a closer look.

Only my hand on her arm stopped her from venturing farther into the crowd and becoming lost among the monsters and people already here. But she was an unclaimed human mate. *My* human mate. I couldn't allow her to wander freely.

But she turned to look at me, and everything I wanted crashed away. I didn't hold her interest here. She glanced at my hand on her arm and she shrugged it away. I wasn't enough. She might never accept me now that I'd spent up my usefulness freeing her from her prison.

I held her gaze for a moment, but she gave the slightest shake of her head, and I didn't try to stop her again as she melted into the crowd. I'd watch her, protect her, save her if she needed me to.

That was my duty as her mate. Even if she didn't want me to.

I sighed as I walked to the flight of stairs Jason had run down. The interior to the nightclub was so different now. I didn't like how understated it was, but I couldn't deny it was still elegant, although the lack of crimson bothered me on some level. When it had been mine, the décor had been much bolder.

Now it was sleek. Almost sterile. But I shrugged. It was also none of my business. And I didn't care.

As I climbed the staircase, I looked out over the patrons, trying to spot Maeve. Her hair was like a beacon as she sat at the bar, chatting to the bartender. At least he'd watch her. He paused briefly and met my gaze as though he knew I'd wanted his attention. When he gave me a quick nod, I relaxed.

I knocked on the door of the first office once I reached the second floor. Sebastian had his head in his hands but looked up as I stood in his doorway.

Then he was immediately on his feet. "Fuck. How did you get here? Are the Ancients following you here? Have you brought trouble to our door? Where's Ciara?" He let loose a torrent of questions and I waited a beat to ensure he'd finished asking them before I responded.

I was also a little taken aback by his tone, but maybe that was to be expected. He hadn't expected me to just show up in his club, and he was clearly worried I'd endangered everyone here by doing so. The Ancients had been here before, too, and nearly killed his mate, if the things I'd been told were correct.

"This seems a little too convenient." His eyes reddened when I didn't immediately answer him. "Are they after Kayla again?" He moved forward as if to make his way to the door. "I need to take her offstage. She's a fucking sitting duck." He shook his head. "I knew it."

"T'inquiète pas, mon ami. Don't worry." The addition of *my friend* at the end was probably a stretch, but we were far more friends than enemies these days, surely. Our cause was a common one. I hesitated. "I mean, I don't know if they're coming, but I'm not drawing them here. I'm not working with them." After the renewed chance at life Nicolas had offered me, I wouldn't betray him.

"Then what?" Sebastian leaned his ass against the edge of his desk, but his pose still wasn't relaxed. He was ready to spring into action at any moment, depending on what I said next.

He didn't trust me, and I didn't blame him.

"It's a long story. We were looking for the information to kill the Ancients or render them ineffective, and we thought we'd become trapped in a hidden witch room. But there was a portal to the old mausoleum and we escaped."

Sebastian raised an eyebrow. "Sounds very convenient. All roads lead to the family mausoleum, huh?"

I shrugged. That was the truth. Although he only knew of the portal to the gardens. They'd used that once when they'd come to reclaim Nicolas's mate from me.

"Any proof of the existence of this witch room?"

That was an impossible request. "I didn't stop to take pictures, if that's what you're asking." My tone turned derisive before I swept the satchel I'd filled from across my body, "But I did grab some of the books and artifacts to bring to you and Kayla. I thought Kayla might be able to help." I tossed the bag toward him. He caught it easily before emptying the contents carefully onto his wide desk.

My ghost had guided me a little on what to bring, and at the thought of her, guilt gnawed at the edges of me. Once again, I'd abandoned her in the place of her death.

Sebastian grabbed his cell phone and made a couple of quick taps on the screen before pressing it to his ear. "Hey. You want to come up here, Francois just walked in and he's brought some stuff I think you might want to see."

He was clearly talking to Kayla, but now that I'd given the magical items to Sebastian, my mind was once again on Maeve.

As if someone had read my mind, there was a tap on the door behind me, and the bartender stood in the doorway with Maeve.

"This belong to you?" he called, and Maeve wrinkled her nose as she looked up at him.

"Actual person right here."

"I know," he said, "and I'm not paid enough to babysit you downstairs."

Sebastian beckoned her into his office, but when he looked like he might speak to her, I spoke first.

"Can I get you anything? Something to eat? Access to a shower?"

She had started to shake her head when I first spoke but her eyes lit up at the end of my questions, and the shaking turned to nodding.

"Actually, a shower sounds amazing." Her stomach grumbled and she pressed her arm across the front of it. "And maybe some food at some point." She laughed softly, and I tensed with the effort not to sweep her body against mine to feel her pressed there.

"Sebastian—"

He held up a hand. "All in good time. Kayla's on her way up and I'm sure she'll take…" He trailed off and glanced at Maeve with curiosity. The he looked at me, his gaze pointed.

My cheeks warmed, but I was pretty sure vampires never blushed. "Maeve," I supplied. *Mate*, my head screamed. *Mate.*

"Well, I'm sure Kayla will take Maeve and find anything she needs to be comfortable. Kayla understands what this is like."

I nodded. Kayla had also been human. But wait, did that mean Sebastian knew?

"Do you…?"

He nodded. "It's pretty obvious." He winked. "Plus I've been in your shoes."

I moved a little closer to Maeve. I didn't need to stake out my territory but the instinct to be as close to her as possible was overwhelming. "So what's the plan?"

Sebastian sighed. "Like I said. Kayla's on her way up…"

"From where?" Maeve cut in. Pride swelled my heart. My mate truly knew no fear. Either that or she had no idea she was talking to the Dupont regent.

To be honest, it was probably the latter. I hadn't exactly introduced them. "Maeve, this is Sebastian Dupont. He's the brother and regent of Nicolas Dupont, King of New Orleans."

Her mouth dropped open. "Shit. It's true." She watched Sebastian for a moment as he chuckled at her reaction. Then she dropped into a messy curtsey. "I mean, your honor. How nice to...pleasant to...honorable to meet you." She glanced up. "I..."

Sebastian laughed harder. "Francois, help your mate out."

As I took her hand and drew her to stand by me, ignoring her protests about her status, he continued to speak.

"As I was saying, Kayla is coming. She and I have left the house for the moment. Regardless of how many guards I hired, it felt like we were sitting in a big bullseye. Downstairs feels easer to defend. There's an apartment down there and we have magic."

"That sounds sensible." Honestly, I no longer knew what was sensible. Luckily, before I had to say anything further, Kayla entered the room.

She glanced at me, a side-eye of suspicion as she gave me an extra wide berth on her trajectory to Sebastian. He gathered her into his arms, and she turned to rest against him as she looked at Maeve and me.

Sebastian nuzzled at her ear, and she smiled. "Francois has brought you some presents, my love," he said softly.

"Oh?" She lifted an eyebrow as she looked first at me then she turned to her mate, so close that their lips almost touched.

I wanted that. Fuck, I wanted it. It was the very thing I'd searched for my whole life. I'd craved that kind of love since even before my madness. The madness had only amplified what I needed most.

Sebastian maneuvered her back around in his arms so she could see his desk. "He found these at his father's house."

I nodded, grateful that he'd removed me from the situation. I'd lived there but it never truly been my house. Always my father's.

"At Émile's?" Kayla spat out my father's name like it was a dirty word, and I nearly laughed. It was the dirtiest word I knew.

"Yep. He brought everything you see here." Sebastian looked at the desk, and Kayla stepped away from him to sort through some of the things. When she grabbed the spell book Maeve had found, she smiled.

"I think I might know what this is." She began to flip through the pages, pausing only to lower her head and smell them occasionally. "This is powerful magic," she murmured. "Fucking great I no longer have a soul to taint."

Sebastian leaned forward and picked up the black sword before looking at me. "This?" He lifted both eyebrows as he held it.

"Don't blame me." I held out my hands, palms forward. "The wolf wanted that."

Kayla glanced at me then looked at what Sebastian was holding. "Now that's interesting," she said. "Ciara has some of the best instincts I've ever known. I wonder what attracted her attention to it?"

I shrugged. "Not a swordsman. I don't really know. But none of this stuff is *good* stuff." I referenced the black magic rolling off it.

"Oh, I know." Kayla's smile wasn't strictly *good* either, and I grinned. Maybe she'd be a good friend for Maeve— someone we could rely on. "It's a weapon, though, and maybe it's one we can actually use. We still don't actually know what works on the Ancients. All suggestions are welcome." She shrugged as she glanced at the items on the table again. "But fuck, we need to tighten the wards."

After Sebastian placed the sword back down, she turned to him, and they began a conversation so quiet I needed to strain to hear it. That was my cue to leave, then.

"Maeve, can I take you for some food and to find a shower? Sebastian and Kayla live in the apartment downstairs and Sebastian has said we can head down." He hadn't... well, not in so many words, but I didn't intend to take my mate anywhere less secure than where the regent felt safe to keep his mate.

I only hoped Nicolas was already down there. He was the man I really wanted to see.

Chapter 16 - Maeve

We headed downstairs, Francois's hand clamped around my upper arm, vise tight, like if we got separated and all he kept hold of was my actual arm while my body got swept away in the rest of the crowd, that would be enough.

No one seemed to get out of our way. In fact, people crowded ever closer as if to look at the newcomers wandering through Nightfall. And although Francois lowered his head and we stuck to the shadows, it would be unlikely that no one at all recognized him.

Someone jostled against me. "I'd like to fuck the clunge on that. Fuck. I wonder if the carpet matches the curtains?"

My ears were attuned to picking up differences in speech after all of the recordings I'd listened to for my blog, and I swung my attention toward the British accent that had spoken, but whoever it was had fallen quiet.

I shuddered. Some men were disgusting, the way they talked about women.

Francois stiffened and his face started to change. A growl started to work its way through him, vibrating his chest, and he seemed about to snap to defend my honor—if it had even been me they were talking about.

I tightened my hold on him, just wanting him to keep it together while we got somewhere safe, although him defending me warmed my insides.

Not like this, though. He seemed to come from a more…refined time, and I wanted to hang onto that image after what we'd all just been through.

Despite his madness, there was definitely more of the Regency gentleman about him than drunk asshole at the local rundown bar.

I pressed my hand over his as though to secure his grip. I liked to have him so close—regardless of what Ciara had said. Forget *said*. She'd warned me. Tried to warn me off.

But what could I say? I'd always believed in the supernatural, despite every naysayer or person who wanted to tell me what a fucking crazy bastard I was. I'd believed in my gut then, and something in me believed in Francois now.

I couldn't explain it, but I liked him, only it felt deeper than that, I trusted him. Like I would do anything for him.

And that thought was scary because I didn't know *why* I felt that way. There was nothing rational behind it. It was as though my heart had gotten loose from my brain and was making its own decisions, but when had my heart become involved?

I shook my head. I was tired, I was dirty, I was hungry. And I was clearly overdramatizing my life. Surely I had enough going on with my very sudden submersion into the supernatural, without imaging myself into a sweeping love saga?

Just as I was talking sense into myself, Francois guided me behind a curtain that had looked like a wall from a distance away, and then pushed through a door and down some stairs.

I stopped, the movement abrupt, and he looked at me, curiosity in his gaze. But I shook my head and heaved in a deep breath, then another, until I couldn't count the breaths anymore and my chest rose and fell rapidly as my focus failed. I wobbled, and Francois wrapped his arm around my waist.

"Maeve?"

I didn't answer.

"Mon ange?" Concern underscored his questioning tone.

"I..." But there wasn't enough air. Only the twin scents of damp earth and an air tainted with copper like in the cell where Ciara and I had been held.

I drew away from him and rested my forehead against the wall for a moment, focusing on the cool paint against my skin as I talked myself down. This wasn't the same as being in that cell. I was safe here.

I was with Francois. I was safe with him.

When I turned to face him again, I smiled, my lips stretching, even though my eyes threatened to water for no reason. "I'm okay," I said—more so I heard the words myself than to reassure Francois.

I'd been telling myself I was okay, despite what anyone else thought of me, for years.

He didn't say a word in reply. Instead, he simply held out his hand. I twined our fingers together and it was like coming home. Everything felt right the moment my palm rested against his.

My breathing slowed to normal and my chest loosened.

"Sorry." I couldn't explain but I could apologize.

Francois squeezed my hand in reply, the gesture reassuring. And again, I had no reason as to why I found his presence reassuring. I just *did*. And after the time I'd just had since I arrived in New Orleans, I was going to grab this random feeling of peace and hold onto it with both hands, even if it was a vampire bringing me that peace.

I relaxed. I'd just roll with it.

He led me down the staircase and we walked through a doorway into a large common area. Then it was Francois's turn to stop abruptly.

"Hello." His tone was clipped, and his hand tightened like he was suddenly unsure of himself.

The vampires on the sofa were snuggled close to each other as they watched their movie, but I didn't look closely at what it was because as soon as Francois indicated our presence, the vampires both stood, the male advancing with a growl low in his throat.

The female vampire with him grinned as she swatted him lightly on the arm. "Give it up, Kyle." Amusement danced in her eyes. Then she extended her arm. "Hi. I'm Sam, and this grumpy guy is Kyle."

I nodded and accepted her hand. "I'm Maeve. I think Sebastian said we could come down here to refresh and maybe eat…?" I made it into a question, although I wasn't sure why.

Sam exchanged a glance with Kyle and then they both looked between Francois and me.

"How the hell…?" Kyle's voice was gruff. "Where's Ciara?"

"Oh…" I waved my hand. "She's upstairs."

"And now you're just back?" There was an element of mistrust in Kyle's voice as he looked at Francois, and I pushed away from the two strange vampires, seeking comfort from Francois's presence instead.

"Yes." Francois answered. "Three of us. Ciara, Maeve, and me. All back. And Maeve is hungry."

"I think I can probably find you something in the kitchen," Sam said. "Is Chef still trailing around between Baton Rouge and New Orleans?"

Kyle nodded but didn't say anything as he ran his fingers over a raised scar on his head.

"Excellent." Sam capped her hands. "There might even be beignets as part of dinner. But first come with me. I can show you to a spare room where you can get washed up and change your clothes."

I sighed with relief then gasped as I ran through what she'd said a second time. "Change my clothes? I only have these. Can I do laundry?"

Sam laughed softly. "I'm sure we can hook you up with an outfit. We have a few women here. We've been looking for you. Kayla has been trying to unpick the wards and spells…" Her gaze softened. "As soon as I get you situated, I need to see Ciara. Is she okay?"

I nodded. "I think so."

"She's home," Francois said, and Sam nodded.

"Okay. Come with me. I'll get you some clothes and Kyle can see to the food."

I glanced at Francois, almost like I was seeking his permission to go with this vampire I'd just met, but he seemed more at ease than I'd ever known him to be.

Apparently, grumpy, mistrustful vampire aside, we were with friends. He smiled and nodded and released my hand. I'd barely even noticed that we'd been standing there like a conjoined Tweedledee and Tweedledum.

"This way." Sam glanced over her shoulder before she walked down a corridor. "The private bedrooms are down here."

"This place is pretty big." I couldn't keep my curiosity inside.

"Yeah. It's magic—literally." Sam looked around. "I couldn't understand it at first, really. I didn't have the best introduction to supernatural life, but things are good now. I have Kyle." She finished talking with a smile on her lips, and I didn't probe further. It wasn't any of my business.

It was good to know she hadn't had the easiest start either, though. Mine certainly didn't feel all that great. Being abducted by the oldest known vampires was possibly quite the claim to fame, though.

"I've always believed." I came to a stop behind her as she opened a door and entered an impossibly airy bedroom.

"Really?" She lifted an eyebrow. "They're quite protective of their privacy."

I nodded. "My Granny had the sight or something. She used to tell me bits and pieces of lore about various supernatural creatures. I've been looking for actual proof all my life."

"Well, you've found it now." Sam laughed then pointed to a door in the corner of the room. "The bathroom's through there. I'll send some clothes down and come back for food when you're done."

I thanked her and she left the room, closing the door behind her.

I'd never seen a shower like it. Double width, rainhead shower above and various other jets from the walls. Starting the water and figuring out how to work everything individually was a bit like piloting the next space shuttle, but eventually the beat of warm water soothed muscles I hadn't even realized were tense, and the delicate scent of orange blossom soap filled the air around me.

When I was done, I wrung my hair out before twisting it into a towel and balancing the resulting turban on my head. I wrapped a second towel around my body, and tucked the corner between my breasts to secure it.

Sam had mentioned clothes, but I didn't know where I was supposed to find them. I cracked the bathroom door open and peered into the bedroom then stepped onto the luxurious carpet just as the bedroom door opened and Francois crept in, his expression nervous, his hands full of clothes.

"I brought these." His announcement was unnecessary as he placed the pile on the bed.

I walked closer to look at what he'd brought.

"All of the women have sent something so you can see what fits," he explained.

I nodded as I reached toward the clothes and touched the top item. "It's so soft."

"Mm." Francois nodded, but his attention wasn't on the clothes anymore. He was looking directly at me, and my cheeks heated. Without warning, he reached out and cupped my cheek. "So soft," he agreed.

I leaned into his touch, the movement instinctive, and he brought his other hand to cup my other cheek before meeting my eyes. Whatever he saw there made him brave. He leaned forward, but he moved so slowly that my heart hammered wildly in my chest as anticipation thrummed through my veins and my lips parted.

When his mouth finally touched mine, I sucked in a breath. It was like touching a live wire, the shock of our connection hot and fast. He wrapped his arms around me, and I pressed against him, trying to eliminate the space between us. I'd expected to be nervous, but I wasn't. Where before, I'd struggled to coordinate my breathing when I'd been kissed, this was easy. Natural.

"Mmm." The noise of pleasure slipped from me, and Francois answered me by touching his tongue against my lower lip. I grinned as I replied in kind, deepening our kiss until our tongues tangled together and our breathing grew heavy.

The towel slipped from my head and Francois tangled his fingers into my hair, bunching it into his fist as he angled my head to kiss me again, harder and with a desperation that I'd never known but eagerly met. His lips were soft against mine but there was no doubt he meant every movement he made.

His other hand pressed against the small of my back and his lips left mine as he nibbled along my jaw before dropping his mouth to my neck. Then he paused, and I waited, holding my breath. Surely he wouldn't…? I didn't know what he'd do, though.

I didn't know if I would stop him, either.

"Mon ange…" There was so much pain in his words.

His touch trailed over my breasts and my towel dropped away, leaving me naked against him. He bent lower and sucked my right nipple into his mouth. I closed my eyes and buried my hands in his hair, partly steadying myself, partly keeping him in that exact position. Fire ran through me, lighting each of my nerve endings, and I throbbed with need for him.

"Mon ange," he said again, and his eyes burned red as he looked up at me. "We can't." His voice was hoarse. "Not now. We shouldn't. It should be…" He glanced at the bed. "You need to know it's special."

I didn't want to know. I only wanted Francois.

I wanted his touch. I might burn alive if he didn't touch me. I whimpered as he skimmed a hand up the outside of my thigh.

"We need to wait." But he drew his touch ever closer to where I wanted to feel it most.

"Please." I'd never even asked before, and now I was dangerously close to begging. "Please touch me."

He paused, his fingers curled against my skin. "Are you sure? My control…"

"I trust you." I placed a palm against his cheek and met his eyes. "I trust you not to hurt me." I guided his mouth back to mine and sank back into our kiss, barely even feeling it as he guided me to the bed.

I lay down, my legs already parted, the invitation unspoken but obvious, and he swallowed loudly. "You test me, mon ange."

For a moment, guilt played with my thoughts, but I pushed it away. My desire was more important. *Francois* was more important.

"Please, Frankie." I whispered the name I was pretty sure only I called him, and he reacted right away, the tip of one of his fingers resting lightly against my clit.

I gasped at the sensation of the light touch then gasped again as he rolled it one way then the other, gathering moisture from my greedy body.

"I must only touch you," he whispered as he moved against the bed, as though seeking more himself.

"Okay." I agreed with him, but it wasn't enough. I worked my hand between us to cup the bulge in his pants.

He bucked against me as my hand closed over him. "Not me."

"Why not?" I drew his zipper down, my sudden need to feel him in my hand urgent and not one to be ignored.

He covered my hand with his, directing my touch, despite his protests to the contrary. He wanted this. I worked the button of his pants until it came loose, distracted as he claimed my mouth in a kiss again.

He groaned when I wrapped my fingers around him and smoothed the precum already at the tip of his cock over the skin there, and he started to move slowly, setting a rhythm that I met as he continued to tease my clit. Those were the light touches that drove me crazy. It was as though he could read my mind or he'd seen me during my most private moments.

His touches remained soft and consistent and I surrendered myself to him completely, moving my hand up and down his shaft, reveling in how hard I made him. My body ached to be filled by him, but even as I considered that, he thrust harder into my hand, seeking something.

The pressure against me grew, and my muscles began to tighten as though I was reacting to his increase in excitement as much as the feelings he ignited in me. My breathing grew more rapid until I could barely catch my breath.

Then I stopped breathing entirely and hung in the moment as my body released, my muscles pulsing. Francois panted against my hair, before he thrust forward one last time and warmth filled my palm and coated my wrist.

I turned my face toward him, and he pressed his lips to mine, an urgent kiss giving way to a lazy one before he chuckled.

"I didn't expect…"

I shook my head. "Neither did I." I ran my fingers lightly up his still-hard cock and he shuddered. "Later?" The excitement and expectation in my tone surprised me, but one experience with this man would never be enough.

He nodded and pressed a quick kiss to my forehead. "Later," he agreed. Then he scrunched his nose. "But right now we're supposed to be joining the others for a meal, and I need to get you cleaned up again."

My stomach rumbled, spoiling any protest I'd been about to make about leaving the room, and I rolled awkwardly from the bed. "I'll just hop back in the shower for a quick wash."

Two minutes later, and fresh from working the space age shower again, I rejoined Francois in the bedroom.

He was standing by the bed. "I brought you some clothes." His cheeks colored as he spoke and he gestured toward the pile of clothes that had been neat when I first saw it but was now mostly rumpled.

I blurted out a laugh. "Yes, I know." I wandered closer and looked at some of the items before finally selecting a dress. The fit didn't really matter if it was just a simple pattern. I pulled it on and Francois looked at me.

"Stay by my side," he murmured. "I don't know if there are any unmated males here, and you are—" He paused and took a long, deep breath. "You are very enticing. I can still smell your arousal."

I squeaked as he took my hand and whisked me from the bedroom. "Wait. What? You can *smell* my arousal? And you're taking me to a room where *other vampires* will also be able to smell my arousal?" This suddenly seemed like a very bad idea indeed.

I didn't care how hungry I was. My state of arousal was still very much my own business. But I followed him back to the communal area anyway, and I drew in an appreciative breath of air saturated with tomatoes, herbs, and garlic.

A group of vampires sat around a table, a plate in front of each of them, and a huge, steaming bowl of spaghetti graced the middle.

I paused. There was something wrong with this picture.

"Are you coming?" Francois gently tugged my hand.

"Yeah." I lowered my voice, although that was pointless, given vampire hearing. Still, I had the illusion of discretion. "But I didn't think you guys ate."

He laughed. "We can, but we don't need to. We're all here right now for your benefit, though. I'm sure you don't really want to sit alone? And apparently Nicolas's chef is happy. It's rare that he gets to cook."

I shrugged. So, vampires were weird. And they could eat. I made a mental note of that as one of the lengths they obviously went to so they fit in.

As I approached the table, Ciara came racing through the door, dragging a male vampire behind her. Her eyes were back to their usual shade of blue, but she looked at the table like she'd never seen food before.

"Spaghetti!" she yelled. "I'm starving." She looked at me. "My wolf still likes to eat." Then she glanced at the man following her so closely he could have been in her pocket. "Oh, and this is my mate, Jason. But first, food!" She sat in one of the chairs and dragged the bowl of spaghetti toward herself.

"You might want to get in quickly, Maeve," Jason said. "Ciara can *eat*."

With a roll of her eyes, Ciara relinquished the bowl, pushing it back in my direction. "Here you go. You take your turn first."

"Thank you." I hesitated before I gave in to the temptation of so much food, grabbing the tongs and piling my plate high. Then I helped myself to come of the artisan bread and a sprinkle of cheese.

Every other vampire at the table took only a small serving and they mostly pushed it around their plates or twirled single noodle strands around their forks for the duration of the meal, but the conversation that bounced back and forth across the table spoke of familiarity and family. For the first time in days, I relaxed.

Chapter 17 - Francois

I watched Maeve as she ate, the unfamiliar sensation of a smile playing over my lips. There was something indescribable about watching my mate satisfy her hunger in such a safe environment. If only I could have provided for her in this way, but that part was to come.

Surely earlier in the bedroom, her behavior had indicated acceptance of me? Memories of how it had felt to touch her rolled through my mind, and I moved restlessly in my seat, looking for a comfortable position.

"Francois." I looked away from Maeve as the familiar voice commanded my attention.

Nicolas and Leia stood in the doorway, and Nicolas's expression was downright murderous, his eyebrows almost touching, his eyes a dull shade of red. He had his hands curled into fists, but he probably had claws more than fingernails, if his face was anything to go by.

He jerked his head in a gesture that clearly meant I should go with him, and I stood, hesitating a little as I looked at Maeve. I didn't want to leave her. She was almost mine. Maybe. Probably.

I bit my lip as I glanced at Leia.

How could I ever have thought…? I shook my head. That didn't matter now. I'd been wrong and everything was still as it should be now.

Except I hadn't bonded with my mate, yet.

"And Sebastian." Nicolas's voice was little more than a commanding bark. "In fact, all of you. With me."

He was only talking to the men, from the glances that were exchanged at the table, and Kyle and Jason both stood with reluctance as Leia glided to the table to take one of their seats.

Leaving Maeve with the women wasn't so bad, except they could say anything about me—and it would all be justified. None of my past covered me in glory. Part of me wanted to hear what they said so I could defend myself, but the rest of me didn't want to hear any of it. Something about even being near Maeve seemed to balance me. I could only imagine how much more stable I'd be once we'd properly bonded.

I was already a different being.

"Come on." Sebastian waited for me in the doorway and gestured down a corridor I hadn't used before. "We're wanted in Nic's office."

I smiled at Maeve, although she paled slightly as I stepped away.

"Will you be back soon?" Her vice didn't waver, but it was quiet.

"I hope so, mon ange." I smiled a smile meant just for her, but Ciara flashed her fangs at me. Being accepted again wouldn't be easy, and hovering here wasn't helping my cause. "I need to go see Nicolas." This time, my smile was apologetic, and I offered a small bow. "Mesdames."

Then I hurried after Sebastian, trying not to think of Maeve's wide eyes as I turned from her.

When I entered Nicolas's office, he was standing behind his desk, his arms folded, and his gaze narrowed on me. "You look well, Francois." His statement was full of suspicion, and his next question explained why. "Have the Ancients got you on a new drug regime?"

I shook my head.

"Virgin blood?"

I shook my head again.

"So how?"

So much suspicion, and I couldn't exactly blame him. Sebastian already thought I must be here as a spy for the Ancients, and why would they really think otherwise? I'd never given them any reason to trust me and I'd been abducted before I could truly work for their side.

"I've met my mate." I looked for a spare seat, but the other men had sprawled across them so I remained standing like I'd been summoned to see the principal—or my father. "I've found my mate." I rubbed a hand over my face. "I don't know how it's working, but she already seems to have some sort of influence on me. I just hope it holds."

Nicolas narrowed his eyes. It might have been suspicion or out and out disbelief, but he changed the subject rather than pursuing the fact I might now be working for the Ancients. "I want to know everything you found out while you lived with them."

I snorted. "Lived with them? You make it sound so luxurious."

Sebastian half-stood. "Watch your tone, Francois."

I held my hands up and backed the couple of steps to the nearest wall. "No tone," I said. "I was as much a prisoner as any of the women."

"And?" Nicolas raised an eyebrow. "What do you know about them?"

"Well." I broke off on a chuckle. "They certainly don't want anything to do with a vampire tainted by dead man's blood." Nicolas simply watched me and I shrugged. "Oui. Hard to believe right? First, they planned to use me in place of my father. But then they realized my blood wasn't pure enough so they…je pense…I think…planned to raise him. They told me I needed to find a book he'd stolen from them." I paused and Nicolas made a continue motion with his finger. "I found the book."

"Great. Is it here?" Sebastian nodded to the satchel I'd brought with me from the house, but I shook my head.

"Non. We hid it, but we had to leave it."

Sebastian scoffed.

"Non," I said again, firmer this time. What good was even working with these assholes if they didn't trust me? "Ask Maeve. She knows where it is." I brought my palm to my forehead as I remembered. "Even better, ask Maeve what the spell says. Her memory is so good that she'd been able to remember it to share with Kayla in case we can use it. She memorized nearly the whole fucking book."

"She what?" Nicolas looked properly interested for the first time.

I nodded. "You heard me. Maeve is pretty much a walking black magic spell book right now, mes amis."

"And Maeve is…?" But Nicolas sounded too casual to not already know.

"My mate." I was short, fierce, in my reply. If anyone threatened that, they'd feel the full force of my wrath. My madness would come rushing back in a heartbeat.

"You need to invoke your mate bond. It will get rid of your sickness immediately and should give you a power boost." Every word from Nicolas was a royal command, and I narrowly prevented myself from rolling my eyes.

Wasn't that what I'd been trying to do for years? I hadn't succeeded... Of course I hadn't succeeded. None of those women had been my true mate, but I hadn't known what I was doing.

Clutching at straws—that had been what I was fucking doing.

"Bien. I know about the sickness part. At least I've always hoped my mate will cure the sickness with her blood, but I think you're wrong about the power boost. Maeve is simply a human who has found out about the supernatural world. She doesn't have any power to offer." Part of me wanted to keep her out of our world. She was an innocent and didn't belong here.

It had always been a dangerous existence but more so now that the Ancients had risen. As much as I wanted her by my side, I wanted to protect her and keep her safe.

Nicolas nodded. "You're wrong."

Some of my self-control slipped. I'd done so fucking much for these people who had overthrown my family, and they didn't even appreciate it.

"We both know Leia was human, and you wanted her, too. You wanted her for yourself, and what was that for, if not to boost your power and cure your failings?" It was the first time Nicolas had spoken to me so harshly, and even though I might have deserved it from him the past, I didn't deserve his derision now.

"You will not—" My voice boomed around the small office as I pushed myself from the wall. standing at my full height as the tension strained at the skin of my face and my fangs ached in my gums. "You will not talk to me that way in the club I used to own, the city I used to rule. My mate is more than a power boost. She is to be protected at all costs." I launched myself forward and swiped the laptop from the desk opposite me. It crashed to the floor and Kyle leaped from his seat.

He grabbed me in a tight hold, walking backward as he wrangled me farther away from the king.

"Francois." Jason stood as well, a hand out in front of him. "Francois. Calm down. Being this angry won't help anyone. When is the last time you fed?"

I shook my head. I didn't care about feeding. I only cared about Maeve.

Sebastian looked at Nicolas. "Want me to get Kayla? We can get some blood in him. See if he calms down?"

Nicolas shook his head. "This is beyond anonymous virgin blood and doses of Kayla's antidote for the dead man's blood addiction now. The only thing that will work now that Francois's body has recognized his mate is invoking the bond." He looked at me. "Which should be done immediately to help save us all."

"Bon." I sneered, not meaning anything was good at all. "I don't see how you think my mating will help keep everyone safe, Ni-co-las." I separated out the syllables and almost sang them at him in the way I had when we were nothing more than children and I'd wanted to annoy him. "But I don't see how me completing the bond with *my* mate will help your situation at all."

Nicolas threw his hands up, his frustration evident. "Because we're in this together, Francois. We're each made more powerful as another one of us gains power. It's about the whole being greater than the sum of its parts. You're with us, Francois, and you're one of us." He glanced just to the side of me and nodded. "You can let him go, Kyle. We need to discuss how we can defeat the Ancients."

"We can't do that yet." My voice was a growl as I rubbed my hand over the areas Kyle had pinned me. He was a strong bastard. "We need to get Maeve to Kayla first so they can discuss the spells Maeve has memorized. She needs to write them down or recite them to me so I can write them down. I think the clue is in those."

"Okay." Nic nodded. "That's step one of the plan, then." He gestured to Sebastian. "Make sure Kayla's room is stocked up and ready to go tomorrow. See if there's anything she needs from the shop. I can send someone out there to get it."

"Can I go?" The desire to get back to Maeve was an itch on my skin that wouldn't be relieved.

Meeting in the office just to decide to meet with Kayla tomorrow was a waste of my time, and why I'd never had this kind of bureaucracy when I ran things. It had been so much easier to only rely on myself. But I couldn't ignore the fact it was nice to have so many others to turn to. I could see the benefit in having a group with the same objective. And the safety in numbers.

"You can go," Nicolas agreed. "But think about your mate bond."

I didn't even deign to look at him. What the hell else did he think I fucking thought about?

Chapter 18 - Maeve

Sitting with the female vampires was…interesting. If I hadn't known they were vampires, I wouldn't have…known. I'd never expected them to be as human-seeming as me. Granny had never imagined that sometimes the monsters were even more dangerous by appearing so harmless.

More than harmless. An image of Francois appeared in my mind. He was so much more than harmless. He was seductive, his voice inviting me to touch him.

To love him, a tiny voice in my head whispered.

But I ignored that. There was no way I could love a vampire. And certainly not one I'd just met. I'd only ever wanted to prove their existence.

Part of me still did what to prove that… My thoughts ground to a sudden halt. *Part* of me wanted to prove it? All of me did, right?

It was all I'd ever wanted, to end my days of just being a kook. A weirdo with a paranormal blog. Another person sitting at home, making a collection of tinfoil hats.

But now there was another pull inside me, a desire to help the vampires remain hidden…to *protect* them. Because what was the alternative? Humans with pitchforks and flaming torches?

Automatic weapons and flamethrowers, more like.

And the vampires would fight back because…who wouldn't? If I proved their existence, I'd be starting a war that would play out in every country all the world. Could I take on that kind of responsibility?

I sat farther back on the couch and let the women's chatter wash over me. I wasn't sure I even wanted to think about it right now. And especially not knowing that there were other types of paranormal beings. I glanced at Ciara. An actual wolf-vampire hybrid.

But these were more than stories to me now, more than a belief or even a specimen. They were all people with lives and loves of their own.

I closed my eyes briefly, before a door banged down the corridor, and I opened them again to see what was going on. Francois strode into the room, and my breath caught at the stark beauty of the man, even though his anger was clear to see.

I stood as I took in the dull red of his eyes and the slightly sharper edge to his cheekbones—not because I was concerned, though. My interest was merely professional curiosity, the part of my brain that still hungered for the information I'd sought all my life. And it had nothing to do with how beautiful he looked like this, either…

"What's wrong?" I asked the question to his back as he walked past, not even close to slowing down.

"Nothing." His answer was stark and short and his tone should have put me off and sent me scurrying back to my safe seat on the sofa…but it didn't.

"There *is* something. It's bad for you to keep things inside."

He laughed, but there was no humor there. "Trust me, I should have been keeping a lot more in for a very long time."

"No." I grabbed his hand as it swung behind him with his stride, and his fingers closed around mine for a moment.

"Maeve." But it was only mild warning in his tone, and I clutched his hand tighter when he might have tried to shake me loose.

"Where are you going?"

"My room." He laughed shortly again. "Well, anywhere that isn't in the same space as a Dupont vampire. Even if the room I end up in isn't truly mine."

He slowed as we approached a doorway, and the room we entered was dark. So dark I could no longer see

Francois in front of me, and I tightened my hold on him like I needed to be sure he was still there.

I felt safe with him. Instinct told me he'd never hurt me. And there was no rational reason for that. Just a bone-deep knowledge that had no reason to exist.

Then he moved so fast that I couldn't react, and my gasp pierced the silence in the room. The wall was hard against my back, and my heart thumped wildly.

Francois's body molded against mine, a knee between my legs, his chest pressed to my breasts as he dropped his mouth to my ear. "J'ai envie de t'embrasser."

My lips parted in response. Even my rudimentary understanding of his language meant that I knew he'd just told me he wanted to kiss me. Memories of the way he'd kissed me before flooded back, and my knees weakened.

He'd kissed me like he wanted me, owned me...like he meant it. I craved the touch of his lips against mine, the feel of his tongue in my mouth, and I grew wet at my thoughts, my chest rising and falling with my increased breathing rate.

His fingers touched my cheek, and his nose nudged mine, but he stopped, and I held my breath as I waited.

"What are you doing?" I finally offered a hesitant whisper as we both stood like time had frozen us in a moment of perfect anticipation.

A low growl rumbled through him, and his eyes glowed the dullest of reds, barely distinguishable from the rest of the dark. "I can't stand to not be around you. I want so much more, Maeve."

I nodded, a movement he surely couldn't see. *So much more.* I wanted all of that, too. I wanted to strip my clothes off and offer myself to him, the ultimate sacrifice. A human tribute for a crazy vampire prince. A giggle bubbled up my throat, but I forced it back down.

Now really wasn't the time to laugh in this man's face.

"I'm really no good for you, but I can't help…" He leaned closer. "I want…"

I closed the gap between us, kissing him before he could talk himself out of the move. I'd never taken control before, but I didn't regret this as my senses swam with awareness of Francois, his scent in my nose, his hands in my hair.

It was like before but so much more. The dark stole my sight but heightened everything else. My body thrummed with twin pleasure and need, and I moaned quietly, surprising myself at my sudden expression of arousal.

But the sound galvanized Francois, and he clutched me closer before dropping a hand to my right breast, his thumb finding my nipple beneath my clothes and stroking it. It was exquisite torture, having his touch so close but not absolute. I pressed closer to him, still offering myself, and as his knee rose higher between my thighs, I ground against his leg a little, craving the movement and friction.

"Do you want me, mon ange?" There was a grin in his words, the hint of a tease—like he might stop if I gave him the wrong answer.

"Always." It hadn't been what I intended to say, but apparently, it was exactly what he wanted to hear and he nibbled a line of kisses along my jaw before devouring my mouth under his, something wild in the way his lips moved over mine this time.

I laid my palm against his chest, coaxing him to become gentler, even though the thrill of being wanted raced through me.

Without warning, he lifted me into his arms and strode across the room. Furniture still barely contrasted against the gloom, but I could make out darker shadows around us. He approached one of the shadows and lowered me onto a soft, blanket-covered bed before climbing on beside me.

His hand skimmed my breasts again, and I waited a moment, looking in his direction, searching the dark for his face. Then his lips crushed mine again and I spun back into sudden bliss. His hands molded my body under my clothes like he was learning my shape.

He nuzzled my neck, breathing deeply as he did. "You're not ready," he murmured. "I can't allow myself."

"Ready for what?" My voice came out breathy and expectant.

He chuckled, the sound a little dark. "Sex with a vampire."

Even in the dark, my cheeks heated. "And what if I am?" Surely, I was more than ready. My body cried out for his touch. I craved him. I arched toward him, trying to pass that message on.

But he moved away, and a flash of panic squeezed my chest. I opened my mouth to protest, but he spoke first.

"Just need to remove these." He sounded distracted, like he was talking to himself, and his fingers trailed along my waistband before he tugged awkwardly at my button. "Damn thing," he muttered.

I almost giggled, but my heart leapt into my throat as he started to draw my jeans down my thighs and that nearly choked me instead.

"What are you doing?" I could barely make my voice heard.

"Rien," he said.

But it didn't feel like *nothing*. It was a whole lotta something as he lay down alongside my bared legs and pressed a kiss to my stomach. I automatically sucked it in, and he chuckled again, but lighter this time.

"Relax, mon ange. I've got you." A tearing sound followed, and cool air hit my clit as he discarded my now ripped panties.

"Hey…" I started to protest—those were good ones.

But I sucked in a deep breath when he pressed a finger gently between my legs, as though he was looking for something.

"Ah… Oui… Still they hide. Such a little bud…"

"Huh?"

"Rien." He brushed me off again before skating a fingertip between my folds. "So wet." He drew the moisture up to my clit and rolled it gently.

Then the sheets rustled as he changed his position again, and his warm breath fanned over my already heated skin as he gently pushed my legs apart.

"Belle, très belle."

I fought the urge to clamp my legs back together as the ends of his hair teased the sensitive skin on the inside of my thighs. He leaned and placed a kiss there, and I caught my breath, holding it as I waited.

I'd never had a man between my thighs like this, and there was something undeniably sexy about it.

But fuck, maybe he'd been right. I gasped at the first touch of his tongue on me. Perhaps I wasn't ready. I reached down for something to hold on to, an anchor, and wove my fingers into his hair as he drew his tongue over me again, touching so many nerves in one small place that it should have been impossible.

He repositioned my legs, wrapping his arms under my thighs as he drew me closer and sucked my clit between his lips, flicking it with his tongue. I writhed against him and forced myself to breath, each exhale a pant before I caught the next gasp of air.

I sighed as he nudged a fingertip at my entrance, the skin there tight and sensitive. He didn't go all the way in, just applied pressure to the edges, and I moaned as I tightened my grip on his hair.

Never before.

My body hadn't responded this way to a man ever, and I'd never wanted like I wanted now. His tongue lapped against me when he released me from his mouth, and I moved, setting the rhythm I liked.

Replacing his tongue with his finger for a moment, he looked up at me. "More?"

"Fuck, yes," I whispered as I continued to move against him, showing him what I wanted. Light and delicate worked for me, but every so often I teased myself as I pressed harder against his friction and drew away again.

Don't stop…don't stop.. don't stop… The chant started in my head but didn't make it past my lips. Instead, I closed my eyes and hid from him, refusing to show him all of me as the familiar sensation of my muscles tightening began to work through my whole body.

I'd done this to myself, many times, but never shared it with anyone, and no one else had ever been in control like now. I drew a deep breath. And this was so much better.

One last flick of his tongue released me, fire sizzling on each of my nerves, my core pulsing, wanting, needy.

I mumbled incoherently as he resumed his lapping, drawing out each throb of my orgasm until my fingers cramped into claws and each new spasm was another shockwave of pleasure.

He pressed a final kiss to the inside of my thigh, and I jolted at the touch of one of his fangs resting against my skin. The sudden danger was heady, and I fought the urge to press against his head so he'd puncture me.

"Sorry," he whispered, his voice thicker than usual, and the mattress moved as he slid his way up to lie beside me, gathering me in his arms and pulling me close to his chest. He drew in deep breaths.

"Are you okay?" I tilted my head to look at him, able to make out the shape of his nose and jaw, and the gleam of his eyes as he watched me.

"Oui." But it seemed to be an effort for him to bring his breathing back under control.

"That was pretty amazing." I spoke without thought but credit where credit was due.

"Only *pretty* amazing?" Although his tone was joking, he paused at the end of his question like my response mattered, and I ducked my head to hide my grin.

The fragile male ego transferred into vampires, too.

"*Very* amazing," I assured him, and I added a reassuring pat to his chest.

My body still sparked with tiny, satisfied pulses, and I almost hummed my pleasure.

"I wouldn't hurt you." He dropped a kiss into my hair. "Jamais."

Never.

"Jamais de ma vie."

Never in his life. I pressed closer to him. "I know that."

"But I *have* hurt people." He swallowed. "Women." Regret laced his tone.

"I know." I couldn't soften it. I *did* know. Ciara had made sure I knew. "I know you did."

He sighed. "So much waste."

"But why?"

"Why?" He sounded genuinely perplexed, and he tightened his hold.

"Why did you do it?" Maybe it was a dumb question. Why did vampires ever kill? "Instinct? Blood?" I shuddered a little. "Frenzy?" It was a term I'd often used in my blog, when nothing else described the scale of what I knew was a paranormal creature attack but authorities provided a mundane answer for.

His chest moved up and down as he gave a big sigh. A world of hurt and regret lived in that sound. "All of the above."

I waited. He didn't seem finished. More like he was finding his way to the right answer.

"And… cure."

The things he and Ciara had mentioned and told me started to filter back. It was like, while I was with him, nothing bad existed. He was simply Francois. Not a mad prince. "Your cure."

He accompanied his sigh with a nod, this time. "My cure."

I stared into the dark, waiting. It was probably the story I'd most wanted to know, ever, and over the years there had been many stories I'd been desperate to discover, but none seemed as important as this one.

None as private and personal, either.

"I always thought..." It was as if he'd begun speaking without considering his words because he halted almost immediately. "My father had always been eccentric. I believed his stasis was further evidence of an incurable madness."

His voice dropped, becoming almost conspiratorial.

"But perhaps now that was just the natural strain of being away from his...brethren. I don't know what they are as a group," he confided. "Brethren is as good a name to describe the Ancients as any. They seem to function as one, on some sort of level. I believe the health of the whole is dependent on their connection and my father suffered from his own self-imposed absence for many years. I thought the madness was coming for me," he whispered.

I tightened my hold on him just a little, offering comfort the only way I could as I pressed closer.

"I took the blood to save myself. I went to a witch to help me. The family witch. I tried a little of the poison as the cure. I knew she was dosing me extra. By that time, I didn't care. I don't know what came first. Was I already mad or was it the dead man's blood? I craved more so I took more. It helped." He looked at me. "But it didn't help at all, did it?"

"No, it didn't help." I kept my voice gentle, but it would do me no good to lie to him. And this huge creature was so gently with me, I wasn't scared to tell him the truth. "Why do I feel this way?" I didn't understand. Why *wasn't* I scared?

"Feel what way?" I had his whole attention.

"I'm not…" I tapped the tip of my forefinger against his chest as I thought. "I'm not scared of you or of telling you things. I want to share with you and share myself with you in a way I've never shared with anyone else." I shook my head as I considered the men I'd known in the past. "It doesn't really make sense. It's not logical."

Although since when the hell had my life made any kind of logical sense? The majority of people would believe I spent it chasing shadows and fairy stories.

Francis's chuckle was a low rumble in his chest. "It's the mate bond."

That word again. "Tell me about it…being mates?"

I thought he wouldn't. He was quiet for such a long time before he spoke.

"It sounds like a cliché," he said. "I've searched for my mate—for *you*—for so long. And I hate that it comes out sounding that way because it sounds almost as if the idea of the mate bond cheapens you in some way—like I would have been happy with just anyone. But that isn't it. You're my other half. My soul. The part of me that has always been missing."

I swallowed. Those were big declarations, but they almost made sense. The way Francois affected me was like something clicking into place. "But now what?"

He swallowed. "That's the question. You know the women you met earlier?"

I nodded, my cheek rubbing over his clothes.

"They were all human. But vampires turn their mates to solidify the bond. It's one of the greatest honors for a male vampire."

I nodded again before I processed his words. "Wait. What? I mean, I know the king's wife—"

"Mate," he interjected.

"And Ciara, but she was a shifter. She was already halfway there…" That made sense. She was already in the supernatural world. Becoming a vampire wasn't such a huge step. "I'd stop being human."

"Oui." He nodded. "But you'd be vampire and you'd be mine. Immortal with me."

My breath hitched. Something in those words… they were laced with temptation. "How? Do you bite me?" The thought should have horrified me.

But instead, it aroused me.

"Oui. And you bite me, mon ange. We share blood. We each become of the other."

I blew out a small sigh, waiting for horror and disgust to hit me, but neither came. The idea that I could belong to someone lifted me, lightening my chest as if I'd carried a weight there always.

"Maeve?" Already, he seemed attuned to each tiny change in my mood.

"I'm just thinking. I've never belonged anywhere before. I didn't exactly fit in growing up. I was too weird and believed in too many things."

"What things?"

"Vampires, shifters, fae. Those things. You, I suppose."

He laughed. "Mon ange, you don't believe in nearly enough. I can show you so much more."

I nearly purred at the promise his words held. He'd just offered to open up the entire world for me. "I think I should do it."

He twisted a little, facing me, his palms curved to my cheeks as he spoke again. "It's not a decision to take lightly. It's permanent, and there are risks. Not every human reacts well to vampire blood or to their body undergoing the change. I've…I've seen their deaths in my lifetimes. I've seen vampires lose their mates that way."

"You won't lose me." I yawned after I spoke, spoiling the conviction in my words.

"Sleep, mon ange. Sleep, and we can discuss it more after you wake."

I nodded and made myself comfortable against him, allowing my eyes to close, my mind already exploring all of the things an immortal life could offer. And with Francois by my side forever, what couldn't I achieve?

A small smile captured my lips as I thought of him.

Chapter 19 - Francois

Merde. The sound of chatting and laughter drifted toward the bedrooms from the common area of the basement home—one of the moments of levity that interspersed more serious moments when everyone considered the threat of the Ancients. The Duponts' relief at the return of Ciara was still palpable.

I didn't want to take part in happy, family life. How had Nicolas created this dynasty out of vampires who almost seemed to be misfits? How the hell could I avoid it?

Except I didn't know what I wanted anymore. I could see the benefits of family   of protection and strength and safety in numbers—but I didn't know how to be myself in this environment.

I was used to being *only* myself.

This many people… This many people who all *cared* about each other… It was alien. My own father hadn't even seemed to care about me. I reached out to Maeve, the gesture almost reflexive as I considered being alone for so long.

I was no longer alone.

As with the previous evening, the table was set, and everyone was sitting there, sharing conversation and jokes. Each mated pair sat together, and my gaze flicked to the two chairs they'd left for Maeve and me. Although each person had a plate in front of them, no one had any food, so it was clear they were only playing this out to ensure Maeve's comfort. That lifted my spirits a bit—at least they cared about my human, my mate.

Maeve grinned as we walked farther into the room, and it was as though the sun had emerged on a rainy day. She lit the room. "Good morning!"

When I would have held back, she grabbed my hand and kept me at her side. The talking stopped as each person here surveyed us quickly.

"I assume the two of you have had a talk?" Leia had never been one to keep her thoughts in her head, but I was lucky we'd reached some degree of understanding, given that the king's mate could very well have ended up as one of my failed attempts to discover my mate.

Every time I saw her, fresh guilt gnawed at my gut, even though everything had worked out for her after Nicolas regained her from me.

"Yes." I kept the word terse, not wanting to go into detail about the things Maeve and I had discussed in the privacy of my bedroom. Those weren't things for everyone here to know.

They could turn everything around and dissuade her from being with me.

Leia lifted a goblet toward me, and I almost laughed at the picture it painted. An ancient cup for a royal long past his use-by date.

"This might make you feel a little better, Francois," she said, and in Pavlovian response, my fangs burst through my gums.

I shook my head, though. I knew what she was offering. Virgin's blood with some degree of whatever they were using to keep my dead man's blood curse under control. But I didn't want it.

I wanted only Maeve.

"Francois." Nicolas's voice was like a whip crack across the room, and I looked at him, watching as his hard eyes gentled. "You need this today. It's going to be long and busy and possibly fraught. Take the assistance we offer you. How long has it been?"

I shrugged. I didn't know. Maeve had helped curb some of my cravings, my madness, but how long could I rely on that? How long before I lost control of myself and bled someone dry?

It could even be Maeve. I'd never forgive myself.

"And Maeve," Nicolas continued. "We have some beignets here for your breakfast."

The women at the table laughed.

"Mmm…beignets." Leia sighed as she looked at the plate. "I remember the days when I could have existed on Chef's beignets."

Kayla nodded in agreement. "He's a genius indeed." She patted the empty seat next to her. "Come and sit down, Maeve. You must be hungry."

Maeve glanced at me as though sensing my remnants of hesitation and shook her head. "No," she started but the gurgling of her stomach gave her away, and everyone laughed.

"Yes," Sam said. "So come and sit down, and convince that man of yours to take what's offered to him, too."

Maeve squeezed my hand. "Come on." She looked into my eyes and there was a plea there.

She didn't mind being with these people. Maybe she even felt at home here, and I owed her that much—a home. It was my duty to provide it for her.

Leia lifted the goblet in my direction again and nodded to the last empty chair at the table as Maeve took the one next to Kayla. As she sat down, Kyle craned his neck to look at her, and I growled.

He switched his attention and shrugged, but his obvious focus on Maeve's neck hadn't escaped my attention.

"Non. I didn't drink from her." I bit that words out, not caring how they sounded. Whether Maeve and I were now mated was no one else's business, but everyone else at this damn table seemed to think they had skin in that particular game.

One day, my life would be my own again.

"Just checking." Kyle wasn't even apologetic, but the knowledge he felt he needed to somehow protect Maeve from me tightened my chest.

"I get my position here is precarious. I am not a Dupont. In fact, I have wronged Nicolas greatly in the past." I emphasized every word. "But I would never hurt my mate."

Nicolas nodded but didn't confirm or deny my words. Instead, he leaned forward. "Would it help at all if Leia spoke with Maeve at some point and explained things as someone who has been through the process? She can tell Maeve what's on the line and what to expect."

"Oh, I don't think that's necessary." Maeve started to shake her head but I spoke as well.

"Oui. Don. I think that's a good idea." Although Maeve seemed to have made her mind up to become my mate, a conversation with Leia wouldn't hurt.

Or I hoped it wouldn't hurt. Leia would have been in the perfect place to sabotage me and she would have had every reason to, but for some reason I didn't think she'd do that. I'd wronged her in so many ways, but she and Nicolas had only met all my previous sins with a kindness that I truly didn't deserve.

I owed it to them to trust them now and welcome and accept this newest offer.

Maeve nodded. "Okay, then. That would be nice. Thank you." She gave a little bob of her head, like she might have curtseyed, had she been standing.

Then she bit into a beignet and a perfect cloud of powdered sugar burst into the air in front her. "Mmm…"

My cock twitched at her noise of pleasure before I finally took the offered goblet of blood from Leia. I didn't want to drink this. I couldn't think of anything worse than not drinking from my mate, but Leia simply shrugged like she knew my thoughts.

"Needs must," she murmured.

I nodded briskly—a bare agreement before drinking deeply. Despite my aversion to it, the blood was good.

Nicolas stood up and touched Leia's hand as he did. She smiled up at him, the look in her eyes one I wanted to see in Maeve's for me.

"I know we all have a busy day ahead of us today," he said, "but before we go to our separate tasks, I wanted to pass on some *good* news for a change."

"What's that?" Sebastian narrowed his eyes thoughtfully as he watched his brother.

Sebastian was made where Nicolas was born, which made him… less, although Nicolas never treated him as such. My father would never have made a child and treated them as an equal like the Duponts had.

I no longer knew if that made them stronger or weaker than the Ricards. I'd always believed them weaker, but my doubts mounted day by day.

"Leia and I are going to have a baby. She's pregnant." Nicolas beamed as he finished delivering his news.

Or dropping his bombshell.

As the others in the room cheered and clapped, a small knot of jealousy rested in my gut. I clapped and smiled with the others—any vampire baby was a cause for celebration.

But I wanted exactly this life for Maeve and me.

When the celebration died down, Nicolas addressed the group again. "We needed to tell all of you, firstly because you're family, and secondly, because I want Leia extra protected in whatever comes up."

"Nic…" she glanced up at him. "There's really no need—"

Sebastian snorted. "There's every need. A new royal heir? We all need to protect that child." He turned his attention to Nic. "I'm at your service, brother."

Nicolas thanked him than looked at me. "Now, would you like to escort Maeve as Kayla shows her where the two of them are going to work?"

His generosity humbled me. He obviously remembered what it was like to be separated from a mate before they'd been claimed. It was like living constantly with the most fragile egg, always afraid that my future would shatter in my hand, no matter how delicately I cared for it.

"It's this way." Kayla led us down a corridor away from the bedrooms. "I think they've deliberately put me away from where everyone else should be in case I start a thunderstorm or blow something up." She laughed. "Although I guess conjuring a demon would be more likely."

She opened a door and a smell of sulfur leaked out from the room.

"Oops." She grinned as she spoke and pinched her thumb and forefinger together. "One of my spells went a tiny bit wrong yesterday. Looks like I didn't quite clean the clean up right, either."

My eyes widened as we entered her room. It was huge. All the way at the back, there were work benches and what looked like a cauldron, and so many dried and drying herbs and plants hanging from hooks in the ceiling.

Closer to the door, bookcases lined the walls and there were a couple of old, dark wood desks with a book or two lying open on each.

"Sorry." But Kayla sounded far from sorry. "I'm a messy spellcaster. But welcome to my domain."

"Very impressive." I nodded as I continued to look around. Nicolas had certainly spared no expense when he took over The Neutral Zone and turned it into Nightfall. A very powerful witch had created these spaces beneath the club—and they were a far cry from the dingy little holes I'd used to detain those who displeased Father.

"We need to get some of those spells written down. See if any of them hold the key to destroying the Ancients. Or if they can at least confirm for us what they were doing here. You do that while I look through a couple of the grimoires you brought with you," Kayla said. "We need the ones that only you know. You know, the ones you're holding in your head."

"Okay." Maeve nodded. Then she looked at me. "I remembered quite a few."

"It will be one of the last ones," I said. "Can we do them backwards?" When she'd said she could remember the spells, I'd only thought about loading her up, not how to extract the correct spell from someone with only a rudimentary understanding of ancient language and magic spells.

"I think I can." She nodded again, a determined set to her jaw. "Let's give it a whirl, anyway."

Kayla pulled a chair from under one of the desks and took a sheaf of blank papers from the drawer. "Can you write them?"

The corners of Maeve's lips tilted in the smallest of smiles. "Probably with more accuracy than I can recite them. If I tried to say them, and Frankie wrote them down, we really would be raining frogs in here or something." She laughed softly.

Kayla's gaze shot to me as Maeve said the word *Frankie* but I just stared at her, daring her to comment.

Eventually, she shrugged and cleared her throat before handing Maeve a pencil. "Yeah, let's give this shit a whirl."

Maeve bent over, and before long the only sounds in the room were the scratch of her pencil tip and the occasional paper swish as Kayla turned a page in one of the books we'd found hidden in the secret rom.

After a while, she stopped and looked over Maeve's shoulder. She pressed her fingertip onto one of the spells Maeve had written down in neat, precise handwriting. "This one," she said. "This is about reanimating a vampire—even one who has undergone final death."

"Father," I murmured. "They wanted him."

"Looks like it." Kayla grimaced a little, her lips pulling taut. "But what's really interesting…" She indicated one of the spells in the books she'd been flipping through. "This talks about draining magic from powerful beings. I think it might be exactly what we need. The Ancients can spell cast, and we need them to not be able to do that."

I chuckled. "Yeah, that ability is really cramping our style, for sure."

Kayla chewed her lip. "Looks like we have some good news and some bad news."

"Oh? Did I remember something wrong?" Maeve frowned at the page again.

"Not at all." Kayla looked at her book again. "The news is in here. We can take away their magic, but it's not something that works immediately. It's a spell that will drain their powers over time, so although it should give us the outcome we want—turning the Ancients into normal vampires so we can imprison or kill them—I don't know how long it will take them to reach that state."

"So they could bring my father back before we neutralize their threat?"

Kayla shrugged. "Maybe. I hope not."

"And are you sure that's what the spell Maeve remembered is designed to do?" I had so many questions. Whatever Leia had given me in the chalice had set my mind on fire. I was alert and interested and engaged. Not distracted or tired.

If normal virgin blood could do this for me, what would Maeve's blood do? I glanced at her, hardly able to dare hope that she might allow me to exchange blood with her.

"Are you *sure* that's what that spell is for?" I clung to the hope that maybe we'd gotten it wrong between us, but Kayla nodded.

"Oh, yes. It's old and it's dark, but it's almost identical to the one in here." She grabbed a large, dusty grimoire from a very high shelf and manhandled it to the desk before I could even offer any help. "Look." She spent a couple of moments flipping the pages.

"But why would they want him?" I still didn't want to imagine it. It was easier to deny that such a man could be resurrected than to entertain the possibility as reality. I glanced at the spell she'd opened the book to. She was right. They were pretty much the same. "I think it has something to do with strength, but I don't get why when they're so strong already."

"Yep." Kayla agreed with me as she leaned against the edge of the desk. "They're this strong and their circle isn't even complete. Imagine if they complete their circle. Once the whole circle is filled, they can pull on divine magic." She shrugged but the movement was anything but careless. "Once they have that…"

"But they haven't needed him." I shook my head. "He was apart from them for so many years." I was really just speaking out loud. My whole life seemed like a lie. "I never knew."

"From what Nic says, no one really knew about the Ancients. Why would you have expected to know?"

I didn't reply. If I hadn't been half-crazed half the time, if I hadn't lived so much of my life trying to numb any and all pain, maybe I could have saved all of us this. Somehow.

"What can I do to help?" I was all in.

"Well, they obviously need your dad but both spells also refer to lineage magic. It's a form of necromancy. Resurrecting the dead through the blood of their descendants. Someone of the same family line."

"I'm the only one," I murmured. "But they tested my blood. They didn't want me because my blood was tainted."

Kayla swallowed and moved to sit in a chair. "I'm not sure it was ever about you, Francois, no matter what they told you. I don't think they ever intended to make you an Ancient. They just wanted your blood."

"To raise his father?"

I'd almost forgotten Maeve was there until she spoke.

Kayla nodded. "I think so. They took Francois's blood, and they can use that to bring Émile back."

I shuddered. The world would be a much worse place with my father back in it.

Chapter 20 - Maeve

I stood nervously in the common area. It was empty, all of the vampires who lived in this basement apartment out working on behalf of their king against the Ancients or keeping the royal dynasty functioning as normal.

Francois was still with Kayla while she tried to examine his blood for herself.

It was incredible—that this whole system of community and even royalty existed alongside human society. Beneath our society in a way, just out of sight. I thought I'd known but I hadn't suspected anything this big or widespread, anything this *rich*.

They had history, wealth, property, tradition, and vampires were cold-blooded killers. Except I trusted them. I was living among them without fearing for my life, without wanting to leave.

Leia appeared from the direction of the bedrooms. "Are you ready?" She smiled as she adjusted her top, smoothing out invisible creases.

"Yep." I smiled. It was still weird to be talking to the equivalent of a queen like she was my friend.

"Come on then. We're going up to the VIP area of the club and Chef is already preparing you a feast. There's nothing he loves more than cooking for a human. The rest of us keep disappointing him by letting our mates turn us." She smiled again, but my giggle was nervous.

Francois wanted to turn me, too. He wanted me to join him as an immortal. And I wanted the same. Right?

I followed Leia up the stairs and back into the club. It was quiet, the stage empty, and only background music played softly as staff set up for later in the day. I'd lost all concept of time from being underground, only following a schedule of mealtimes when the vampires told me it was time to eat.

"Do you like the club?" Leia turned around as she spoke to me.

It was just small talk, but I nodded. "Sure. It's very…nice." Who was I kidding? It wasn't like I'd seen very many nightclubs in my time. At least, not to spend time in and enjoy. If I was in a nightclub, I was looking for something paranormal there, following a tip.

She laughed. "I'll let Sebastian know." Then she lowered her voice. "It didn't used to look like this. Francois used to own it, back when his father ruled, and it was very different. It's better now than it was before."

We walked up a staircase where the steps were lit with tiny lights that looked like stars and a chrome banister guided our way. The VIP balcony was plush and luxurious, and the corners were dimly lit, affording anyone who sat up here plenty of privacy.

"This is our table." Leia walked to a table that had already been set for two. "I don't eat very often but apparently this baby is already craving beignets." She patted her stomach lightly and laughed. "I never dreamed I'd be ruled by a parasite." But her tone had softened and the words held no malice.

I sat and drew my chair in, taking a deep breath as I did. The fact that I was living with vampires hit me again. Everything I'd ever wanted to know.

Nothing I could ever tell.

"So, you're Francois's mate," Leia said as soon as we were both sitting down. Apparently, she didn't believe in small talk.

I nodded. "Yeah. He said so."

She lifted an eyebrow. "They're never wrong about it, but you should feel it too. Do you feel anything for him?"

I paused. How could I confess that it was as though I'd known him for years? Like he was the only man I ever wanted in my life? I had so little experience with men…it all sounded so ridiculous and fanciful.

"I think I know how you might be feeling." Leia watched me carefully as she spoke. "It's the same for all of us, to be honest. We all get swept up in feelings that we don't understand. I just want to be sure that Francois has explained everything to you." Then she tilted her head. "No, that's not quite right. I'm sure he tells you what he understands of the process. But I wanted to tell you, as someone who has gone through it. I want you to know what I know. What the other women know. I didn't have anyone to talk to me."

I nodded. "I appreciate that." Then I laughed. "I still can't believe any of this is real. I mean… Shit. Of course it's real. I've been trying to convince people it's real. I just never expected…"

Leia laughed too. "I get that. But in a way, you had a head start. I had no idea about vampires. I had an alcoholic father drinking the profits from our family bar and a house that was falling down around my ears when Nic found me and kissed me."

"He what?" I spluttered a little. "But…but…"

Leia raised an eyebrow.

"Consent," I finished, although if Francois had grabbed me and kissed me, I couldn't have guaranteed I would have cared about consent. My heart had already given that man consent to do anything he wanted to me. My head wasn't stupid enough to not know that.

But it was more than simple consent. It was absolute trust, no matter how risky or unlikely that sounded.

"It goes against modern thinking, for sure," Leia said. "And there were other questionable things about how he engineered being with me, but what about vampires is truly modern? It's a whole different culture. It's a possessive one, a territorial one, and they're long-lived. They've seen a lot of life, and when they find their mates, they get a whole new lease on that. Everything in their world shifts." She shrugged. "It's amazing, actually. The feeling of security and safety and of love and being loved that I have right now. I'm not sure humans can ever experience it. I certainly never did."

"You mean there's more?" Surely my feelings now were already as good as they were going to get. There could be no superlative.

But Leia nodded as she tucked some hair behind her ear and gestured for me to eat the breakfast that the server brought to the table.

"I can't eat all of this." I laughed as I surveyed serving dishes piled high with bacon, eggs, hash browns, sausage patties, and grits.

"Don't forget the beignets as well." Leia sniffed the air appreciatively as the server approached once more. "I think this baby has very good taste." She helped herself to one of the sweet pastries and smiled. "So." She got back down to business as I put food onto my plate. "What do you know about being a vampire mate?"

"That I'd be turned, that we'd be together forever, and that Francois thinks I'm a cure?"

She chewed slowly, like she was thinking. "Has he mentioned it can be dangerous? Not all humans make it. I nearly didn't."

Looking at her now, that was hard to believe. She was so full of life and vitality. Especially when compared to some of the human myths of vampires being undead and decaying.

"Could I…could I just cure him? Without the need to be a vampire?" Sudden anxiety gnawed at my gut. I didn't want to die. I quite liked my humanity as well. Before I'd come to New Orleans, I hadn't been living a bad life really. I had my own place and I was independent.

But the corners of her mouth pulled down and she shook her head as she tore off a corner of her second beignet. "You can't feed him without being turned. I mean, you can. But you'd end up as a thrall and eventually, you'd die. No matter how much care Francois took to keep you alive. And it's no life at all. Maybe I should have brought Sam." She looked toward the staircase as though she expected Sam to appear. "She was a thrall before Kyle rescued her. But that's really her story to tell."

Being a vampire or not being a vampire. That was heavy enough. But if I chose to not be a vampire, I couldn't save Francois from his madness without ending my life. I swallowed at the starkness of that choice. Him or me.

I was quiet long enough that Leia spoke again.

"Are you okay?" Leia touched my hand. "Please don't think I'm trying to put you off. This is an amazing life. And the sex is out of this world. The whole connection is like nothing I can describe to you. But there *are* risks and I want you to know those risks. This should be your decision and to make the right one, you need all of the information. Especially because Francois…" She bit her lip. "He has extra needs. Extra history. Extra baggage. He's come a long way, but all of those things still exist."

"This is a heavy choice to make." The words were out of my mouth before I could stop them, my doubt on full display.

She nodded but didn't speak.

"I don't know what to do."

"And I can't advise you. Not really. I can only give you information." She sighed. "I wish I could tell you what to do, make it easier. But everyone has to make their own choice on this. We all did." She looked at the stairs again as she spoke, as if she could see each of the women I'd met there.

"And your decisions worked out okay for all of you."

She nodded.

"But it might not for me."

She didn't move at all this time. No acknowledgment either way.

My throat dried. Everything had seemed so clear before. I could stay with Francois forever and cure him of what he thought was wrong as long as I let him turn me into a vampire. And when he held me in his arms, that really seemed like the only choice.

But right now, here eating breakfast, I was scared and unsure. Uncertainty skittered inside me. I didn't want to die. I'd risk everything, gamble on a future that I didn't know existed.

"There are four of you." I cycled through the women's names in my head. *Leia, Kayla, Sam, Ciara...*

She nodded. "Yes, there are."

"And you all survived being turned."

She nodded again like she was aware which direction my thoughts were headed.

"The odds don't seem exactly in my favor." Four times. Four times, Nicolas's family had already been lucky. Their luck had to fail at some point. What if I was that point?

I nudged my breakfast plate away. My stomach had tightened into a tiny, hard ball.

"I'm sorry," Leia said as she watched. "I'm sorry if I've made this difficult for you."

"No, it's not that." The urge to run was strong. I could just leave, right? I wasn't a prisoner anymore. I could go and forget all of this.

My chest hollowed, and I sucked in a breath to try to fill it. Of course I couldn't just leave. Francois. His name echoed around my head. I already felt so connected to him. How could I be without him?

And he was depending on me. He needed me. I'd never been needed like that by someone before.

No one had ever needed me to give up my life for them, anyway. And the pull to do exactly that was like nothing I'd ever felt before. The intensity to give up everything for one man scared me.

"It's a fight-or-flight response," Leia whispered. "But that's okay. You have a lot to think about."

I nodded, unable to find any words. My head was too full of all the thoughts to get any of them out. I wouldn't have made sense if I'd tried.

"You want me to take you back downstairs? Or we can go out and wander around New Orleans a bit." But she grimaced as she spoke. "Although Nic probably wouldn't like that with the way things are at the moment."

"It's okay." I half stood. "I can find my way back downstairs." I needed to think. Or find Francois. Or…leave. But I pushed that last thought out of my head.

"I'll stay here a little while longer." She tipped her bagel in my direction. Whether she was staying because she really was feeding her baby or because she had enough discretion to offer Francois and me some privacy, it didn't matter. I was simply grateful.

My steps were heavy as I returned to the basement. My head swam with my thoughts, and I wandered into the living room and sat down. I didn't want Francois to die or succumb to the madness everyone kept talking about.

But saving him was a huge responsibility. Was it one I could bear? I swallowed against bile as it crept up my throat from a roiling stomach. How could I not bear the responsibility? I needed to save him. If I could, I had to.

Surely?

How the hell could I not?

As if conjured by my thoughts, Francois walked into the room, a book open in his hands as his eyes scanned the pages. He sat at the other end of the sofa, and for a moment, I didn't move, trying not to alert him to my presence as I studied him.

Would I give him up? Could I?

"Je sais que tu es là, mon ange."

I know you're there, my angel. His voice always melted me. More so when he spoke to me in French.

He looked up and set the book to the side, not even bothering to mark his page as he closed it. "What's wrong?" His brow furrowed as concern etched itself in every line of his face and the tightness of his jaw.

"I… I met with Leia." I didn't know what else to say, but he nodded like something had made sense.

"Je vois. I see."

But did he? Did he really?

"I could die." My words came out a whisper. Maybe humans faced our own mortality every day. But not quite like this.

"You could stay with me." His words were an equal whisper but full of the kind of torment I'd hoped to never hear. Especially not from him.

It was as though he was losing everything he'd ever lived for. Everything he'd searched for.

"I'm old now, Maeve." He closed his eyes briefly. "Old before I found you. Yet I did find you, and that has made me lucky. But I'd never force you, never take what you can't give freely. I've learned many lessons in my life, and that's the most important one. I can't make something so just by wishing for it." He tightened one of his hands into a fist before smoothing his forefinger over where his knuckles bulged white and tight against his already pale skin. "I can survive on the blood Nic and Leia provide. They infuse it with something Kayla makes."

"I'm not sure it's my place to stay." I started to stand. If Francois would be okay without me, on whatever blood they provided for him, maybe he didn't even need me anymore.

But the thought of leaving him tore at my heart. Panic at the idea of not being with him prevented me from walking away. I couldn't leave him. I just didn't know if I could be what he wanted.

"No." His hand on my arm stopped my movement. "You don't need to go anywhere, mon ange. We can try to be together as we are now. There will be challenges—the instinct to bite you and claim you as my own will be strong, but I can do it. I'd do anything for you. Please stay with me."

I breathed out as I settled back down. There was a third solution. It wasn't as cut and dried as staying or going. Saving him or leaving him. We could stay exactly as we were.

Some of the tightness in my chest eased and I shifted my position to settle against him, immediately blanketed in familiarity as he wrapped an arm around me and held me close.

He pressed a soft kiss against my hair.

Everything would work out now. I couldn't be this comfortable with a man for it all to fall apart. The circumstances under which we'd met could have been better—I stifled the sudden urge to laugh. Yeah, they could have been *way* better, but at least we *had* met.

Maybe karma or fate or whatever existed after all. And maybe it was on our side.

Chapter 21 - Francois

I tightened my hold on Maeve, trying to fight the desperation crawling through my body. It had been a long time since panic had seized me in a grip this strong. I'd searched so long for my mate, searched when other vampires hadn't bothered at all.

I'd wanted her. And now I had her.

And she was rejecting me.

Or that was what it felt like.

She was willing to forsake all of the gifts I could provide—immortal life, abundant wealth… Once, I would have added prestige and position to that list, but I really no longer had either. I existed at the whim of Nicolas, and I had to be grateful for that.

Except today, I wasn't.

Not when I wanted to give my mate everything. Hadn't I told her everything? Did I need to say more?

I glanced at Maeve, looking at the profile of her nose as she rested against me. Love for her welled inside me. So long. It had been so long and I'd made so many mistakes.

No, I couldn't say any more.

I needed to treasure her exactly as she was and throw away my own selfish desires for my life...*our* lives. I couldn't do anything to influence her decision. It wouldn't be fair.

And how often had I tried to force my decision on others before? That had never worked out well.

I couldn't force Maeve. She was my true mate and I couldn't do it to her...but where exactly did that leave me?

It left me even more dependent on Nicolas and his family. I hated being grateful. It was exhausting—to continuously remember that you had someone else to thank for everything and live your life accordingly.

I squashed the bitterness trying to take root inside me. I couldn't blame Maeve, and it wasn't Nicolas's fault.

But it had to be someone's fault because fucking life just wasn't fair. It was another hit. Again and again. I had the rest of a cursed immortal life for this kind of punishment.

The bitterness tasted ugly.

And I'd made promises I might not be able to keep. What if I lost control when I finally took her to my bed properly? What if I lost my control? I could kill my mate the way I'd killed so many before.

The thought was unbearable.

But I couldn't deny it was possible.

I'd defy any vampire to keep his instincts at bay while loving his mate. Even now my gums ached and I longed to taste her.

I moved abruptly, needing to put some space between us but not wanting to be too far away.

"Come to the kitchen, mon ange." If nothing else, I could still feed my mate. Well, perhaps. It had been many years since I'd ventured into a kitchen. I hadn't needed to.

"Okay." She sounded unsure, and I smiled to try to assuage any worry.

"I need to brush up my skills if I'm to love a human."

Her smile faltered for a moment before brightening again. "And what am I to eat?" She sounded so shy that I dodged forward and pressed a quick kiss to her forehead, holding my breath so as not to take in any more of her delicious scent.

I paused before I answered, though. This could all go horribly wrong. Then I couldn't help my grin as memories of my mother rushed back. "A dish my mother used to cook. I think it reminded her of her childhood. A time before she was turned. She ate it whenever she was sad, even when she had no need of the food."

"Comfort food? Sounds like a plan." Although Maeve smiled, my heart squeezed. Was she sad? In need of comfort?

"Are you sad, Maeve?" I needed to know.

I led her to a barstool as I spoke, but instead of answering, her eyes widened as she looked around the gleaming white kitchen space. "Wow. This is a better setup than most restaurants, surely?"

I shrugged. "Je ne sais pas." I didn't know.

She laughed. "Of course you don't, and why would you? You don't eat. But didn't Leia mention a chef?"

I paused as I reached for a saucepan. I'd forgotten about Chef. He didn't like anyone else in his kitchen. Then I glanced over my shoulder at Maeve. Admiration was plain to see on her face, and it was admiration for me.

I'd deal with Chef's temper later. I'd deal with anything for Maeve.

And at least with Chef in residence, the kitchen was well stocked, so I didn't need to worry about not finding the things I needed and losing the admiration I'd just gained.

Seeing Maeve impressed with me... Someone *so important* being impressed with me. It was everything. I'd forgotten. Or maybe I'd never known it. Perhaps the respect my position had always commanded had simply been driven by fear of my family name. Where I wouldn't have cared before and didn't care then, it mattered now.

I didn't want Maeve's fear. I wanted her admiration and respect. I wanted her love.

I wanted forever.

But I'd start with tonight.

And I'd start with aligot.

Except… I'd neglected an important step. As I arranged the potatoes on the counter, I looked at Maeve. "Do you like potatoes? I should have asked before."

"How very remiss of you." But there was a teasing curve to her lips. Then she nodded. "Yes, I like potatoes. And cheese…butter…cream…" Her eyes widened as she tracked my movements while I grabbed ingredients. "Hang on… Are you just making me mashed potatoes?" She laughed.

I raised my finger and pointed at her. "Non! Not mere *mashed potatoes*. Nothing so simple for my mate. Have you ever had aligot?"

She shook her head.

"Ah, then you're in for a treat, mon ange. It's a dish from the old country. France," I added when she drew her eyebrows down. "My mother used to make it when there was something wrong or she was sad." Which had been far too often looking bad. "It was a salve for all ills."

"Your mother ate?"

I nodded. "Yes. It was almost a reflexive behavior. She didn't need the food for nutrition and she didn't need to eat. But I think it was the comfort of an old familiar motion."

"I think I can understand that." Her expression dropped a little.

"Something you'd miss?" I tried to sound lighthearted but it was just one more thing she expected I was taking away from her.

"I can't imagine it." She said it like a confession while she leaned forward to watch what I was doing.

"You'd be able to eat again. Not right away, but we do retain the ability. And imagine it—eating solely for pleasure." I looked away, not wanting to apply too much pressure.

Even though I ached to apply *all* the pressure.

Love me. Choose me.

As I cooked the dish, boiling the potatoes and making the mash and folding in the garlic and cheese until it hung from the spoon in wide, aromatic ribbons that would taste as delicious as they smelled.

She breathed in. "Smells amazing," she said.

I bit back my tiny smile. "Simply providing for my mate," I murmured.

I was so lucky to have found her. Even though I'd been searching, that would never have been a guarantee. I hadn't even been looking in the right city. Fate had truly brought her to me.

She was so beautiful. I was actually falling in love. Nothing I'd ever expected. I hadn't known, and I hadn't presumed or dared hope.

"Are you going to eat as well?" She tucked a lock of that red fire behind her ear.

"Of course," I said like it was a total no-brainer.

If I couldn't share blood with my mate, even when the urge grew stronger each day, then I'd share her meals. I'd eat actual food until my body couldn't process anymore so I could share a ritual with her.

I served the aligot into two bowls, huge mounds of potatoes, and Maeve laughed.

"Really? How much do you think I eat?"

"I would hate for you to be left…unsatisfied."

Her cheeks pinked as soon as the words left my mouth, and she dropped her gaze. I set the food on the bar in front of her, and walked around to the stool next to hers, ignoring the delicate scent of her arousal as I did.

She wound the aligot onto her fork like it was noodles, laughing as it was slow to tear away from itself before she took her first mouthful. Then she closed her eyes and made a low moan of appreciation. My cock jerked at the sound. I'd make her aligot every day if she made those kinds of noises when I did.

We spoke as we ate. Things I'd remember, things I probably wouldn't, but I'd be glad to hear her stories again and again as she distracted me from what she was saying by resting her hand on my arm or laughing without restraint.

"How do you know Nic and his mate?" Her eyes shone curiously as she glanced up from winding a particularly long stretch of cheese around her fork.

I laughed. "You could call is history."

Her gaze sharpened. "History?"

I smiled and nodded. "We go a long way back. Our fathers were…"

"Friends?" she supplied and I laughed, shaking my head. "Far from it. No, I used to believe they were peers, but perhaps they were more different than I ever realized. Nicolas's father was…" I stopped, almost unable to believe what I was about to say. "He was good." Then I shrugged.

"My father was rarely good. He was mostly bad. Sometimes with a side of evil, I think." But despite that, he'd been my father, and his behavior hurt even now. "But Nicolas and I… More likely we are best described as *frenemies*. All our lives."

She laughed then.

She was carefree and she was beautiful.

Radiant.

Vitality shone from her.

Even this was enough. It would have to be. To sit beside her and simply soak her in. It seemed selfish to ask for more than her presence in my life…even though I *wanted*.

Silence fell as she chewed thoughtfully. After she'd swallowed the mouthful of silky potato and cheese, she met my gaze.

"Have you managed to learn anything new about the spells or what we need to do?"

Before I could answer her, Sam and Kayla came through the door, their chat and laughter bursting the bubble I'd created for Maeve and me. The time that I'd carved out simply to enjoy my mate was at an end.

"We need an ingredient," Kayla said, and part of me bristled that she was answering the question that Maeve had asked me.

But as if she knew, Maeve took my hand, entwining our fingers as she listened to the rest of what Kayla had to say.

"I can't brew the spell to unravel the magic because I need the final ingredient."

"Is it hard to get?" Maeve moved forward on her seat. "Is it something I would have heard of?"

Everything to do with our world seemed to fascinate her, which made it ironic that she would resist when I wanted to bring her in and immerse her completely. But I couldn't think about that. I needed only to be grateful for what I did have after so long without.

Kayla's mouth tugged into a grimace. "Yeah. It's not the easiest. We need powdered leaf of the corpse plant— Rafflesia arnoldii. It only grows in the South Pacific, and only a few countries."

"Have you tried talking to Temple?" Sam asked as she opened the fridge and perused the blood in there. "When Kyle and I were on a mission for Nic recently, Temple put us in touch with a botanist who helped us bring down a nest of rogue vampires with some sort of concoction. I have no idea what was in it," she added, as she grabbed a mug.

"Sam!" There was a note of outrage in Kayla's tone. "What the hell, dude?"

Maeve snorted but Kayla was too focused on talking to Sam to stop her stream of words.

"How come you didn't tell me about this before?"

Sam shrugged, not fazed at all by Kayla's frustration. "You didn't ask."

Kayla sighed then grinned. "I didn't know to ask. But I could use a botanist because I need this powdered leaf. And I need it…" She folded her arms and tapped her foot as Sam continued to move casually around the kitchen, not a hint of hurry in anything she was doing. "I need it as soon as possible to finish this spell."

"Okay, okay…" Sam grinned and blew her hair off her forehead. "I get the message. I'll go give Temple a call now." She grabbed her mug from the microwave and sauntered back to the living room, already pulling her cell phone from her pocket.

"What about the rest of the spell?" I returned my attention to Kayla as she lifted herself onto one of the remaining barstools.

"Oh." She waved a hand. "Another ingredient I haven't got yet is the blood of one of the Ancients themselves."

"What?" That sounded impossible. Forget a corpse plant and its powdered leaves, forget Temple and his botany connections. "How the hell do we get hold of their blood?" Did those decrepit, desiccated beings even have blood?

I shuddered. How would any of us get close enough to bleed one of them? They wouldn't be vulnerable until we'd done the spell and surely we needed them vulnerable to harvest their blood…which we needed to do the spell.

It was like some kind of impossible Escher painting with no end and no beginning.

"Ah." Kayla leaned closer, her eyes gleaming as she spoke. "*That* element, I have a plan for." Her face fell a little, her eyes clouding, and a small pit of dread settled in my chest. "But it requires bait."

"Bait?" I screwed my mouth up in distaste. I didn't like even saying the word. There was something sinister in it.

And plans with bait never seemed to have a guaranteed outcome. Too much was left to chance. Well, maybe that was unfair. Things worked if all the dominoes fell where they were supposed to.

"What bait?" Maeve asked. I'd been so lost in my thoughts I'd almost forgotten Maeve was also listening, even though her fingers clutched mine ever tighter.

"Us," Kayla whispered, the only clue that she didn't feel good about this, either. "Me, Sam, Ciara, and you."

"What?" I repeated the question from before, only louder and with more outrage this time. I'd only just found my mate. No way was I risking her as bait in some sort of plot to bring down the most powerful vampires in existence. "No way is that happening. Not now, not ever. Not on my watch."

As the last word left my mouth, the others entered the kitchen.

"What's going on? Why are you yelling at Kayla?" Sebastian's cheekbones were already becoming more prominent as he prepared to defend his mate from me.

I held my hands out. "Sorry." There was no point in enraging him further but neither could I sugarcoat what was happening. "Kayla has a plan to defeat the ancients using the women as bait."

"What the fuck?" Sebastian turned his attention to his mate, his anger barely cooling. "What did this asshole just say?" He jerked his thumb toward me in case anyone in the room was in any doubt as to who the asshole was.

Usually, that would have grated, but I was too irritated by Kayla's proposal, and I hadn't even heard the whole thing.

As if the other guys had taken valuable seconds to process the idea that Kayla was planning to endanger their mates, the yelling didn't start for a few moments, and then there was no way to make out individual curse words, although Maeve shrank back from the sudden atmosphere of angry vampire.

I put my arm around her and pulled her closer. "Shut up, you fuckers." My voice boomed out of me.

"Thank you, Francois." Kayla nodded at me as though I'd silenced everyone for her benefit rather than to keep Maeve from being scared. Then she turned to Sebastian, Kyle, and Jason, where they still stood in a small group, emanating vibes that said not to push them on this. "Guys, with all due respect, this really isn't your decision. It's a decision for *us*." She turned to Maeve. "Are you willing to trust me and help bring down the Ancients?"

I tightened my arm around Maeve again, willing her to say *no*, trying to telegraph my need for her to refuse. Kayla wasn't being reasonable. There had to be another way.

But to my horror, Maeve nodded.

"Yes," she murmured. "Let's do it."

"What?" I looked at her but I didn't get chance to protest further as Sam walked in and Kayla spoke immediately.

"Sam, you going to help with my plan to finish the Ancients?"

Sam didn't even ask for details. "Fuck, yes."

Kayla looked at the guys. "That's three out of four," she said. "Want to take bets on what Ciara will say?"

Jason frowned and jabbed his finger in the air toward her. "Don't you da——"

"What Ciara might say about what?" Ciara strolled into the kitchen and paused to give Jason a kiss on the cheek before pulling away and looking at him. "Are you okay?" She glanced at everyone else. "What's going on?"

"We're discussing how to defeat the Ancients," Kayla started.

"And we're not doing it." Sebastian stepped forward. "I'm regent here, and I say fucking no way."

But Kayla only shook her head, a small smile on her lips as she watched Sebastian. "I think you're superseded by your king, my love, and he wants to bring down the Ancients by any means." She looked at Ciara. "You in?"

"Oh, yes." Ciara's eyes flashed briefly, a reminder of her shifter side, and I withheld a shudder. Hybrids were almost mythical, and there was always something strangely feral about her that worried even me.

She wasn't a vampire mate that I wanted to be on the wrong side of. None of these women were. Each of them had powers that were almost unheard of in mates, as if the Duponts were creating a new breed.

Except Maeve.

My mate was still human.

Still fragile.

I couldn't take the risk. "You can't—"

But Kayla shot me a look, her eyes narrowed. "We do this as a group," she said. "It's the only way. The Ancients know that if they take a mate or two or more, you'll come for them. Your mates are too valuable to you. It's akin to summoning you. So if we're out there in the open, The Ancients will come for us. They won't be able to help themselves. I also suspect they underestimate us." She rested her hands flat against the bar, her spine ramrod straight as she spoke, aware that so many in the room disagreed with her stance. "We only need to trap one of them and find out more, and then take what we need. It's essential for the spell and for getting rid of all of them for good so they no longer threaten us or our existence."

Chapter 22 - Maeve

Oh my God, oh my God. I swallowed against rising panic. What the hell had I just agreed to? I was a fucking human but all of the other females—actual vampires—were standing there looking like she-woman or something, and I couldn't exactly be the only one not to agree to put myself on the line.

Fucking peer pressure.

Forget proving the existence of vampires. I was now so entrenched in the paranormal, I was about to put my life on the line for a second time. I was goddamn making a habit of sacrificing myself for their cause.

I took a deep breath in and blew it slowly back out, and Francois gripped me so tight that I shifted against him, trying to find a comfortable position or encourage him to loosen his grip.

"It's okay," he murmured against my hair, and I nodded, not wanting to speak in case I gave away my fear and uncertainty.

But how the hell could I even help? Sure, everyone here thought I was Francois's mate, but Kayla was a witch,

Ciara was half-shifter and Sam… I paused and studied Sam. She was a fucking badass if nothing else…

I had literally nothing to add to this mission at all. No powers, no strength, no shifting ability. I was actually a liability. I didn't even have knowledge.

Not beyond what I'd gleaned from Granny and my own observations, anyway. But even I wasn't dumb enough to think that believing things was the same thing as actually knowing them or being able to do them. I wasn't a badass or a witch or any sort of vampire hybrid.

I was literally useless and never more so in my life before.

Francois had said I could remain human. He was happy to allow me that, and although I wasn't sure I wanted to be a vampire and risk my life by being turned, it seemed there was no safe option anymore. Every path I looked down to continue my life forward, I could die.

And maybe this life required me to give in and succumb to the paranormal, the supernatural. Perhaps I had to be other.

But that wasn't what I'd ever wanted. I hadn't wanted to outlive my peers by being immortal. I hadn't wanted to remain young while everyone I loved grew old and died. I'd watched that happen to Granny, and I hadn't intended to watch the phenomenon on into forever. It was hard to lose people.

And there was no one I could endanger by telling them about this world. I would have to just walk away from everyone I knew. I'd be alone.

Alone with vampires.

I ignored the shiver running through me.

I'd be the vampire.

Francois cleared his throat. "I don't think this is a good idea."

Kayla turned, her mouth open like she was about to start shouting at him, but he held up a hand.

"Écoutes," he said to her. "Just listen. Maeve is human. She can't be expected to be bait for the Ancients. She's not as robust as you are and she doesn't have the experience." He was measured and calm, but he'd put each of my fears into words.

"She's coming, Francois. She's already agreed. She knows the importance, even if you don't. She's a…" Kayla paused and watched the pair of us assessingly. "As good as a Dupont mate," she finished. "We're all in." Then she moved away from the bar and beckoned. "Come on, girls. Let's leave the guys to it. We have things to discuss."

Francois held me against him briefly, and I breathed in his already familiar scent. Everything about him spoke of safety. My trust in him was absolute.

I couldn't say the same about the others, yet.

He pressed a kiss to the top of my head. "Mon ange," he whispered.

Then he released me and I fell into step behind Kayla, dread roiling in my stomach. I followed her to her spell room, and she sat in one of the chairs alongside the bookcase before gesturing to a sofa and a couple of other easy chairs I hadn't really noticed on my last visit.

"Right." She started with any sort of explanation and before anyone had really made themselves comfortable. "Obviously I've got a plan." She grimaced. "As much as I can have, anyway."

Sam nodded. "Like all the best plans." A wicked grin captured her lips.

"So, what are we doing?" Ciara played with the ends of her hair, brushing the tips over her cheek as she spoke, the act so casual, she could have been discussing take-out choices rather than potentially life-ending endeavors.

"A girls' night on Bourbon Street."

Sam whooped. "About time, man. I'm so sick of being caged up down here. Kyle and I are used to a little more freedom, for sure."

Kayla nodded. "Definitely free tonight. I'm going to amp up our scents, and we are going Ancient fishing. We won't need to do a thing to find them. They'll find us." She nodded when she finished speaking, like that was her whole idea.

"I don't think I get it." Was I the only one still in the dark? Despite how dumb it made me feel, I probably needed clarification. Not knowing exactly what was going on truly made me dangerous to them, even if they were connected by some sort of hive mind and seemed to already know the plan. Did vampire powers stretch that far? Maybe I hadn't ever really known anything at all. All those years of research were adding up to a fat lot of nothing.

I nearly laughed at the realization.

"How will this actually work?" I sat forward in my chair, trying to ignore my rising embarrassment. It was like being a new student who'd been studying a different text.

Kayla smiled, but it didn't make me feel any easier. "Because of you."

My stomach rolled over, and nausea clawed at my throat. "Me?" The word emerged cracked from my suddenly dry throat.

She nodded. "Yep. In fact, I'd go so far as to say it might *only* work because of you. Your human scent is fucking delicious." She took a deep inhale as though to prove her point and her grin became embarrassed. "Sorry." She shook her head then continued. "We can smell an unmated human virgin from miles away."

I automatically pressed my thighs together. "Sorry." My cheeks heated.

Sam laughed. "Don't be. I'm surprised one of the Ancients didn't make a snack or a pet out of you sooner, to be honest. But don't worry. Even though you might feel like a target, we won't let anything happen to you." Her cheekbones became more prominent as she said the words, turning her feral but proving she meant business.

Kayla leaned forward and lowered her voice. "If we're all agreed, I think we need to do it tonight. The guys will only try to change our minds." She waved a hand. "And I'm not really prepared to listen to Sebastian flapping about this." The she chuckled. "They always think they know best."

After the other women voiced their agreement, I nodded mutely because it turned out no one else was really the bait—that was just me. Fear clutched at me with cold fingers as they stood. What if I couldn't do this? I might let everyone down. Or I might die. Neither outcome was a good one for my future.

"Battle stations," Kayla said. "Let's dress for a night out."

Actual excitement laced the air, and it wasn't just the anticipation of battle or bring the war to a close. They were excited to be going out.

"It's been so long." Ciara sighed dramatically. "I think Jason would keep me on an actual leash, if he could."

"That's enough bedroom talk." Kaya grinned. "There are definitely some things we don't need to know about."

But there were far more pressing concerns than giggling over innuendo. "I don't have anything to wear." It was probably the first time in my life I'd said that and genuinely meant it.

I literally had nothing to wear for a night out on Bourbon Street. Even if it was a night out I wanted to attend.

"No worries. Wear something of mine." Kayla made the breezy offer as she opened the door to Sebastian's and her room, and an unfamiliar masculine scent caught in my throat.

There was something that was oddly enemy territory about it, but it didn't seem to bother anyone else.

Kayla threw open a door and gestured inside, and what should maybe have been a bathroom was instead a closet the size of the bedroom again. "Choose whatever you want," she said.

It was like walking into a department store. I glanced at Kayla. Surely none of her clothes would fit me.

She waved a hand in a shooing motion. "Pick something."

When I didn't immediately walk forward, she entered the closet herself, turning to eye me critically before she perused the shelves and hangers.

"Now," she murmured. "I think we're looking for sexy... Sexy but functional. In case we need to fight or run."

Holy crap. Both of those things were scary. Firstly, Kayla expected me to pull off *sexy* when I was more used to *geek chic*, and secondly, that I might really need to fight or run. Regardless of Sam's promises of protection, it might really come down to those two things. Me fighting and me running. In all honesty, the evening could end in me dying.

I swallowed, unsure of what to say, but I didn't have to say anything. Kayla turned to me, her arms full of clothing and she jerked her chin toward the bedroom. "Come and try these on."

As I slid into the skinny jeans, ones it looked like I'd spray-painted on by the time 1 turned to the mirror, some of Kayla's attitude had seeped into me. I borrowed her power and strength, standing taller somehow in the low-heeled boots, even though the silky cream-colored sleeveless blouse was more revealing than I'd usually wear, a deep vee showcasing my cleavage.

I turned, studying myself in the mirror, and Kayla nodded, her approval clear.

"You just need to put your hair up now," she said. "Make sure there's nothing blocking the scent of your skin. Let me just see if I've got some hair ties…" She started to rummage in a drawer.

"No. I'll do it." I needed a moment. "I think I have some…" I gestured to the door. Anything I had was probably in Francois's bedroom but my nerves were screaming and I needed to settle them alone. Anxiety prickled over my skin.

"Okay." Kayla nodded slowly. "We'll go as soon as we're all ready."

I left the room and walked down the hall, picking up my pace as adrenaline buzzed through me. Francois's room was dark and cool when I entered, and I closed my eyes, breathing in the scent of the man I was quickly coming to depend on.

More than simple dependence. There was something much deeper than that. An innate trust. A belief that he would protect me above all else. Francois wasn't a good guy...Not if I listened to the opinions of everyone else.

But he was good to me.

"Mon ange...?" His voice was soft and questioning as he seemed to detach himself from a shadow at the edge of the room.

"Oh." I shouldn't really have been in here but I wanted to be surrounded by him for just a moment.

I turned toward him, and before I could say anything else, I was in his arms as he pressed my back to the wall and his lips were on mine, claiming my mouth with a force that was both brutal and soft—like I was something more fragile than he'd ever known.

He withheld most of his strength, protecting me from the unrestrained passion of it.

I surrendered to his kiss, twining my arms around his neck as his tongue sought mine, and I aligned myself against his body in wordless offering.

When I broke the kiss, my breathing was uneven and ragged. "We can't. We don't have time…" But I *wanted*. Every time he kissed me, I wanted him more.

He rested his forehead against mine. "But your scent… You desire me, Maeve."

I nodded, unable to deny it.

"Then don't worry." He slid his hand down to trace his fingers along my waistband. "I'll be quick. Just a taste."

I almost moaned and my knees weakened. The memory of his head between my legs started a slow steady beat of wantonness inside me.

His gaze met mine in the gloom, his eyes a dull red. "Let me?" he implored, and when I should have shaken my head, I nodded instead.

How could I ever refuse this man anything?

He lowered the zipper on the jeans and popped the button open, and I giggled as he drew them inside out to take them off.

They stuck around my boots and he blew out a frustrated sigh. "Oh, for a decent skirt," he muttered. "I know how those work."

I giggled again. "Well, those all work the same. Just lift up."

He turned his gaze back to mine, his smile wicked. "Oui. Indeed."

I tried to relax and play it cool, even though my heart raced at the nature of our discussion and my cheeks warmed. "And here you are trying to get into my pants."

"Get my mouth on your pussy," he corrected, and my breath caught in my chest.

No man had ever spoken to me that way before, and it was base and coarse and dirty…and it was *real*. This man really did want me.

Cool air moved against my skin, and Francois pressed his palms against my thighs. I parted them immediately, looking down at him on his knees in front of me, like he was at prayer.

Worship. The word drifted through my mind, leaving me breathless again.

He leaned forward and simply rested his cheek against my leg, his breath skating over my skin, and I grew wet with anticipation.

A low groan rumbled through him. "The things you do to me, mon ange. I can smell your desire." He pressed a kiss to my skin before the tip of his tongue flicked against me, and I tangled one of my hands into his hair.

I closed my eyes, waiting…expecting him to tease me a little more but he pressed his fingertip against my clit and I stiffened, letting out a gasp.

"There it is," he murmured. "I swear they move. Little things that like to hide."

Before I could reply, he touched me again, but this time with his tongue. I whimpered, and he murmured something in response. Then he sucked my clit into his mouth and I gasped again, unable to control the sounds I was making.

"I want to be closer." He suddenly took hold of one of my legs, his fingers clamping around the back of my right thigh before he lifted it over his shoulder. Then he did the same with my left leg so I sat against his face my back still resting on the wall as he lapped his tongue over me, smoothing and stroking as I began to rock, seeking more friction and control.

My fingers tightened in his hair and he groaned against me as I tugged a little.

His hands moved to my ass and he pushed me closer against him, speeding up his movements as waves of pleasure crashed through me, increasing in intensity as I surrendered to the tightening of my muscles.

I couldn't catch my breath properly. All I knew was Francois and the way he was making me feel. I gasped each inhale, barely having time to exhale before I gasped again. Time changed, slowing even as it sped up and spun away completely, and I craved release.

I drew in one last breath before my core pulsed, my body throbbing like desire had a heartbeat all of its own.

He didn't stop immediately, setting off aftershocks with small laps of his tongue, teasing my already sensitive flesh as I squirmed against him, unsure what I wanted. It felt so good for hm to keep touching me... So good.

But also, my legs were Jell-O. If I didn't move soon, I'd just be a puddle of colored gelatin slime on the floor.

"Stop," I whispered as another spasm twisted my body and a soft sigh escaped my lips.

"Mm?" His hum made me twitch again, but I giggled, high after feeling so good.

"It's too sensitive." I ground the words out, focusing on each one, trying to ignore all the things Francois made me feel.

"If you're sure?" He glanced up at me, his hair tousled from the way I'd mussed it for him, and I grinned at the question on his face.

"Absolutely." Oh my god. Fuck, that had been amazing.

He helped me regain my footing, my dismount not at all awkward as he supported me. Vampire strength had its benefits, that was for sure. When he grinned again, the tips of his fangs showed, but instead of revulsion or fear, my desire spiked again, curiosity making me braver than usual as I reached out to touch one.

He jerked back and I retracted my hand awkwardly. "Sorry." Then I stood straighter, searching for my courage as I took in his form when he stood, noting the bulge at his crotch.

"Your turn?" And my voice only squeaked a tony bit. What the hell was I offering? What would he accept?

"Oh?" He joined me leaning against the wall, and he dropped his hand to his own waistband, his gaze never straying from mine.

It was a challenge.

I swallowed, the noise audible.

"I can smell your fear," he whispered. "And combined with your desire, it's delicious, mon ange." For a moment, his eyes were a blaze of red. Then they dimmed again.

But I'd seen a predator, and it had excited me.

I covered his hand with mine. "Yes." It was nothing more than a breath as I lowered myself to my knees.

There was something very sexy about a man who wanted me.

Francois cupped the length of his cock beneath the fabric of his pants, and I ran the tip of my forefinger down the length of it.

He hissed a sudden breath. "Tease."

I bit my lip. Was I?

Francois stood so still that I repeated my movement before pushing his hand aside and fumbling for the zipper.

"I have buttons." His voice was soft, but my cheeks burned.

Oops. "I knew that."

He chuckled.

What the hell was I doing? I was usually pretty confident. I knew my shit… But faced with one hard cock and I was reduced to a bag of nerves.

"Touche-moi, mon ange."

I shivered. Being told what to do was kind of sexy, and I only chewed my lip, appearing undecided, for a moment. Of course I was going to touch him.

I undid his buttons, keeping it slow. It was probably sexier and it gave me time to compose myself. When his cock sprang free from the confines of the fabric, I hesitated for a moment.

I'd never really studied one before. I hadn't had the opportunity. "Beautiful." I spoke the word without intending to, and his cock stiffened further as though in response to my praise.

I grasped his shaft lightly, wrapping my fingers around it as I stroked softly upward. A bead of precum glistened at the tip and I leaned forward, instinct driving me to lick it off with a quick swipe of my tongue.

He rested a palm on my head, the weight of his hand pleasing. I opened my mouth and licked around the top of his cock before sucking the head into my mouth. The skin there was so soft, so warm.

I closed my eyes and bobbed my head lower, sliding my tongue down the underside of the shaft, gliding my way down. Not all the way, though. That wasn't going to happen. He was bigger than I'd anticipated.

I cupped his balls for a moment before I worked my hand in tandem with my mouth, enjoying him sliding in and out of my mouth, worshiping him as he had just worshiped me.

He didn't make a sound, but his grip on my hair increased, and I licked around his head again, swirling my tongue over him before returning to sucking again, settling into a rhythm. I moaned as he swelled a little more in my mouth, becoming harder, making it more difficult but rewarding me for my attention.

Power flashed through me. I had this man. This vampire was mine. He liked the things I did to him, and I wanted to do more.

I licked away more precum and glanced up at him, making startled eye contact before I closed my eyes again and focused. His scent surrounded me, and as he'd often told me he could smell my desire, maybe I could also smell his.

His cock grew bigger and warmer, and I moved faster, still guiding myself down with my tongue.

"Maeve," he gasped out, his rare use of my name almost disturbing my focus.

But instead of responding, I held steady, taking as much of his cock as I could, wanting to please him.

He swelled one last time then he pulsed, cum filling my mouth before I swallowed. As I drew slowly away, licking the soft skin clean as I went, he shuddered at each soft touch. I finished with a gentle kiss right at the tip and he groaned.

"Sensitive?" I asked, but turnabout was always fair play. I ran my fingers lightly over him, and he shuddered again.

"Stop. No more teases." But he grinned.

I stayed kneeling beside him, resting my cheek against him as I watched his cock. "I'm not sure you'll ever fit inside me." I'd been thinking out loud, but he chuckled softly.

"Challenge accepted."

I met his gaze. "Challenge accepted?" I understood the words, but I'd been serious.

He nodded. "You were made for me. You're my mate. Nature will take care of the rest. I won't hurt you. You'll see."

"But I've never…"

"I know." He didn't need to say any more, and we both fell silent again.

He knew and he'd look after me. That was all I needed.

"Am I making you late, mon ange?" His voice was lazy, like he didn't actually care, but the question galvanized me into action.

"Shit. Yes, you are."

He laughed at my sudden outrage. "I think it took two of us to make you late."

I nodded then shook my head. "You're just a very bad influence. I need to get dressed." I scrambled to grab my jeans and turned them the right side in. "Damn it. Where are my panties?"

Grinning, he slipped his hand into his pocket and withdrew a crumpled piece of lace. "This little thing?"

"Yes!" I gave a frustrated chuckle and grabbed it off him. "I need to get back to Kayla."

He sighed. "All right. Let me help."

He bent to retrieve my boots and as I watched his movements, surrounded by the intimacy of what we'd just done, I fell for him a little more.

Chapter 23 - Francois

"Are you sure this is all Kayla said for us to do?" Kyle cracked his knuckles as he glared at all of us and around the bar in general.

His stress was contagious, and I fidgeted with the beer coaster in front of me, tearing at the thin cardboard layers and ignoring the stale smell of the beer that had soaked into it.

"Yes." Sebastian's tone invited no argument. "We're only here as a safety measure. We're going to see how many Ancients come, and if it looks like too many, we split them up. Between us, we should get the blood of at least one."

At least Kayla had conceded to being helped. I didn't think any of us could have stayed in the apartment under The Neutral… I cut my thought off. It was no longer The Neutral Zone. It was now Nightfall. Sebastian's club.

Not mine.

The only thing truly mine now was Maeve.

And my senses swam with her. I could still feel my mouth on her pussy, and her scent filled the air. Whatever Kayla had given her to amplify it had worked.

Far too well, in my opinion.

She was a true beacon. There was no way the Ancients wouldn't come. Her scent was the sweetest perfume. A siren call. I'd wanted to do so much more than taste her, but to have done anything else would have put Kayla's whole plan in jeopardy.

Maeve needed to remain unmated and a virgin for her scent to be the one that attracted the Ancients here. That wasn't my only consideration, though.

"What if…" I stopped speaking. I almost didn't want to put my thought into words.

It was the fear I kept squashing down so I didn't have to acknowledge it.

But Sebastian looked at me. "What if what?" He was rarely truly friendly, and this occasion was no exception.

"What if what, Francois?" Jason was friendlier. But then we'd been living together when the Ancients abducted me.

Technically, he'd been my babysitter or my jailer, but part of me hoped he'd also been a friend. I didn't have very many.

"What if they have too much power?"

Sebastian raised an eyebrow. "What do you know?"

I shrugged. I shouldn't have started this, really. I didn't know anything, and I couldn't give them anything new. I only had my fears.

"I'm worried about Maeve," I said. "And here's something none of us has considered. What if they did something to me while I was with them and now they can somehow use me now to further their cause?"

Sebastian opened his mouth but Jason spoke first. "Some sort of sleeper agent? Do you really think so?"

I shrugged. "I don't know. I…I don't feel any different. And I know all that I owe to Nicolas…" I looked at Sebastian as I spoke.

I didn't want him thinking that I'd be in any way disloyal. This evening was already fraught enough, with every mate on the line. Each of the men here was operating on a hair trigger, so perhaps it had been a silly time—a fucking stupid time—to mention my worry that I could be some sort of sleeper agent for the Ancients, but I owed it to the Duponts to always be honest.

What if something the Ancients had done to me forced me to turn on Nicolas and his family? My blood ran cold, chilling me. Father had always controlled me. Mostly by coercion. Sometimes by force.

But the rest of his family, the remaining Ancients, they were capable of so much more. They'd taken my blood and they'd fed me. They could have done anything to me, and we would all be naïve to at least not consider it.

I never wanted to go back to being controlled by anyone. Initially, I'd expected Nicolas to do the same. I'd been the enemy. He should have kept me close. He wouldn't have been wrong to just lock me up and walk away.

But he'd given me freedom, or he'd been trying. If rehabilitation was the same thing. And it certainly felt that way.

"Jason?" Sebastian spoke again. "You got this clown when we split up?" He jerked his chin in my direction.

Jason nodded. "Yep."

"Like the good old days, oui, mon ami?" I beamed a wide grin just for Jason's benefit, and he chuckled in response.

"Still not really your friend."

But I knew different. Out of any of these guys, Jason was the closest one to a friend I had.

"Okay. We can't keep sitting here. We're too obvious. And I think I need to move Kyle away from the door—he's genuinely scaring away customers now." Sebastian half smiled as he spoke, but I'd just watched a second pair of women enter then immediately leave after catching sight of Kyle's glowering, hulked form half in the shadows.

Sebastian was right to split us up and move us farther into the club, even if we didn't have immediate sight of everyone entering.

"Come on." Jason stood. "Maybe I can stretch to buying you a drink to look at while we wait."

I chuckled. "Anything to fit in."

We moved to a different table, and I sat down, still aware of Maeve. Every time I took a breath, her scent assaulted me afresh, keeping me on edge, sparking my worry. Kayla's laugh rang out across the bar, and Jason craned his neck, trying to look around the people in the crowd.

"I hope Ciara's okay," he muttered. "I mean, of course Ciara's okay."

"She's a hybrid." It was neither agreement nor denial on my part. Simply comment.

Jason nodded and smiled. "Isn't she?" Pride shone from him. Then he sobered a little. "I'm glad you've found your mate, too."

"Oh?" I tilted my head. "Now the killing might stop, you mean?"

His cheeks colored. "No, not that. I…"

I chuckled. "I know what you meant. She just isn't truly mine yet, is she?"

He shook his head then nodded as though not sure what response to give. "She is, though. She's more delicate right now—looking after a human will never be easy—but she's yours in every way that matters."

I coughed to clear my suddenly tight throat at his earnest words, and I swiped my finger over my eyes. "Damn New Orleans heat," I murmured.

But since when had any of the Duponts really been bothered about my future? Even Jason. I hadn't expected him to be so earnest and positive about Maeve. I hadn't expected him to *care*. At least not enough to say anything.

"Thank you." I chuckled again. "I feel like I've tried this part a lot." Regret seeped through me at the thought of the ghosts I'd left in my wake. "And I still don't know what I'm doing. Maeve doesn't…" I breathed her scent in again and the regret deepened. "She doesn't know what she wants."

He laughed. "I think that might be normal." I met his gaze. "Firstly—" He waved a hand. "Women, you know? And secondly, what woman ever expected her life journey to include being a vampire? We're kind of a lot to take in, right?"

I nodded. "I expect so. But how did Ciara find it?"

"Oh, she had extra baggage. But better than I expected. But it was a total culture change for her really. Maeve hasn't got a pack in the same way, but it must be similar? Humans live in bonded families, they have friends. What Ciara saw herself as giving up to be with me—her pack, her way of life—Maeve must have some of that, too?"

I nodded. "I'd forgotten." Then I sighed. "It's been so long, oui?"

Jason nodded too. "It's hard to remember the bonds of humans. But we bond, too. It's not so dissimilar."

"But it is for me. I had only Father left, and his kingdom. What you have with Nicolas is something entirely different, something other. The promises you make to your mate include family."

"As do yours now," Jason said, and I wiped my eyes again.

Damn this New Orleans climate. Vampires weren't supposed to get allergies, surely.

We chatted back and forth, occasionally sipping our beers but mostly nursing them.

Then the atmosphere in the bar changed. The temperature dropped and the chatter of the humans lowered as if someone had turned the volume down.

Everything became a little more distant and a little more hushed.

"Over there." Jason nodded toward the doors as two Ancients walked in.

"That's Aleron and Nisha," I said. I didn't like either of them, and they weren't exactly doing a very good job of trying to blend in.

I glanced at my own frilled cuffs. Perhaps this was also my cue to update my look. It wasn't as if I had a reputation to maintain in town anymore.

As they moved farther into the bar, Jason and I wound our way to position ourselves behind them, and I glanced around, catching sight of Sebastian and Kyle going the other way. Nic was somewhere out the back, hidden out of sight—the only part of the plan Kayla didn't know about because he was ready to swoop in and remove all of the women if things went south. Temple was somewhere too, but any one of these shadows could have had his name on it.

Aleron raised his hand and pointed, spotting Sebastian and picking up his pace, but I stepped into the light, considering whistling in his direction. In the end, though, I simply called his name.

"Aleron." He turned. "Oh, Aleron, of all the bars in New Orleans, fancy us meeting each other in this one." I bowed. "How lovely to see you again, mon ami. Last time really was too short."

Aleron growled, the low rumbling sound carrying across the bar, and his face contorted, his eyes grew red, and his hair started to drift in a nonexistent breeze.

"Damn Ancient magic," I muttered.

He and Nisha exchanged a quick glance and then they began to move, Aleron towards Jason and me, and Nisha in Sebastian's direction.

This was our cue.

"Game on," Jason muttered and we ran, charging through the door and out into the steady stream of tourists walking down the street. All we needed to do was keep Aleron busy and out of the way. Or capture him and take his blood. But if the others were able to capture Nisha inside the bar, that would be easier. The women were already there, ready to do their part.

I threw a glance over my shoulder. "Where is he?" There were people in the way now, chattering and laughing and swaying with too much drink as they made their way to the next location for even more.

"Did we lose him?" Jason stopped running, the transition abrupt. "Fuck. That wasn't the plan. He was supposed to stay on us. Should we go back? See if we can pick him up again?"

I started to nod. We had to try. But before I could agree, Aleron landed in front of me, having jumped from the roof above.

He grinned. "Stupid baby vampires. Found you. What game shall we play next? Wait, was this tag or hide and go seek?" He thought for a moment. "I know, how about we try some bondage?" As he spoke, Jason began to rise in the air.

Jason fought, struggling against the same invisible bonds the Ancients had secured me with when they'd abducted me from the apartment I'd shared with Jason.

Aleron grinned, then looked at me, lifting his hand and pointing like I should lift off the ground, too. When I didn't, his eyes widened and lips parted. Oh, he wasn't so cocky now, not so sure of his magic now that he couldn't control both of us.

"What's the matter, mon ami?" I pouted as I spoke, like I was genuinely confused. "Why do you look so sad?" But inside I celebrated.

If he couldn't control me at the same time as Jason, they surely hadn't done anything to me at all. They couldn't have. My worry about being easily controlled by the Ancients, and being used by them against the Duponts faded away.

I darted forward, knocking Aleron off balance and his hold on Jason wavered but didn't release entirely. I aimed a punch at the side of his head, but Aleron dodged and laughed, even as a fine film of sweat broke out on his forehead.

They weren't as strong when they were alone. That was interesting. I aimed another punch his way, and he dodged again, but less quickly this time. If I could just weaken him further, we'd have what we needed.

Hopefully, the others were being as successful with Nisha. There were more to overpower her in the bar, anyway, and there was no way she could control Sebastian and Kyle. Kyle was a force to be reckoned with all on his own.

I aimed a punch again.

"For fuck's sake, Francois. Stop playing with him and end this." At Jason's call, I darted forward again, and yanked Aleron against my body.

I hovered my fangs over his neck only briefly. This was sweet, sweet justice for all the times they'd fed me crap blood. And what a way for a vampire to die.

I pressed my fangs into his skin but before I could draw my first blood, he was gone, and Jason hit the ground with a loud thump as Aleron took off down the street so fast that none of the tourists probably were aware of anything but a breeze as he passed by them.

"Damn it." I reached to help Jason up. "I nearly had him." I hadn't even taken a mouthful of blood let alone weakened him.

"We need to get back to the club."

I licked my lips as I nodded my agreement, and the sweet, coppery taste of blood burst across my tastebuds. Apparently I'd pricked Aleron if nothing else, and his blood… The lights around me brightened then settled, and I could make out all sorts of shapes and figures in the shadows and milling through the crowds.

The ghosts of New Orleans were all revealed to me before they faded and were gone again. I shook my head and snapped back to reality.

If only my ghost were here with me now. Perhaps she'd know what was happening.

The clarity in my head continued. It was as if someone had connected me directly to a power supply, and it could have only been a couple of drops. I could only imagine how Father had felt with that blood constantly in his veins.

"Francois!" Impatience tainted Jason's tone now. "We need to get back to the bar and check on the others. What if his only role was diverting us rather than it being the other way around?"

Shit. I hadn't thought of that. I ran after Jason and we wove our way around the constant stream of people walking toward us. They moved like they were one, oblivious to our hurry.

"We'll go around the back," Jason called over his shoulder as he darted along the side of a wall. "Nic should still be there if nothing has gone wrong."

Premature dread gnawed at my stomach at his words. *If nothing had gone wrong.* I'd only just found her. Nothing could go wrong now.

At the back of the bar, the women were standing beside Nic beside Temple's van.

"Well?" Jason looked at all of them as he reached for Ciara, and I pulled Maeve into my arms, so grateful that she was safe.

She winced as I rubbed my fingers over her arm, and I glanced downward. Two red pinpricks marred her soft skin, and instant rage filled me.

I lunged for the van—that was where they must have Nisha—and I beat my fists against the flimsy metal between us. She wasn't remotely safe in there now that I'd seen what she'd done.

"Francois, stop." Jason grabbed me, but his voice in my ear was a mere annoyance.

I threw him backward, not caring that my friend hit the ground with a crunch. My thoughts were a blaze of red in my head as Ciara ran to Jason.

No one mattered but Maeve.

No one.

And none of them could stop me from getting the Ancients now. I'd destroy all of them. I'd bring down the whole world to keep Maeve safe.

"Francois!" Nic used a more commanding tone, more hypnotic, and I knew what he was doing. "Sam, get over here. You said your coercion extends to vampires sometimes, right? Can you hold him? I have things to do."

As Sam stepped in front of me, talking about something I wasn't even listening to, my muscles began to relax. My anger started to drain away, and I stepped away from the van.

But I didn't forget the reason for my anger.

"Who the hell bit my mate?"

Chapter 24 - Maeve

The bar really wasn't as loud as I'd expected it to be. I'd thought Kayla was planning a really raucous night out. We'd certainly dressed for fifty shades of sexy between us.

Instead, the backdrop to the chatter of the people in here was soft jazz rather than anything Cajun or zydeco and there wasn't a beard or a biker or a flannel shirt in sight.

After so long being surrounded by only vampires, everything here looked so normal, and a pang of familiarity ached in my gut. I wanted normal. Hell, I longed for it.

Except, did I?

If I tried to imagine sitting on one of these barstools and discussing the weather or the latest development in politics, or even what I did for a living, I couldn't. It was as though that lifestyle was no longer an option, as though it had disappeared.

Perhaps there really was no going back, and that was sad. I'd changed, and the world had moved on without me. I'd spent the past few weeks with paranormal creatures and supernatural old guys and now I didn't truly fit anywhere.

But I missed it. Not being chased and attacked and afraid all the time… That sounded almost idyllic. Especially as I'd set myself up for all three of those things tonight.

"Come on. Let's head over here." Kayla indicated a booth at the back. "What do you drink, Maeve?"

"I have no idea." I laughed as I shrugged. It wasn't as though I spent a lot of time out on the town back home in Boston. I was way more likely to be found urban exploring an abandoned building or sitting in a cemetery past midnight.

"Well, choose something." Kayla brandished the drinks menu in my direction, and my gaze fell on the list of cocktails. I'd expected the usual options—long island iced tea or dry martini, but instead, I laughed.

"Oh my God. I think we should all get a different one." I stopped. "Oh, shit. Sorry. You don't drink."

Kayla grabbed the menu and her eyes sparkled as she read the options before passing the menu to Ciara, Sam, and Leia. "But I'm definitely thinking we should order. This is too much fun not to."

"Who's drawing the short straw and actually asking?" Leia perused the menu.

"I think Maeve should do it," Sam said. "But I'll come with you if you feel like you need protection."

I laughed even as embarrassment crawled through me. "I don't think this is the part of the evening where I was supposed to need protection though, right?"

"Very true," Ciara agreed. "So ladies, what'll it be?"

"Nothing for me." Leia curled a lip. "Alcohol isn't sitting well right now."

After I grabbed their orders, I approached the bar.

The bartender smiled as he moved towards me. "What can I get you?"

I grinned, although anxiety fluttered in my stomach, and I didn't know if it was because of what I was about to say or due to the rest of the evening and the big unknown hanging over my future.

Most likely the second one, but I took a deep breath before I spoke, anyway. "Sit on my face, creamy pussy, tie me to the bedpost, and cum in my panties, please." My face burned a little as I finished the order.

"What... No dirty little virgin?" He smiled as a fang peeked from beneath his top lip.

Immediately, I took a step back. Kayla had boosted my scent. Every vampire in spitting distance of New Orleans knew exactly what I was and probably how to find me.

"Relax. Nic already spoke to me. You're among friends."

I nodded. Okay. That was okay. The entire bar was looking out for me, then. I fumbled for my money in my purse, but he shook his head.

"I'll bring your drinks over when they're ready." Then he looked at the other women. "Just try to keep any fighting to a dull roar. My boss will have a heart attack if you destroy his bar."

I nodded again like it was the only movement I could make right now. *Fighting.* That was the part I didn't want to do. Although the others had put safeguards in place—Nic was out back, there were guys in here with us, and apparently even the bartender was on our side if things went wrong.

I rejoined the others, sliding into my seat.

"Well?" Ciara grinned.

"I made the order." I flipped my hair, making the gesture casual.

But I looked around. Shit, I was the only human here. The target. The weakest link. Never had felt so vulnerable. Not in all of the risks I'd taken trying to find the paranormal and prove its existence before. I almost wish I hadn't stumbled into it.

The bartender approached the table. "Ladies." He grinned and held up the first cocktail. "Sit on my face?"

Everyone laughed. "Me." Ciara licked her lips then chuckled. "Although Jason might kill one of us."

I laughed along with the others, but my mind was still distracted. I really wasn't good enough to be here. I wasn't like them. I couldn't do what they could do. They couldn't rely on me, anyway. If everything went wrong with Kayla's plan, I couldn't save any of them. There was just no way.

I'd always been weird in the human world, and I'd gotten used to it. Perhaps I'd even started to embrace it. It was kind of like my calling card. It went with the job. But I was even weird here.

I wasn't good enough in either world. No wonder I didn't have any friends.

"Maeve?" I looked at Sam as she spoke, and she wrapped an arm around me, drawing me to her body. "You doing okay? I know this part must be scary."

I tensed a little. It was rare for anyone to hug me, even like this. A side-arm hug thing. Mom had never even done that. Granny had, though. Huge bear hugs full of lilac fragrance and soft, thin skin when she wrapped her arms around me and pressed one of her cheeks to mine.

I sighed. Maybe it was a blessing she was gone now. I wouldn't have to leave her.

"How are things with you and Francois?" Sam wasn't nosy when she asked, but everyone else leaned forward, like the answer mattered.

But the door to the bar opened and I glanced up then caught my breath. The Ancients were instantly recognizable, their hair so pale it could have been white, and their movements smooth but also slightly awkward. There was definitely something otherworldly about them and they didn't appear to try to hide that.

I swallowed. The secret hope I'd harbored that they wouldn't even come inside, that somehow someone had arranged for all of this to happen where I wouldn't even see it, let alone take part, was killed in an instant. It was going down, and it was going down now.

Francois and Jason moved, skirting the edge of the room, and part of me relaxed. Everyone was on task at least, but I was still front and center. I'd never been so aware of my own vulnerability. Not even when I was alone with Francois and we were intimate—at least then, I still felt safe. I felt protected and loved.

Not here, even as the other women crowded behind me, their physical presence almost overwhelming as Kayla started to mutter under her breath.

"Go to Nic?" Sam appeared at my elbow and tugged me to standing before she even finished speaking. "Do you remember where he is?" I nodded and started to move, fear propelling me forward before I could even think about what to do.

An Ancient female was walking in our direction but in the next moment, she seemed to be right in front of us.

I made a strange yipping sound—the kind of embarrassing noise that would probably keep me awake for many nights in many years to come as I relived it—but Ciara snarled and stepped forward, already slashing with her hand. Her claws ripped a jagged trail in the Ancient's cheek as Kayla's magic began to wrap around her.

The woman met my gaze and smiled, but it was full of malevolent promise, and I shuddered. I couldn't go back. I couldn't let her get me. What the hell was I thinking, agreeing to be bait?

I checked over my shoulder, locating the exit, then backed toward it, keeping the Ancient where I could see her. My back hit the emergency exit door and I fumbled behind me, reaching for the silver bar to push and let myself out. The alarm blared as I did, but the only one who even seemed to notice was the bartender. He glanced up and winked in my direction.

Wind blew through my hair, making a cracking noise like it was alive and had electrified me as I pushed the door wider. Then pain ripped through me, coursing up my arm as something sharp caught hold of me. I ripped away as I fought through the door, my eyes half closed, my hands reaching into the dark.

My arm throbbed.

"Got you." Nic spoke as he pulled me forward, catching me as I fell against him. He lifted his cell phone to his mouth. "Temple, you're up." Then his nostrils flared and he glanced at my arm.

Blood trickled down my wrist and I pulled my arm back against myself, clamping it to my side. Nic didn't get the chance to ask about it because the air around us filled with screams from inside the bar as the door opened and Kayla rushed out, pushing Leia in front of her and dragging Sam behind her. Last came Ciara, loping forward in wolf form. As soon as she left the bar, the screaming died down, and Nic leapt forward and slammed the door shut as Kayla murmured another spell.

"It's sealed," she said.

"Okay." Nic nodded. "Did Temple get the Ancient?"

Kayla shook her head. "No. She was too fast. They're something else, Nic. I need to go back to the drawing board on this one. I need to tweak the plan."

"Okay." He started to agree with her then looked up as Jason and Francois came running around the corner.

Francois swept me against him immediately, and he smoothed his fingers over the bare skin of my arm in his usual comforting way but he grazed too close to the bite mark, and I flinched as pain flashed through me.

I watched him as he looked down, watched as his eyes widened and rage contorted his face.

He sprang toward the van—it was empty but he didn't know that as he beat against it with his fists, leaving dents in the strong metal. I shrank away from the display of violence, but the other vampires ran toward it.

"Francois, stop." Jason took hold of his shoulder, but Francois didn't pay him any attention at all, continuing his violence like an overgrown toddler having a tantrum, except this tantrum could be deadly.

But Francois threw Jason to the ground, his show of strength dangerous and scary as his eyes flashed red and he seemed to growl ugly French words.

"Francois." The king's voice boomed out, and even I listened.

Francois slowed his frenzy a little as Nic turned his attention to Kyle and Sam.

"Sam, get over here. You said your coercion extends to vampires sometimes, right? Can you hold him? I have things to do."

Sam nodded and walked toward Francois, not the least bit intimidated by what she was seeing. Instead, she started talking to him really quietly as she maintained their eye contact.

He stepped away from the van and some of the red color bled out of his eyes. "Who the hell bit my mate?"

He turned to me, but I held up my hands and stepped back. The back end of the van looked like a crumpled aluminum can.

But he only shook his head and made a scoffing noise. Then he was in front of me, using his vampire speed against me for the first time. But as he pulled me to him again, I forgave him. He smelled like home.

He smelled like home, and I never wanted to be anywhere else.

"Mon ange," he whispered after pressing a kiss into my hair as he loosely held my bitten wrist in his hand. "We'll fix this, I promise."

Chapter 25 - Francois

The memory of Maeve's face as I'd lost control of myself and dented Temple's van haunted me. I'd never wanted to cause her fear or revulsion, but it looked as though I'd managed both.

I leaned forward in my seat as we approached Nightfall. The sooner we were back there, the better. We'd be safe inside those wards and then I could start to fix my mistake.

But Maeve! My mate. Someone else had bitten her. Nausea like I'd never known overwhelmed me. I'd never expected to be in the position of a vampire reclaiming his mate.

Preferred mates were double virgins—sexually and never having been bitten. Nicolas's Leia had been both. That's what I'd thought…

But I'd been wrong then. So wrong. Maeve was one hundred percent my mate. A bite from another wouldn't stand in my way.

I glanced around the van, my gaze landing on Sam. But it was possible. She'd been a thrall after all. At least one other had bitten her prior to Kyle. Maybe several others. If I could find nothing else, I'd talk to her and Kyle.

Shit. I shook my head. I hadn't protected her. Even with the full might of the House Dupont—the king and his regent—I hadn't been able to keep my mate safe. How could I have failed?

When we got out of the car, I guided her as though she were elderly, but vampire venom was already coursing through her veins. There was no way to know how that would affect her.

She could die. Some fucking Ancient could have killed my mate.

I shook my head. I couldn't think like that. I smoothed my hand over her back as I guided her through the living room toward her own bedroom—not the one where I'd most recently pleasured her. For this transitional phase, she'd probably want her own space. Or something.

What the hell did I know about women turning into vampires? They all died, right?

"Where are we going?" She pulled away and turned to face me. "I want to talk to the others and find out everything that happened. Did we get the blood we needed?"

What? Why did she want to know that? That was not relevant in the slightest right now. There were far bigger things to think about than how the plan had progressed.

There would always be time for other plans, other missions, other attempts.

There was only one Maeve.

Only she mattered.

I took hold of her hand and drew her along again, and she fell quiet as though surprised by the abruptness of my movement. But I couldn't think of the things I needed to say to make her understand. I just needed to know she was somewhere safe.

We entered her room and she pulled away for a second time.

She paced to the wall and back again, pushing her hair out of her face when it fell where she didn't want it. Then she blew out an exasperated sigh. "What's wrong, Francois? Why are we in here by ourselves?"

Even hearing her voice tested my control. I didn't *want* to control myself any longer. Was there any point in my control now?

I didn't answer that last question. I didn't dare. I couldn't give myself permission to become the monster again, and there was no telling what would happen if I loosened my control.

I couldn't take any risks. She was perfect. So perfect. It was hard to look at her now and not be consumed by need.

Someone else had tried to ruin perfection, had claimed her for themselves.

One of those fuckers had touched her. I fought against the warring emotions inside me.

"Francois? What's wrong?" She stepped forward, right into the space I'd been trying to create for myself.

I forced my focus to her arm before I lifted it and examined her wound. The bitemark was inflamed now, puffy. The vampire hadn't had chance to heal it. Or more likely, they'd wanted me to see.

This was a deliberate claim. A declaration of war.

I remembered that one detail about the Ancients anyway. Their bites had the power to turn immediately. No blood exchange or mating ritual. Literally a wham, bam, thank you, ma'am.

Without the thanks. Just the brutality of change.

And the sight of the bite mark confirmed all of my worst fears. There was definitely enough venom in her system to turn her.

"Are you okay?" I met her gaze as panic flashed through me.

I couldn't control any of this. I couldn't stop the turning or control the events that were about to take place.

"Are you in any pain? Does it hurt?"

She shook her head carefully. "I'm a bit warm and there are some loud noises. I don't know where they're from. Can you hear those? It's almost like they're actually in my skull."

"I'm sorry." There were no other words. I was so sorry. *So*, so sorry.

I should have done better.

She smiled as I tucked her hair behind her ear, and I leaned my forehead against hers.

"I love you." My words were a whisper. It was more than love but they hadn't invented how to say that yet. "I'd do anything for you." I paused, wanting to prolong this moment longer. It was peaceful now. I loved her. That was what I really wanted her to know. Not this next part. I drew her closer. "You're being turned, Maeve. I can't stop it. The Ancients. They can…they're very powerful. They can turn you with one bite."

"What?" She drew back and her eyes were wide, her bewilderment plain to see. She touched her neck then glanced at her wrist. "But it was a second. It barely… I didn't…" She fell quiet and met my gaze again. "It can… I can't… I've read about it. I *know* that's not the way it's done."

"It's a bite from an Ancient, mon ange. The first vampires." I chuckled but there wasn't a drop of humor in my body. "Legend says they're the descendants of gods. They're a power like no other vampire. A drop of their venom can turn a human."

"But I've done all the research. I know about turning. I didn't...I didn't know about them." Tears glistened in her eyes and I drew her close again, closing my own eyes as the front of my shirt grew damp from her quiet tears. "I didn't want this."

Her words struck a chord. She truly hadn't wanted to be vampire. She'd already rejected me once and this felt like another. I pushed away thoughts of myself. It wasn't my time. I could mourn Maeve's choices later.

"Let's make you comfortable." That was really the only thing that mattered.

If I could get her through this, maybe I could fix everything else. Or I could talk to the people who knew how to fix it.

I undressed her and laid her in the bed before undressing and climbing in after her. She curled against me like the movement was automatic, and I held her close as she cried a little more.

"I don't even know why I'm crying," she said as she choked back another sob. "I think it was just a shock."

I smoothed her hair. "Your choices were taken away, mon ange. This is grief." My heart ached for her.

"How long do I have? How much time?"

I sighed. She made it sound like a death. Perhaps for her it was. "I'm not a turned vampire. I was born. My experiences are limited to stories I've heard." I didn't mention all of my personal failures. She knew about those. "I think it's different for every human. Usually the transition takes one or two days. Sometimes a week." I finished on a small shrug. "It isn't an exact science. It sounds strange, but biology rarely is. There are many variables at play, and I don't know when one of the Ancients last turned someone. I haven't read enough of the research yet to know. I'm not sure any of us has." It sounded like such a fucking copout. It wasn't one, though. We really didn't know enough about the Ancients yet.

And now this had happened.

"I couldn't even write it," Maeve murmured.

"Hm?" I moved so I could look down at her as she rested against my chest.

"In my blog. I couldn't have made this up." She laughed a little. "A week, huh? I'll be useless for that long?

Seems like the whole process could be a little more efficient."

"Your body is becoming a whole new being," I reminded her. "But don't worry. I'll help you through it. I'll do whatever I can. I'll stay. Guard you. I won't let anything happen to you. Fuck the war, fuck the Ancients." I paused. "Even fuck the Duponts. Nothing else matters. Only you. All I need is you." Hope gripped me with fervor. I just needed her to get through the transition. I could help her if she did but this hard part, it was all on her, really.

She sucked in a soft breath as I finished speaking then lifted her face toward me. I lowered my head until our lips met in a soft kiss. Her hands cupped my face and for a moment, it was as though she was the force I needed to live. Like I could somehow breathe her in like humans breathed air.

"I want you," she whispered. "I want all of you. Inside me. While I'm still human. Before I turn into someone else. I want to be able to remember now."

I didn't answer right away. Of any words she might have said, those weren't the ones I expected.

Blood filled my cock, and I cleared my throat. "Are you sure?" I wanted her more than I'd ever wanted anything before, and I couldn't guarantee I could control myself any longer. Even just lying here next to her teased at the edges of that control, tempting me to do more. "I might not be able to contain my bite," I whispered as I trailed my fingers along her jawline before letting my fingertips drop to her neck and that pulse point I desired most of all. I wanted to press my tongue against it and sink my fangs into her vein. "I want to mark you as mine for all the world to see. I want them all to know."

She pressed her hand to my chest. "Do it then."

My cock stiffened further at the challenge in her words. How far could I push her? "What?" My voice came out low and gravelly with desire. "Push my cock deep inside you while I sink my fangs into your neck? Make you come until you can't remember what your name is? Make you scream my name like it's the only sound you can make?"

Her breathing grew more rapid. "I want all of that, and I want it to be my choice. I want my last days as a human to be all mine, no matter what decisions have already been made for me."

I didn't ask her any more questions. Instead, I rolled her gently onto her back and kissed her again. When her soft lips parted beneath mine, I touched my tongue against hers and deepened the kiss.

She wrapped her arms around my neck and kept me pressed close to her as I explored her mouth. My cock responded to her soft moans, and I could taste the scent of her desire.

I reached for one of her breasts, cupping it before I stroked my thumb over the nipple. Her body responded to me immediately, her nipple hardening under my touch.

I lapped over it with my tongue before drawing it into my mouth, and she arched toward me, her hands in my hair.

My cock rested against her thigh, and I moved a little, allowing myself to experience just enough friction to tease me.

"Francois." She whispered my name, and I grinned.

I'd told her it would be the only word she'd remember.

"Oui, mon ange?" I nuzzled against her other breast before taking that nipple into my mouth, and Maeve parted her thighs, shifting how she lay beneath me.

It was an obvious invitation. One I wasn't about to turn down. But that didn't mean I had to move fast.

Our first mating should be a true seduction. She needed to have no doubt it was me she wanted or that it was my cock inside her body. I wanted to fill her mind as much as her body.

This moment was all about us.

I started to move down the bed, but her hand tightened, tugging my hair and turning the pinpricks of pain at my scalp into pleasure.

"No." The word was abrupt. Harsh, even.

"Non?" But her pussy... "Just a taste."

"No," she repeated. "Inside me, please."

I hesitated. She *had* said please—and so very nicely. "What do you want, Maeve?" I spoke so softly, so quietly it was almost a purr.

"Your cock."

It jerked at the mere mention and I stifled a groan. Such beautiful words from her lips.

"Where?" I didn't have an iron grip on my control. This was a very dangerous game.

"Deep inside me."

I kissed her again, trying to chase away the visuals of my lips on her neck, trying to prolong these moments.

She drew away. "I'm so wet for you." The innocence in her eyes was gone, replaced by the look of a wanton temptress and she moved invitingly, writhing beneath me.

She pressed her hand between us and her fingers wrapped around my cock, stroking up the shaft, balls to tip, in one long movement. I held still to try to control the shudder she induced.

She stroked me again. "So hard," she whispered. "And I really am so very wet." This time the faux-innocence was spoiled by the way her top teeth pressed against her bottom lip.

I groaned. "But I wanted…" I wanted to touch her, to *please* her.

"Please."

"You say that so well." I kissed her again, my cock swelling with anticipation at all the promise the kiss held.

It was unrestrained and uncivilized, undignified and a little wild. Manners didn't exist as our lips and tongues met. She devoured me almost in the way I wanted to devour her, and the passion she displayed stoked mine higher.

When she wrapped her arms over my back, her fingertips pushing against my skin, I moved my body over hers and nudged at her entrance, seeking my way in.

She gasped and I stopped.

"No. Don't stop." When she pressed against my back this time, her nails pricked at my skin, and I took that as encouragement, pressing forward before drawing back as I encouraged her body to stretch to accommodate me.

Every part of me wanted to ram myself home and claim her, but there was time for that kind of fucking. This was a special moment in so many ways, and I intended to preserve that.

Maeve was my mate. All mine.

I set a steady rhythm, pushing in and drawing back, teasing her by keeping things slow, and she sighed beneath me every time I filled her. Her eyes were closed and I looked down at her, taking in every detail of her beautiful face.

Her eyes sprang open and she smiled shyly. "Hello."

I pushed forward again and her lips parted. Then she tilted her neck, the movement clearly inviting and enticing, and I sucked in a quick breath.

Her pulse beat rapidly in her neck, fluttering as though it didn't already have my attention, and I groaned.

"I'm yours, Francois."

I wanted to bite her so very badly. It had been a constant need—a gnawing ache—since the first moment I'd seen her. I lowered my head slowly, delaying the pleasure of piercing her milky skin with my fangs.

Excitement thundered in my veins as the instinct to claim her rose above all else. It no longer mattered that someone had bitten her before me. She was truly mine. She was offering herself *to me*. I plunged my hand into her hair, the underside of my forearm resting against her cheek, to hold her head steady.

Precision and control were still important. Perhaps especially important.

I rested my fangs on the surface of her skin for the barest of moments, her scent filling my nose. Then I sliced through, and it was like penetrating her with my cock all over again.

Euphoria bubbled inside me but I reined it in. I wanted to be present and not lose myself entirely to the moment.

But the first draw nearly finished me. Her blood was the sweetest I'd ever tasted, and warmth coated my tongue as flavor exploded in my mouth.

I sucked again and swallowed, timing each with thrusting in and out of her body.

A sharp pain in my arm distracted me, and my orgasm approached even faster at the realization Maeve had bitten *me*.

True acceptance.

As I released inside her, she tightened around me in a steady pulsing, the strength of her body gripping me in waves.

After a few more teasing thrusts, I lowered myself next to her and gathered her back into my arms.

"Are you okay?" The thought I might have hurt her chilled me.

She stretched, the movement almost feline, although she never left my arms. "Everything's perfect now," she murmured as her eyes fluttered closed.

I stroked strands of her hair from her cheek. "Go to sleep, mon ange," I whispered. "I'm right here."

Chapter 26 - Maeve

My breath sounds were harsh in the quiet darkness of wherever I was. I reached out, instinct driving me to find someone else to share the sudden loneliness with, but the sheets beside me were cool and empty. No one else was here.

Muffled footsteps shushed outside the door to the hallway before it opened on silent hinges, letting a vertical chink of light slice into the room.

"Mon ange? Tu dors?"

I automatically relaxed at Francois's quiet voice. "No, I'm awake." I struggled into a half-sitting position before reaching for the lamp on the nightstand next to me.

I blinked in the sudden light then smiled at Francois as he approached the bed with a tray. My stomach rumbled at the aromas of sweet pastries, bacon, and coffee.

"I think this should still be suitable for this stage in the transition," he said, "but every one seems so different from what they've been telling me." He grimaced.

"Too much advice?" I was only half teasing. The other vampires seemed to have a lot of opinions between them.

"Oui." He bent and placed the tray next to me. "Chef has sent some food…of course."

I glanced at a plate of perfect beignets and couldn't prevent my grin. "Of course Chef has sent food. It might be his last chance, right?"

"Oui." Francois sighed before grabbing a beignet for himself and tearing the corner off in an angry bite. Then he sat down, perching on the edge of the bed. "How are you feeling?"

I paused as I considered his question, almost running through a mental checklist before I gave him my answer. "Yeah, actually. I feel great." It was kind of amazing. I hadn't expected to feel so good. "Maybe being a vampire is going to suit me?"

But he frowned. "Are you sure?" The concern lacing his voice was sweet but unnecessary.

"Yes. A bit sore between my legs, if that's what you mean?" I raised an eyebrow at him. "Might benefit from a kiss better?"

He chuckled drily.

"The pain in my arm is gone."

He leaned forward and rested the back of his hand against my forehead and lifted my arm as though he was a nurse about to measure my pulse rate. He examined it then looked at me.

"Your fever is gone, too. And where's the bite mark?"

"Hm?" I glanced at the smooth skin. The holes were completely closed as though they'd never been there in the first place. "Oh, it's gone. That's good, right?" I lifted my arm and showed it to him like he hadn't already seen.

He took hold of it again and ran the pad of his thumb over the smooth skin as though the bite had simply become invisible and he might be able to feel the evidence of it if he just touched me.

He furrowed his brows. "How did you heal it? It's completely gone. But so fast…" He met my gaze again. "How did it happen?"

I shrugged. I hadn't done anything. The process had taken control of it all. "Part of my transition? Does it matter? It's gone now. There's the whole vampire turning magic thing going on, right? My body remaking itself or whatever." I twisted my arm to look at it again. "Nope. We didn't miss anything. Just my normal arm." Just as I fucking liked it, really. Wearing an Ancient's bite hadn't filled me full of joy.

He touched my forehead again then cupped his hand around the side of my neck. "And you're really not hot at all anymore." He moved the tray out of his way like he needed to reperform a full exam. "Lie down, mon ange."

I swatted him gently away. "What are you doing? I feel great. Isn't this a good thing? Look, bring the tray back and I can finish eating, you can relax, and later..." I paused, hoping to build some suspense. "Maybe I'll let you do that thing with your tongue again." I grinned expectantly, but he didn't take the bait.

Instead, he turned more still than I'd ever seen him. It was as if he'd just vacated his own body and I hardly dared move, myself.

"Francois? Are you okay?" I resisted the urge to wave in front of his face. I'd never seen that done in a way that didn't seem rude. But the gesture was never more appropriate than it was here.

In a blink, he was back with me, and he looked at me as his eyes grew wide. "You're not turning. You're not becoming a vampire. How is this even possible? Your body has rejected the venom." He stood abruptly, but I grabbed his forearm and yanked him back to the bed.

He hit the mattress hard. "Oof." Then he narrowed his eyes. "But you've gained strength, I see." He leaned forward, peering into my eyes like I somehow lived inside my body now and he was trying to see the real me. "Do you have a thirst for blood? Would you like to slash a human neck open?" A hint of fang peeked above his lower lip at that last suggestion.

I laughed and shook my head. This whole thing was ridiculous. None of my research had ever suggested that people bitten by vampires—two vampires, in fact—and weren't killed by said vampires just carried on living their normal lives. And on top of everything they'd told me, transition was almost inevitable, surely? "This is silly. I feel fine, I look fine. I am fine."

He shifted closer and drew the sheet from my body, revealing all of me to him. His eyes heated at my nudity, and anticipation rippled over my skin. After last night, his attention was welcome.

In fact, I *craved* it.

He touched me, skimming his fingers and palms over my skin, and I pressed toward him.

"Maeve." He rarely used my name, and he pushed out a frustrated breath. "I'm not groping you. I'm looking for anything amiss. I want to make sure you're as well as you think you are."

I blew out a sigh of my own. "And what if I want you to grope me?"

He looked at me for a moment then shook his head and chuckled. "We'll have to get to that. And I have no idea how you've done it, but I think you're still human—even with that extra display of strength."

I tilted my head like I was considering what he'd just sad. But I didn't really care. "Right now, Francois—" I spoke slowly to get his attention and like I was explaining something to someone having trouble grasping the concept. "I'm naked." I smiled. "And I don't want to think about vampires or Ancients or even mates. I just want you. It's like I can feel you here." I cupped my hand over my chest where a strange new awareness of something was growing.

It made me both jittery and satisfied, although right now the jitteriness was winning out over the satisfaction. I needed to do something.

I needed to do Francois.

"It's making me want you even more." I toned it down for him, but I was pretty sure he got the message.

His eyes flared a vivid red, and he sprang toward me, pressing me to the bed and parting my thighs with his knee as his lips claimed mine.

I grinned and pulled back, nipping his lower lip as I did. "Oh, no. Turnabout is fair play."

Almost without thinking about it, I flipped us over. Then, before he could react, I straddled him and ground a little against the hard ridge already evident in his pants.

He reached up, pressing his palms over my breasts. "I feel a little overdressed," he murmured.

I shrugged. "We can fix that." And I took his shirt in my hands and tore it open.

"Mon ange," he grumbled. "That was my favorite one. They don't make them like this anymore."

But I moved over his hard cock gain and he fell silent, closing his eyes as he parted his lips.

"What was that? I didn't hear you."

He shook his head. "Nothing." He breathed out. "Just keep doing…that."

"Gladly." I rolled my hips again before placing my hand on the buttons keeping his cock in his pants.

I nudged my hand over the bulge and it jumped at the touch.

Francois opened an eye. "Please," he murmured, and I grinned as I unfastened his pants and took his cock into my hand, enjoying the weight of it as I lightly caressed the soft skin.

"Lift." The command dropped from my lips as I rose and he followed me with his hips so I could push his pants farther down his thighs.

He dropped back down and I took hold of his shaft before running my hand to the base and positioning myself above him. Then I hesitated. What the hell was I doing? I'd been a virgin until last night, and now I was up here changing positions and behaving like I knew what I was doing?

But I hadn't grown up in a vacuum. I knew what to do. More importantly, my body seemed to know what to do, and I was already moving up and over him. I was wet already…*so* ready, and I teased my clit with the head of his cock, smoothing it over my body in soft strokes that made sparks jump inside me.

Francois murmured and pushed his hips up, and I chuckled.

"I've got this one, thank you." But I took pity on him and positioned the tip of him by my entrance.

I slowly lowered myself, stopping as I allowed my body to accommodate him, basking in the feeling of fullness he brought me. I didn't move immediately once I had settled onto him, instead taking a moment to look at him and the desire in his expression as his hands moved over me.

This man wanted me in a way I'd never been wanted before.

I lifted up and he began to thrust with his hips.

I giggled. "Someone's impatient."

But I didn't stop him. We moved together in rhythm, and I worked my hand between us to smooth my fingertip over my clit. He groaned as he saw what I was doing, and his thrusts became more forceful, nudging my finger against my body until I began to tighten and fought to still move in time.

He gripped my hips, helping to lift me, and I applied more pressure to my clit, chasing my orgasm as he chased his.

My breath came in ragged, irregular inhales until I almost couldn't suck any more air in. I held still as Francois slammed upwards one more time, and my whole world throbbed, breaking me apart before I snapped back together.

He grunted and his cock twitched inside me, and I flopped forward to lie against his chest, his cock still hard inside me.

"Wow." It was the only word I could say. It was the only word that summed everything up.

Just...just wow.

He smoothed a hand over my shoulder, stroking me in idle circles and swirls, and I relaxed under the casual gesture.

"Do we even have to move?" I asked.

"Mm… Peut-être." He made a considering noise. "I suspect we should. Just so the others know you're still alive."

I groaned. "But I was having such a good time."

He answered my lazy frustration. "And we will have a good time again, mon ange. Again and again and again…" Then his hand landed on my ass. "But until then, we should get up."

"Ugh." I slid off him and walked to the bathroom. "I'll get ready."

***

When we walked down the hallway from the bedroom, everyone was already sitting in the living room, like some kind of family meeting was taking place, but they all talking stopped and everyone turned to look at me as I entered the room at Francois's side.

Nic stood. "What the hell happened?" He looked at me, his eyes narrowing, but Francois reached for my hand, and I took it.

This was a weird situation, still being human in a room full of vampires. It wasn't the easiest thing to discuss either, when I had *no idea* what the hell had happened. Probably better just to let Francois deal with this conversation.

"Je ne sais pas, Nicolas."

Excellent. I squeezed his hand. Francois had made a truly excellent start—if telling his king he didn't know was the correct answer.

"As far as I can tell," he continued, "The poison is gone from Maeve's system." He turned and gave me a confused look. "She still appears to be human, although her strength is increased."

The room erupted with the sound of eight vampires all talking at once as Francois and I stood and watched them. But as I watched, I suddenly didn't care about the loud voices and the random gestures, and the room full of passion and vampire strength.

Francois had been right. I may still have been only human, but I was different. I was changed. Before I was bitten, I was weak. Now, I was strong, confident in my life, and happier than I'd ever been.

I had everything—my humanity and my vampire.

"Wait!" Kayla held up a hand. "I'll be right back." She hurried from the room, and we all watched as she headed off in the direction of her spell room.

She didn't seem to have been gone two minutes before she was back, a particularly grimy book clasped to her body. She placed it onto one of the tables and opened the old, tattered cover.

Sebastian approached her and stood behind her, looking over her shoulder. "What's that?" he asked. "It looks like it might be contagious. Have you sanitized it?"

Kayla grinned. "I think we'll all be just fine, don't you? There's a clue in the word *immortal*."

He laughed. "So what is it?"

"It's a book about supernatural creatures. I found it at a black market stall when I was making a potion to ward off some trolls from a fae area of the bayou."

"Ward off?" Sebastian raised an eyebrow.

Kayla shrugged. "Ward off…kill…the end result is the same."

I shivered a little. Kayla sounded like a very powerful witch if she commanded the dark arts.

"Why do we need the book?" Francois stepped forward but didn't let go of my hand.

"Because…" Kayla turned some more pages. "Aha!" She jabbed the page with her forefinger. "Listen…*A Venator – Latin for Hunter.* Venators are descended from a clan of shamans who gave their lives to fight vampires. They're human, but as they mature, their powers slowly come to the surface. Usually they start to realize their potential at around thirty. Their first power is strength." She glanced at Francois then me. "Then improved hearing, and third is improved sight. After that, they inherit the full power of their blood oath." She looked at me again. "I guess your process got sped up by the vampire venom."

I laughed and shook my head. Now *this* was the craziest thing I'd ever heard, and I'd heard some batshit crazy stuff in my life. What the hell was Kayla talking about?

"I'm not some sort of hunter." I laughed again.

Kayla raised an eyebrow. "You aren't? What exactly have you been doing your whole life?"

I shrugged. "Trying to find proof of…oh." I stopped talking as she nodded.

Kayla bent back over the book again. "Since the Shamans started to disappear, there have been fewer venators than there were before…"

"Wait." Sebastian held up a hand. "How old is this book?"

Kayla lifted an eyebrow. *"Old."*

"So we don't even know if there *are* any shamans, let alone these venator things. I mean, shit. First Ancients and now witch-doctor-created vampire hunters. The world's gone crazy." He paced to the other side of the room and Nic laughed.

"The world is the same place it's always been. And we've been here for hundreds of years. We can be here for hundreds more."

"Anyway." Kayla looked at both guys. "It says here that the only way to kill a venator is to behead them…" She was quiet a moment, her eyes scanning the page as she read ahead. "And I don't really think we need to read the rest." She finished with a bright smile and closed the book quickly. "So, anyway." She pointed at me. "You equals venator."

I looked at Kayla for a moment, expecting her to laugh at her joke. Then I glanced at the other vampires in the room. Each of them watched me, their faces blank.

I looked at Francois. He still hadn't let go of my hand, but his eyebrows drew down, his confusion evident. "Mon ange?"

I blurted a laugh, almost a hiccup, really, and another, until the laughing was too fast and powerful to control and the first tear emerged from the corner of my eye, but I still couldn't stop. I laughed again even as I struggled to suck in a breath. As Francois drew me carefully against him, the laughter turned to loud, ugly-sounding sobs, and I buried my face into the front of his shirt, my hands clutching the fabric at the back.

The room stayed quiet, as if I was playing out my confusion for an audience, and I fought to bring my crying under control. Even when I'd finally quieted, I remained standing against Francois, hiding myself as I pulled together the last remnants of my composure.

When I turned around, I smiled tightly. "Sorry."

"You never need to apologize." Francois rested his hand on my shoulder, and I nearly grinned.

There was something amusing about being told I never needed to apologize. Like maybe ever again. And it most certainly wouldn't hold true.

"Are you mated?" Nic's question was blunt and abrupt, and his tone was curt.

He'd already moved into royal figurehead mode and was protecting his dynasty and territory.

Leia laughed and rested her hand on his upper arm as she met my gaze. "I think, my love, that there are some things that are none of our business." She grinned and my face heated.

Well, shit. They were all going to know I'd just had sex for the first time.

Sam appeared beside me and looped an arm around my waist. "It's okay, Maeve," she said then lowered her voice. "We were all virgins once."

That was true enough—and they'd all been aware I was a virgin, anyway. They all probably knew my change in status without us having to declare it.

All of the girls laughed, and I glanced at Sam. "What's funny?"

Leia shrugged but took the lead answering. "It's the way things are around here. We were all virgins before we turned."

Maybe I'd known that on some instinctive level, or maybe one of them had told me—Ciara, maybe? But it didn't actually make any sense. Each of these women was beautiful inside and out. There was almost no way they wouldn't have been approached by a guy before a vampire just stumbled into their lives.

"Yes, we *have* mated." Francois spoke like he was making a grand announcement. "Maeve bears my mark."

He lifted the hair from my neck, and everyone leaned forward to look.

I closed my eyes briefly. It was like being meat on a market. But my eyes sprang open again when the only sounds in the room were gasps.

"There's nothing there," Jason muttered, but he stepped forward to have a closer look, even lifting the hair at the other side of my neck.

What did he mean? Francois had bitten me. I touched the side of my throat, searching for a tender point or somewhere raised or uneven, but there really was nothing there. My fingers skated across smooth skin.

"Francois?" I glanced at him. "What does this mean? I can still feel you…here." I touched my chest in the same place as before. It was like he had left part of himself inside me somehow.

His eyes widened as he touched my neck, too. "Mais…rien." He tried again. "Nothing there." Then his eyes widened and he fumbled with his cuff, trying to push far too much lace out of the way.

He gave up and whipped the entire shirt over his head instead, and my knees weakened at the sight of him. The craving was back.

He lifted his arm and exhaled—the relief in the sound obvious.

I glanced at his arm then looked again, finally seeing what he'd been looking for. The bite I gave him. The skin was puckered and slightly raised, my teeth-marks already immortalized in his skin.

"*She's* claimed *you.*" Leia laughed, although the confusion mixed with her amusement was evident.

We all looked at his arm again as Francois held it out, pride clear on his face.

Kayla returned to where she'd left the book on the table and started flipping through the pages again. "Hang on, there's something I missed." Her eyes widened as she quickly scanned one of the pages. "Okay." She looked up. "Okay," she said again. "It's a bit weird, but if a venator bites a vampire, they can become soulmates. The vampire's soul is reborn in the venator. If one lives, so does the other. But…" She swallowed and cast a quick glance at Francois almost like she was nervous. "If you don't drink from Maeve, you'll become human again. It's her bite that kills vampires and only her blood can keep you in your current state. That's what creates the soulmate bond. My, my." She stepped back. "I've never seen a finer line between love and death. And I thought being turned vampire came pretty close."

Well, fuck. I could potentially kill everyone in this room.

My whole body seemed to heat with the intense shame of that news, and I backed away, already looking toward the exit. I needed to go. Just leave. Now.

I could hurt one of them and maybe I wouldn't even mean to. It was what I'd been bred for, apparently— vampire killer. No wonder I'd spent so much of my life trying to find them. At least that made sense now. But why hadn't Granny told me? Perhaps even she hadn't known. It didn't really matter now.

I tried to slide past Francois, my mind spinning with too many thoughts, but he reached for me then pulled me against him. I pressed my hands against his chest to push him away, but I didn't want to hurt him. I couldn't use all of my strength just now in case I did.

"You need to let me go," I said, keeping my voice low. "I could hurt you. Kayla just said I'm capable of killing you. All of you." Oh, God. I didn't know what to do. I needed to go and I couldn't. I was trapped.

"Maeve." Again Francois used my name, and again I stopped and looked at him, my head suddenly—blessedly— quiet. "Stop. I'll never let you go no matter what. Didn't you hear Kayla? We're bonded. We're not just true mates. You're my *soulmate*. There's nothing you can do to get rid of me now."

Chapter 27 - Francois

My heart beat for the woman in my arms. So much more than my true mate. *Soulmate.* The word echoed around and around in my mind. The keeper of my soul. *That* was what I'd been searching for all this time. I'd hurt so many people and done so much damage. But I was finally here.

Maeve was in my arms.

There was no one else. I wouldn't want someone else anyway. There never had been anyone else.

There was irony in a hunter as my mate. I'd always been the hunter, the predator, and I'd hunted so many. They'd been my prey. They never stood a chance.

Only now everything was equal in a way. The woman I loved held the power to kill me. She could hunt me. I was her prey.

I almost laughed. After everything, it was exactly what I deserved. And yet I knew I was perfectly safe with her.

"Calm down, Maeve. Everything is all right." I could feel her mind racing like a buzz of activity inside me. Something frenetic and panicked. "I'm not going to leave you. I'm by your side. We're in this together."

Nicolas sighed and sat on the sofa.

I almost laughed again. I'd never seen him look so defeated. Not when battling the Ancients. Not even when battling *me*.

But one tiny human woman, my mate, and he looked as though his world was ending.

When he raised his gaze to me, it was tired. Conflicted. "Do you trust her?" he asked. "Do you trust your mate?" He didn't look at Maeve as he spoke, as though these weren't easy words to say.

Maeve had lived among us for weeks. We'd rescued her, protected her. *I'd* loved her. Now Nicolas doubted her. He was going against his instincts whichever way he jumped. Vampire mates were always above reproach.

Perhaps until they were also vampire hunters. Had there ever been such a pairing before?

I met Nicolas's eyes. "With everything that I am." My trust in Maeve was unwavering. This news didn't affect that. In fact, knowing what she was and the power she held and that she'd still chosen me as her soulmate… That filled me with a new sense of worth.

I was worthy. A vampire hunter had deemed me so important that she wanted to keep me with her for all time, going against centuries of instinct of her own.

She moved in closer to me as if seeking shelter. Like she didn't realize she was potentially the most powerful being in this room now.

The apex predator, where before she'd probably feared all of us.

"Maeve?" Kayla addressed my mate, but she got all of our attention. "What if we use *your* blood?"

"My blood? What for?" Genuine confusion laced Maeve's tone. But a lot had happened since we'd come to find the others, and even I wasn't quite following Kayla's train of thought.

"I think…" Kayla bit her lip as she paused like she was pondering her next greatest plan. "I think I could modify the spell against the Ancients so we don't need their blood anymore. You're a vampire hunter."

"But my blood *heals* vampires. You just said so yourself." Maeve started to shake her head.

"But what if it didn't?" Kayla's smile began as mischievous but took on something with a touch of evil. "Maybe my modification would reverse that."

She was talking about the darkest of magic. The kind that would have left a black stain on her soul—if she'd still had one.

"I think—" Kayla looked at Maeve appraisingly, a new consideration of my mate in her eyes now that she knew what she truly was.

But there was no fear there. Probably someone with as much command over magic as Kayla seemed to have developed since she'd turned would have little to fear in any situation.

"I think I could create the ultimate weapon to stop the Ancients. With the right spell and your blood, we should be able to strip their powers even faster. Maybe more." She finished with another flash of that predatory grin.

I opened my mouth to speak. It still sounded dangerous. I didn't want Maeve anywhere near the Ancients. Regardless of anything else, she was still human.

"It could mean the difference between life and death, Maeve." Kayla's tone turned wheedling. "And not just for us." She looked around the room, including everyone in her statement. "But for many humans as well. We don't know what the Ancients have planned. We don't know what they're going to do. What about the people you know? The people you grew up with? What about them? You could save them all."

"Potentially," I said. "You're talking in possibilities. We don't know that this will work any more than the last plan *didn't.*" I emphasized the last word. If that plan had succeeded, we wouldn't even have been discussing this now. "And Maeve was also front and center of that attempt, if I recall correctly, oui?"

"Francois." Maeve spoke quietly as she rested her hand on my arm then stepped around me. "I'll do it. I'll do anything I can to keep all of you safe."

Kyle laughed, but it was sudden and out of character. He so rarely spoke, and when he did, it was only the most efficient of commands. His mating was possibly even more perplexing than mine because his mate seemed to adore him. Yet he was the very personification of a charmless man.

"Keep us all safe? You do realize that we're the very creatures you're destined to kill?" He rubbed a hand over that ugly, ridged scar that ran over his scalp. "And I have no idea who you are."

Sam swatted at him. "Quiet, Kyle. Maeve isn't a killer. She helped us out last time and she was still the same Maeve. Nothing has changed except we've all found out." She reached toward Maeve again as she spoke. "We know you, Maeve. You didn't sign up for any of this, and you must be even more confused than the rest of us. First you knew about the supernatural world, then you were abducted into it, and now you're one of the biggest puzzles within it." Her gaze softened. "Don't worry about the things Kyle just said. It's just biology. You're still our friend."

My affection for Sam grew as she defended Maeve, her eyes blazing with conviction. Kyle stepped back, retreating as his mate spoke, and triumph flooded me at the chastened man. At least some of the people here had Maeve's back, and if Sam was one of those people, then she had powerful allies. Sam was a true fighter after everything she'd been through.

"Okay." Kayla picked the book up again. "Come with me and we'll see about getting this spell together. I don't think we have any time to waste." She turned and started to walk to her spell room. She looked over her shoulder, not even breaking her stride. "Maeve and Francois, you're with me. The rest of you can do whatever gossiping you're dying to do."

"Research," Sebastian called after her retreating form, and she laughed.

I took Maeve's hand again, and we followed behind Kayla as she took the familiar hallway to her witchy workspace.

"I'll try to make this quick," she said.

Maeve squeezed my hand, her anxiety on display, but it only increased my admiration for her. She was scared and she was willing to do this anyway.

Inside her room, Kayla led us to the far side and she started opening cupboards and reaching onto shelves. She pulled out a metal bowl decorated with scrolling script I couldn't read.

The words almost seemed to move as the light shone on them. Then Kayla produced a blade and set it onto her workspace next to the bowl.

Maeve sucked in a breath.

"It's okay," I whispered against her hair. "I'm right here." But as I looked at the blade, I wasn't sure it was as okay as I said.

Kayla ignored us, busying herself by reaching for various sprigs of dried herbs and chopping them into small pieces. Their sharp aromas drifted into the air, filling the space with the smell of vitality and life. A jar Kayla had taken from a cupboard seemed to contain things that looked like wizened dried fingers, but I didn't look too closely.

She removed two of them and chopped them with a huge cleaver, each strike almost an act of violence as bone glistened white under shriveled flesh. I tore my gaze away until the hacking sound stopped.

She emptied the small pieces into the bowl with the herbs before smashing the contents with a heavy-looking pestle. The mixture turned a dull gray, and I looked away again as my stomach revolted—which was ridiculous.

I wasn't squeamish.

Kayla looked at Maeve. "Hand," she held out her own hand ready to take Maeve's.

Maeve glanced at me, and I would have done anything to take away the fear in her eyes.

"I signed up for this," she said like she was reminding herself rather than telling me.

"But you can change your mind." I didn't look at Kayla—she probably felt differently. But I didn't want my mate forced into anything.

Maeve placed her hand in Kayla's, and she closed her eyes for just a moment before looking at me. The fear in her gaze was gone, replaced by determination, and I nodded. There was the strength I knew she had. Pride swelled inside me. Maeve was so much more than I ever could have hoped for.

Kayla held Maeve's hand palm up and murmured some words as she grasped the handle of the knife and held it above the pad of Maeve's thumb. Without warning, she plunged downward and made a clean slice across her palm to the base of her pinky.

Maeve didn't even flinch, but her face whitened as Kayla squeezed her hand and blood welled all along the new split in her skin.

Kayla spoke some words in a different language as the blood pooled in Maeve's palm before she gave a sharp twist and emptied the blood into the bowl below, not spilling even a drop.

The contents of the bowl fizzled and steamed as the blood hit the ingredients Kayla had already added. Then the mixture smoked as it turned color from the red of the blood to a vivid purple. The scent in the air changed, too, becoming cloying and sweet, like decaying honeysuckle.

I watched as the potion bubbled and Kayla continued to squeeze Maeve's hand to encourage more blood to fall. Then she wrapped Maeve's hand with a white bandage and spoke a few words before pushing Maeve in my direction.

"Stand back," she said.

She drew herself up to her full height, her back ramrod straight, looking every inch a dark witch as her face filled with shadows and contrast. The atmosphere in the room changed, becoming dark and oppressive, and Kayla's voice was a low growl as she cupped the bowl in her hands and swilled the contents around.

When she started chanting, the sound was barely audible, but it quickly built to a deafening roar, and even from where we'd moved to, it was obvious the consistency of the mixture was changing, becoming crystalline and forming shapes.

When she finally fell silent, six arrowheads lay in the bowl, and she parted her lips to speak before collapsing over her work bench, her face pale.

"Oh, no!" Maeve ran forward. "Kayla! What happened?"

"Don't touch her," I bellowed. "There could be residual dark magic inside her."

"But why has she fainted?"

"She's used too many of her reserves. She just needs rest." I'd seen it before but not often. Witches didn't usually give so much of themselves to their spells because a reaction like this left them vulnerable. It was a good thing Kayla was somewhere safe, with those she trusted.

"I'm going to get Sebastian to come for his mate. Are you happy to stay with her?"

She nodded. "Of course." She hovered near Kayla, not touching her, merely turning her attention between the witch and the arrowheads that had been created.

"Touch nothing," I reminded her.

"I won't."

I already knew she wouldn't, but it helped to hear it. Then I left the workroom and hurried down the hallway. Nicolas's office was in one of these rooms. I headed toward the sound of male voices. They always sounded so serious.

I knocked on the door but didn't wait for a reply before I entered the room. They all sat motionless, watching me.

"This is the part where you all yell *surprise*, non?" I sat in the only remaining seat.

"Non." Nicolas stood and walked to perch on the edge of his desk. "This isn't a party, Francois. How did the spell go?"

I frowned. "Always so serious." Then I sat forward and looked at each vampire. "I think Kayla has created something very special." The amount of energy she must have poured into that bowl to deplete herself completely told me that much. "She needs Sebastian, but Maeve is watching over her. The spell was a very powerful one and she's fainted."

"Fuck me," Sebastian murmured as he headed for the door. "Why didn't you start with that?" His footsteps sped to a jog as he disappeared through the door and I looked at the others.

"She's created arrowheads. Six of them."

Nicolas nodded. "One for each Ancient. That means we'll only have one shot per vampire. If the arrowheads do what Kayla has spelled them to do, they should melt away their magic and leave them vulnerable to the usual methods of final death."

I nodded, unusually excited about this part. Bloodlust usually ran strong in my veins, and the mere thought of battle would send me out to create fledglings to act in my army.

But this wasn't a show of force. This was almost a battle of wits. And one of expertise if each arrow needed to strike true.

We wouldn't win by my usual brute force methods, and apparently I needed to place my trust in Nicolas again.

Only it wasn't so easy this time. I wasn't worried about myself. I'd survived years with madness running through my veins. But I wasn't sure I could survive without Maeve, and if the Ancients got wind of what she could do or what we were using her to do, she was in danger.

Chapter 28 - Maeve

Sebastian had entered Kayla's spell room like someone had set him on fire and told him to run. His eyes had burned dull red, and his cheekbones had been sharp.

But the sight no longer unnerved me. Either I'd seen it often enough or my new knowledge of my lineage helped to take away my fear. Possibly it was a little of both.

He'd sighed when he saw her. "She used too much energy," he said as he strode toward her. "She needs to take more care." But his voice softened as he said that last part, and his love and concern for his mate was clear.

"Francois said not to touch her in case of residual magic."

He swung a steely gaze in my direction. "I'm taking my mate to rest."

I stood and watched as he scooped her from her awkward position then cradled her against his chest. He dropped a quick kiss into her hair.

"Can I sit with her until she wakes up?"

"Yes. I should get back to the others." His reply was gruff but I might have also detected relief there. "We're still working out how best to get close enough to the Ancients to target them with the arrows."

He'd set Kayla on the bed, made her comfortable, and left me sitting in the chair beside her. What if he and Francois were wrong?

I watched her closely at first, but her condition didn't change. She simply lay in the bed and slept. I rested my head back in the armchair as fatigue stole over me. It had been a busy time recently. Abduction, vampire bites, transition to vampire *hunter*. I closed my eyes.

When I woke up, I checked on Kayla. She was still exactly as I'd left her. Shit. I'd slept. I was supposed to be watching over her, and I'd slept. Thank God Sebastian or one of the others hadn't come in and found me.

Perhaps it hadn't been long. I leaned forward to check on Kayla again when I stopped. Something…something was wrong with me. My head throbbed like drums were beating inside it, like multiple hearts had taken up residence in my body.

But they weren't quite heartbeats. They were slower than anything I'd ever heard in a human or probably in the vampire lying alongside me. It was as if the heartbeats were suspended in time or running in slow motion.

Kayla woke with a gasp, sitting upright as soon as her eyes opened. "Shit," she breathed. "What the hell is *that?*" Then she turned to me, her eyes wide. "They're here."

Kayla didn't stay for even a second in her bed. "I need to get back to my spell room." Then she was gone, using her vampire speed to move through the apartment.

I left the room to find Francois. He needed to know the Ancients had arrived.

Fear propelled me forward and my breath came in rapid spurts. My thoughts were a buzz of white noise, and adrenaline thrummed through me.

I ran through the sitting room and down the other hallway before the sound of male voices behind a closed door brought me to a stop.

I burst into the office, and didn't even pause for breath. "They're here." I used the same words Kayla had used when she woke up, but we all understood what they meant.

Nic took the lead even though I'd really directed my statement to Francois. "How do you know?"

"I can hear them." I stopped and thought about it. "Kind of. I feel them more than hear them. It's like their heartbeats are inside me as well as inside them."

"Mon ange." Francois stood, his eyes dark in his face. Bleak. "You must go to the bedroom and hide. Maintenent. Now. Run! Hide!"

"No way! I can't go anywhere and hide. I have to help. I have to stay and fight." I couldn't do anything else.

My blood was the thing that was going to start killing them, and I had to ensure we took out as many as we could. Otherwise, this nightmare would never end.

The Dupont vampires would be constantly at risk of being hunted and picked off or wiped out otherwise. Perhaps other vampire families too. Maybe humans. I had no idea what the Ancients might do, and I couldn't take any chances.

"Maeve, listen to me." Francois' cheekbones sharpened, but I wasn't afraid of him anymore. He had more control after drinking my blood, so maybe he'd been right all along.

And I had more control in this situation.

My hands found my hips as I stood my ground. "I don't think so, and you can't make me." I sounded like a petulant teenager but the sentiment was so much more than that. I could stand against these vampires independently. I was a vampire hunter. "I'm so much more useful than you think."

"You're my mate." He ran his hands through his hair. "I can't risk you." Usually his mussed-up hair made me crave him, but this time I only wanted to fight with him to get my own way. I wasn't being unreasonable. I was realistic.

"And I'm also powerful in my own right. I'm going to fight." I wouldn't be fought with on this.

Before he could argue against me again, Kayla barreled into the office, her speed making her entrance even more dramatic than mine.

"Here are the arrows," she said. "I've attached the heads I made to the shaft. We can use them like this." She looked at each of the men. "There are six arrows. Nicolas, Sebastian, Kyle, Jason, you'll each have one. You'll take the last one, Francois, but you need to wait until I've unraveled the magic of the first four before you target the fifth Ancient. Their magic is held together by powerful bonds, and this delay will ensure all of the bonds are broken. As soon as you shoot the final Ancient, I can cast the spell that will take them to their final death."

I shivered. Something about the way Kayla explained everything so calmly still made me feel like a cold-blooded killer, like I should have a TV show made about me or something.

For a moment, I mourned my blog. I'd thought I wanted to know all of this. Right now, as we discussed killing the oldest beings on Earth, I just wanted my naivety back.

Francois gripped his arrow and took one of the bows that Kyle collected from a closet in Nic's office. He wasn't saying anything anymore, which was a bigger indicator that he was nervous than anything else I'd seen.

"I'll be right there," I whispered. "I'll protect you." Those words were among the truest I'd ever spoken. I had the power to protect him.

He was my soulmate.

Before any of us could say anything further, there was a loud bang from upstairs, and plaster flakes rained down from the ceiling.

"They're fucking inside my fucking nightclub," Sebastian growled.

"Have you just missed this whole conversation? They're *here*." Kayla turned to him frustrated.

"We can rebuild. We've rebuilt before." There was something reassuring in the way Nic spoke to his brother. "But now, we need to fight. We got this?"

Sebastian nodded. "You know I'll always serve you."

"I do know." Then Nic led the guys out of his office, and their mates met them, forming each of the pairs before they split off in a predetermined pattern before Nic led the last of us up the stairs and into Nightfall.

As we reached the top of the stairs, fear trickled through me. None of this was under my control now. It was like the climb on a rollercoaster and the pause before the drop. Everything inside me tensed, but I kept my gaze steady and my step didn't falter.

No one else could know I was afraid.

We charged through the door at the top, into the main nightclub, where a fight had already broken out, but Nic did immediately join it. A bright light shone on the stage, and Kayla was illuminated there, but she wasn't performing.

She was chanting.

Only it wasn't much different to someone singing, and it was one of the most beautiful sounds I'd ever heard. Haunting, too. Almost distractingly so.

The yelling and fighting around me increased. There were men and women here who must have formed part of Nic's army. Since spending time with the small group of vampires, I hadn't had a lot of reason to consider how far the wider population stretched, and I didn't have time to ponder it now.

Then all sound deadened, and the movements seemed to happen in slow motion. I saw each of the small details in the room as my senses honed and sharpened.

Then I saw the female Ancient. Not just any female Ancient, but the one meant for Francois and me to take. Her eyes locked with mine, and she was on us with supernatural speed. Faster than any I'd seen a vampire display before.

"Clémence." Francois's word was a whisper as he pressed closer behind me, but the vampire pushed me aside before I could do anything. I glanced back as Francois started to struggle with the Ancient and as I turned to join him, someone grabbed me from behind.

The scent of death and decay and fresh earth surrounded me, reminding me that these vampires were unlike the ones I'd grown used to spending time with. These vampires were the ones from horror stories and legend.

"Aleron!" Francois shouted to the vampire that gripped me, but he couldn't do anything.

The female he'd been fighting seized his moment of distraction and wrestled him into a fresh hold. He struggled, but he couldn't get free.

Aleron yanked my arms hard behind my back, and my shoulders burned. "Francois," he said. "If you don't join us to help in raising Émile, I'm going to snap your mate's neck." His breath fanned across my skin, bringing with it the increased scent of death, and that galvanized me into action.

Strength I didn't know I had—even now—roared through me, and I ripped from his hold, whirling on him while he still didn't know I was free. Without thought, I bit into his neck, ripping out a section of flesh while blood spurted into my mouth.

I contained my gag as I pushed him from me and he slumped to the floor. As I stepped away from him, Kyle let loose an arrow that embedded itself deep into the fallen vampire's chest.

I spat the remains of him from my mouth as I stalked toward Francois, picking up the arrow he'd dropped as I approached.

The room came into focus around me, offering me glimpses of everything I needed to see most. Each of the

Ancients lay on the floor, an arrow in them, except for the one holding Francois in front of her like a shield.

"You need to put the arrow in the final one now, Maeve," Kayla called from the stage. "I'm not sure how much longer I can hold everything as it is."

I looked at Francois, and his eyes were rounded and sad. "You need to go through me to get to her, mon ange. Straight through my chest. It's the only way."

I shook my head. No. I'd only just found him, only just discovered so much about myself. I wasn't about to sacrifice all of that.

Besides, he clearly had no faith in all I could do. Or he was being a big drama queen at the final hour.

"No, Francois. You'll never die at my hand." I looked between him and Kayla, at the desperation on Francois's face, and the determination and fatigue on Kayla's.

Sweat beaded on her forehead. Time was running out.

"I love you, Frankie."

He closed his eyes but the ghost of a smile lingered on his lips, and my own mouth tugged in affectionate return as I threw the arrow with all of my newly gained strength.

Chapter 29 - Francois

I opened my eyes as the arrow my precious Maeve had thrown—*thrown*, without the aid of a bow—hurtled toward me. It would have been easy to close my eyes again, and ignore certain death, but I'd caused so much death in my time that I needed to face my own.

But pain only pierced my shoulder, radiating outward as the arrow pinned me to Clémence.

"Francois, what have you done?" Her words were a groan in my ear as she slumped against me.

Her unexpected weight took us both to the floor, and I twisted as I fell, watching Maeve rush at me from an unusual angle.

The Ancients began screaming as one, an unearthly wail echoing through the nightclub, and Maeve yanked at the arrow, snapping both ends off before withdrawing the shaft from my shoulder.

I winced before scrambling away from Clémence, who continued to wail, eyes wide open.

"Sorry," Maeve whispered to me as she helped drag me away from the Ancients.

On the stage, Kayla lifted her arms like she was making some kind of sacrifice to the ceiling, and she delivered her last words in a booming roar that vibrated through the whole space.

The wails stopped abruptly and each of the Ancients crumbled to ash, littering the floor with piles of the pale gray powder.

Sam whooped! "Yeah! Although you stole all of my fun, Kay. I thought we were going to take them out by more…traditional means." She squeezed her fist as she mimed extracting a heart from a chest.

Kayla grinned. "I found a spell that looked much more fun, and now I'm definitely burning that page of my grimoire."

Sebastian chuckled as she leaned against him as the pair approached Maeve and me. "Definitely sounds like a spell that shouldn't be out there doing the rounds if it could reduce us to ash."

Her grin widened. "Oh, I did modify it a little. The results wouldn't usually be quite this dramatic."

Sebastian glanced at her, the pride in his eyes obvious. When they came to a stop in front of me, I looked up at them. I was resting against Maeve, but something was wrong inside me.

I'd never felt like this before, but I'd also never been pierced by a magical arrowhead before. I probably just needed to wait for my healing to kick in.

"How are you doing, Francois?" Kayla's brow creased with concern. "You don't look so hot."

Maeve glanced down. Pushing my hair back from my face, she gasped. "What's happening to you? You look *old*."

"It's the arrow," Kayla said. "It entered his body, and he's of Ancient bloodline. The magic has affected him, too. He needs to feed to heal—from his soulmate. Your blood heals him, remember?"

I shook my head. "No, time heals me. I just need rest."

"Not this time, buddy." Nic stood above me now. "I've never seen anything like this."

A sense of dread settled in my stomach at Nic's words, its weight like nothing I'd known before. I was immortal. Vampires healed. I'd found my soulmate. I wasn't ready.

I'd changed.

I didn't want to die.

"You need to feed to heal," Kayla repeated.

Above me, Maeve sighed, and she stroked her soft hands over my face. "I have the power to save you, Francois. Let me."

"But not… Not like this." There was a desperation inside me to keep our connection private. "Non."

"Exactly like this. However it needs to be." As she spoke, she moved my head from her lap until I was lying flat on the floor.

My shoulder throbbed, the pain radiating out from where Maeve's arrow had penetrated my body. She positioned herself beside me, an arm wrapped over my chest, and lowered her mouth to mine, placing the softest of kisses on my lips.

"I love you," she whispered. "Now take what you need." Then she moved upward until her neck was positioned over my mouth instead. "Is this right?"

Instinct took over, and I angled her head as I needed it, trailing the tip of my tongue over her skin. She shivered and her pulse beat stronger. I could almost smell the blood coursing through her veins. I wanted that blood inside me too.

My fangs descended from my gums, and I touched her neck with the tip of one.

"Yes," she whispered. "Yes."

She pressed her body closer to mine and as her warmth seeped into me, I bit down, my fangs gliding into her with an ease that almost surprised me. Her blood filled my mouth, coating my tongue, and I drew deeply, taking the nourishment I needed, connecting with my mate on the deepest level possible.

Power rushed through me, my strength returning, and Maeve moaned as I drew on her blood again.

She moaned and my cock hardened at the sound. I wanted to roll us over and pound into her... But we were in public. Way too public, even if everyone had moved away and were distracting themselves clearing up the aftermath of the fight.

Even if the club had emptied out, I didn't want to fuck my mate on the floor of Sebastian's nightclub.

She deserved far more than that. And she deserved far more than a quick fuck.

She'd just saved my life.

I wrapped my arms around her and stood up, my movements smooth again, my lips still at her neck. She sighed, her contentment clear.

Relying mostly on muscle memory, I sped from the club floor and down the stairs, reaching my bedroom in record speed. I let go of her neck as I lay her on the bed, and I lapped my tongue over the puncture marks to start their healing.

She whimpered and I smoothed my hands over her breasts, feeling her nipples harden beneath the fabric of her top.

"Do you want me?" I whispered, even though the answer was obvious. I slipped my hand inside the front of her pants.

"What are you doing?" she whispered back, even though that answer was obvious, too.

I chewed my bottom lip like I needed to think. "Well, I've heard that going in dry hurts, oui?" I tried to keep the crude words seductive and low, then chuckled as I continued to touch her.

She barked out a shocked laugh. "Such a charmer."

"Oui?" I took her words as a challenge, already thinking of my next dirty words.

I tugged her shirt higher with my spare hand then flicked the button at the top of her fly and undid it. "I'm going to be inside you so hard and fast. I'll be balls-deep before you know it."

She arched toward me, pressing her clit harder against the tip of my finger. I sought more of her slick wetness then found the small, swollen piece of flesh again. Female anatomy would ever be a mystery.

Why did their bodies insist on hiding the parts that brought them the most pleasure?

"You want me to tell you what I'm going to do to you, mon ange?"

Her eyes flickered open briefly as she looked at me, meeting my gaze before she closed her eyes again, hiding her feelings from me. "Yes." The word was little more than a gasp.

"I'm going to fuck you until you see stars."

"Until I can't even remember your name?"

I chuckled again as I rolled her clit under my finger. "Until you *only know* my name."

"Yes," she whispered.

"You're overdressed again," I said, and she shimmied her hips as I stripped her pants and panties.

"Touch me some more."

I removed her shirt and she lay naked before me. "No 'please'? I'm going to have to tell your mom that you demanded I touch you and didn't say please." My tone was lightly chastising as I flicked her right nipple then leaned over and took it in my mouth.

"S'il te-plâit." She crooned her plea in French and my cock jerked.

"You get me so hard." I nuzzled her neck again, and she fumbled between us.

"So hard," she agreed.

I rested my finger back against her then withdrew it and she moaned.

"Don't stop."

"I want to taste you. I love the sounds you make."

She parted her lips on a small gasp, her hips already moving, ready for me. "Please."

The small word brought a smile to my lips. "That's better."

I moved down her body before I lifted her legs and parted her thighs, making room for my head between them. Her hands were already in my hair, her fingertips pressed against my scalp when I flicked my tongue over her then repeated the motion.

Then I sat back and inserted a finger inside her. She pushed against me as I started to press it in and out of her, nudging her clit with my knuckle on every return. Her breathing changed, becoming more irregular and she buried her face in the pillow to her left, muffling the noises she made.

I stroked her most tender spots until her breaths became rapid, one running into the next and the next until she sucked in a final one and pressed against me as her body shuddered and her inner walls gripped me in waves.

I waited for her pleasure to pass before I lowered myself over her. "Bien. Now I just need you to do that again. Come on my cock."

She exhaled slowly and met my gaze for the first time. "Is that a challenge for you or for me?"

"Both." I grinned. "I never leave a job half done."

I pushed my cock inside her, stretching her body for me as I always did, before sliding smoothly back out. She whimpered as I glided against her all over again.

"Don't stop." Then she bit her lip like she hadn't intended to speak, but her words spurred me on.

I sped up my movements, chasing my own orgasm as I remembered hers, and she gasped her pleasure beneath me, offering me her neck again as I reached under her head to bury my hand in her hair.

"Bite me." I pressed the underside of my forearm to her mouth and excitement took hold of me as she licked the skin there, her tongue soft.

Then she clamped her teeth around me, claiming me as her soulmate again as I slid my fangs back into her, drawing her blood in a matching rhythm to the thrusting of my cock deep into her body.

She was mine. Completely mine.

And I was hers.

My balls tightened, drawing up against me, and I sucked in breaths I didn't need. Without warning, she released my arm and moaned as she contracted in more waves around me, and I held still above her as she brought my orgasm too.

I thrust inside her a couple more times and she giggled. "That was nice."

"Just nice?" I pushed back in again, and she giggled harder, the force of the movement evicting me from inside her.

"Sorry. I just laughed you out."

I shrugged. "I'll be back."

She laughed harder. "So charming." Then she grew more serious. "But I hope you'll be back. I like this."

I nodded. "I know."

I kissed her, the soft kisses she always enjoyed best before I rolled to her left and gathered her against me.

Her breathing was still rapid and her heart beat fast. "I can still feel you here." She touched her chest above her heart, where her skin still gleamed from our exertions.

I ran my fingers down the side of her body and she stiffened slightly under my touch. "Ticklish?"

"Nope. Not ever." She sounded so definite that I laughed.

"Really. Another challenge?" I was going to like spending my life with my mate.

My life…I glanced at the woman in my arms. A mere human mated to a vampire. "Maeve?"

She moved her head so she was looking at me. "Mm?"

"Would you like…Would you like to get married? I know it's what humans do…" I stopped talking. It wasn't what vampires did. What was I suggesting and why was I suggesting it?

But impulse drove me to bind this human to me for our entire lives, and immortality was a long time. I wanted it to be a celebration as she knew that binding. We weren't only true mates.

We were soulmates, and that was different.

We could be different than the others.

We didn't simply have to be mated. We could be *married*.

She nodded, her hair teasing against my skin as she did. "Yes."

"Yes?" I behaved like I'd never heard the word before.

"Oui," she said, smiling now.

"Oui!" Now that I definitely understood. I drew her up over me, and she laughed before lowering her head to mine and pressing our lips together in a kiss.

Chapter 30 - Francois

Several months later

"There's no one here." Maeve peered farther into the gloom of my old home.

So many memories rushed at me. My old life all felt so long ago. It was as though I'd lived many lifetimes here. I'd been a child, hiding in my mother's skirts. I'd been mad, hopped up on dead man's blood, I'd been a lowly spare instead of a true heir, I'd been regent in Father's stead.

Father.

Regret tinged all of my memories of him. Regret for what might have been rather than what I'd lost.

An Ancient. But what had he left, and why? He'd been ruthless all my life. And unfeeling, but now I'd never know what he thought set him apart from the others like him, but it was unlikely to have been a desire to be better. To be better at being bad, perhaps.

He never did like being told what to do.

I pushed thoughts of my father from my mind. He was truly the past.

Then I laughed at Maeve's confusion. "Of course they're here." I could see my ghosts more clearly now that I was healing—now that Maeve was healing me.

They walked around as though they owned the place and they spoke to me in clear voices.

"You look well." Ah, there she was. The one who'd always been with me.

I nodded. "I am."

"Then you've found your future?"

I nodded again. Her words inspired guilt. I'd found my future, but I'd denied the ghost her future when I was still searching for mine.

But she smiled as she spoke. "It's about time."

"And what about you?" I worried about them. All of them. Earthbound and trapped.

"Oh, I don't know. There's something very gothic about being an inhabitant of a decaying mansion in the bayou. And I'm not alone." She indicated the others, still moving about their business as though they'd forgotten they were dead.

"You're not going to the light, ma petite?" I'd called them all *ma petite*, never distinguishing between women as I tore through them in search of my mate and my cure, and using the habitual term of endearment now sent a cringe through me.

But she didn't appear to notice. Instead she shook her head, a sweet smile on her face. "What light, Francois? Do you see *a light*? I think this might be as good as it gets."

Maeve gripped my hand. "What are they saying?"

I turned to her. "I think I have a renovation to do. We're the lucky owners of a haunted bayou mansion."

Her eyes grew sad. "We can't help them?"

"We can modernize. Make their surroundings more pleasant?" I didn't have much to offer beyond that. I'd made some awful mistakes that I couldn't undo, but I could hopefully make things a little more bearable. "Maybe we can even move back here so they aren't alone."

Maeve nodded. "I can see a time when that would be okay."

Nicolas knew some very good tradesmen if the refurbishment of the nightclub was any indication. I'd need to speak to him.

"Bon. C'est décidé." It was decided. "We'll be back soon," I promised the ghost.

Maeve turned slowly like she was inspecting the room. "I still can't see them. Bye," she called anyway.

The ghost laughed. "We'll see you all soon."

I took Maeve's hand and led her from the house.

"We need to get back to the Regent's house," she said.

Nic and Leia had moved there when travel between Baton Rouge and New Orleans became more arduous for Leia.

"I promised I'd be around for her delivery. And it feels like…" She paused and touched her heart then her head. "It feels like now would be a good time to be around."

I nodded. Over the past few months, I'd learned never to doubt Maeve's instinct when it came to reading vampires. The girls enjoyed her newfound abilities, but the guys were less impressed, with Kyle in particular preferring to keep his distance.

We drove back to the house and joined the cluster of people outside the master suite of rooms.

Every time Leia shouted out, Maeve rested her hand on her own belly, like she could protect the small life inside her from knowing about what was to come.

We hadn't told anyone yet. It seemed too soon, and I could barely believe it. My own heir. When I considered being a father and a family with Maeve and my child, happiness filled me to such a degree that there was almost no room for any other emotion.

Eventually, everything in the room fell quiet but the plaintive cry of someone much smaller than any of us filtered through the closed door.

My heart squeezed. Another born vampire. Nicolas Dupont was continuing the Dupont legacy, just as I was continuing the Ricard one. Perhaps our children would be better friends than we had ever managed.

Nicolas pushed through the bedroom door. "It's a boy!" he declared, and Sebastian pulled him into a fierce hug.

Kayla produced a bottle of champagne and some glasses. "I know this isn't traditional in vampire circles," she said, "although perhaps not all of us are drinking—" She glanced meaningfully at Maeve. "But it feels right to wet the baby's head in a human custom because we're all evidence of what happens when vampires and human join."

The women nodded as they accepted their glasses.

"To many more," Ciara stated as she leaned against Jason and looked up at him.

He chuckled. "Might take some practice."

She shrugged. "I'm not averse to that." Then she grinned. "Not averse at all."

Sebastian released Nicolas. "Any ideas on names?"

Nicolas shook his head and turned to reenter the bedroom but I stepped forward and touched his arm. He glanced at me.

"May I see Leia for a moment?"

His eyes narrowed, but the expression was brief and quickly gone. "Okay," he conceded. "But she needs rest."

I nodded. "Absolutely."

He stood back and allowed me to pass him. I pushed the door behind me, but didn't close it fully. I was no danger to Leia now, and everyone knew it, so taking a little privacy wasn't too much to ask.

Leia was sitting in her bed, a tiny bundle in her arms, and I peered at the small face peeking out of the soft blanket swaddle as I approached. "He's beautiful. Très, très beau."

She smiled in response, but I still hung back. Perhaps Leia's and my relationship would never be an easy one, and I couldn't blame her for remaining wary of me, but I had to try. There were some things I needed to say.

"Leia?"

At the sound of her name, she shifted her focus from her newborn. "I just want to show him to everyone and let them see what I've done. Is that wrong?"

I laughed softly. "It sounds entirely reasonable." Then I cleared my throat. "Can I just have a moment of your time before you do?"

"Are you okay?" Her immediate concern tightened my throat. I didn't deserve concern. Especially not from her.

I nodded. "I am. I'm just...just...sorry." The last word came out cracked and broken. "I'm so sorry, Leia. I'm sorry for taking you from Nicolas. You were never meant to be mine, and I'm sorry I couldn't see that. I understand so much more now. Maeve..."

She shook her head in the smallest of movements, and my heart dropped. I'd come seeking some sort of forgiveness, to make amends, and there was none of that here.

But then she spoke. "We have no need of sorrow here, Francois. We're both well, aren't we?"

"But your father..." I'd done the most appalling thing.

Tears shone in her eyes. "I know. But he had his demons just as you did." She looked down at the baby in her arms. "We're not going to repeat the mistakes of the past, are we? *Jean* doesn't seem like quite the right name for him—my father was never a very honorable man, so honoring him now seems odd. But maybe Nic will have an idea." She glanced back at me. "You don't need to seek forgiveness from me, Francois. You've proven you're a changed man."

I blinked back at her, and tears pricked my eyes, too. I'd never dreamed that I could be forgiven for the things I'd done.

I hadn't deserved to find my mate or secure my future, either, but somehow all of those things were true now.

I was doing my best to fix the mistakes of my past and I finally had a future.

And my soulmate.

Made in United States
Orlando, FL
14 August 2022

20997499R10253